THE RELUCTANT QUEEN

KEN COFFMAN AND KRISTEN LOLATTE

Other books by Ken Coffman

Steel Waters
Alligator Alley (with Mark Bothum)
Twisted Shadow (with Mark Bothum)
Glen Wilson's Bad Medicine
Toxic Shock Syndrome
Hartz String Theory
Endangered Species
Fairhaven
Mesh (with Adina Pelle)
The Sandcastles of Irakkistan
Fiancetto
Buffoon
Real World FPGA Design with Verilog

The Reluctant Queen ©2020 Ken Coffman and Kristen Lolatte
All Rights Reserved

ISBN Print 978-1-949267-54-9
ISBN eBook 978-1-949267-55-6

Cover Photograph by Wayne Fournier, www.thruthesoberlens.com
Cover Design by Guy Corp, www.GrafixCorp.com
Chapter icons by Brian Antoine Woods, www.BrianAntoineWoods.webs.com...
except for Happy Birthday, Apples, Travelers, King Queen Checkmate and The Letter by Enya Waterbury

STAIRWAY≡PRESS

APACHE JUNCTION

www.StairwayPress.com
1000 West Apache Trail Suite 126
Apache Junction, AZ 85120

Kristen's Dedication

To my mancub who will always be my mancub.

To Mr. Jenness who found and fanned the flame of writing in high school, and who unknowingly passed the torch onto Ken many years later.

To Wayne and Beth who helped to create magic and beauty out of thin air.

To David and Elizabeth who are forever and ever in my heart of hearts.

To those special souls who always help me to stay true to who I am and keep me on my magical path without judgment.

Ken's Dedication

To fallen friends Douglas Paasch, Justin Gideon Harrison, Lee Tegen and Greg Kotsolovos.
RIP, my brothers.

Happy Birthday

SHE WAITED AS long as she could, but the call of nature could not be ignored forever—she had to use the bathroom. Maybe if she tip-toed and was really quiet on her shiny, black, patent-leather shoes...

His eyes were open, though just narrow slits. Sitting with his thin body buried deep in a plush recliner, he was in the dark room sipping Jim Beam—pouring inch after inch into a crystal glass at a regular rate of an ounce per hour.

At six, she could read and had made out the words one-by-one, *Kentucky Straight Bourbon Whiskey*. It smelled vile and tasted worse; she could not imagine why anyone would drink it when there were so many other things that tasted good, like chocolate milk or cream soda. The Crinoline slip under her frilly skirt was noisy over her leggings, but she tried to be quiet like a mouse, edging along the wall as far from him as possible. Sometimes—like an ostrich—if you did not make eye-contact, you could be invisible. Truly invisible and she really, really didn't want to bother him.

With a soon-to-be-revoked credit card, he'd paid a small fortune for her sixth birthday party in their foreclosed mini-mansion—with a clown, magician, confetti, a banner and balloons everywhere—but instead of happy, he was in one of his dark moods.

After slipping into the bathroom, she pressed the lock-button as the door closed so it was not obvious it was carefully and securely locked.

After maneuvering the skirt and leggings, she tinkled in the toilet, then flushed and ran the water to pretend to wash her hands. She studied herself in the mirror.

"You are a pretty, pretty little girl," she muttered. "An angel, Daddy's special princess."

She slapped her cheek.

"Good girl, bad girl. It's all your fault. It's all my fault. I'm sorry, princess."

She slapped her other cheek and stared at their rosy glow, now matching. All around, the voluminous bathroom was beautiful with hardwood crown molding, pink wallpaper and incandescent lamps over the mirror filling the room with light. It was a perfect room in a perfect house without a speck of dust or fingerprint smudge. If the maid ever missed anything, there were fireworks.

Maids never lasted long before they were replaced.

Gathering her courage, she took a deep breath, then slowly opened the door and peeked out. Her father had not moved, though the level in the whiskey bottle had fallen an inch.

Her mind was filled with the question.

When it was gone, would he go to bed or open another bottle?

His silent eyes tracked her as she slid along the wall, but soon she was outside in the back yard and running.

Though everyone in the neighborhood had been invited, no one had come to her party. Almost no one. The Shelton twins had come, but they didn't count because they were stupid and ugly and weren't going to miss a free meal.

No, that's rude, Fiona, they shouldn't be blamed for being the way God created them.

Rotund and homely.

2

Giggling, the girls took turns stuffing Vienna sausages into each other—as many as their gaping mouths could hold.

Disgusted, Fiona turned away.

The magician had set up a card table covered with a black felt cloth. The cloth was stained and looked like moths had been nibbling on it. A tattered tent card said, *Doctor Wonder.*

As the Shelton twins gathered, he fanned a deck of cards.

"Birthday girl, I will perform an amazing feat for you. Pick one, any one, and don't show me."

She eased one from the middle of the desk.

Nine of Clubs.

She knew this trick—her father had bought her a *magic* deck when she turned four. The cards were tapered, just a little. Watching carefully, she saw *Doctor Wonder* rotate the deck. Surreptitiously and feeling sly and evil, she rotated her card instead of slipping it directly back in the deck like she was supposed to.

She watched his face carefully as he sorted through the cards over and over to find the slightly wider one. Slowly, realization washed over his face. He could try for a thousand years, but he was not going to find her card. He clenched his jaw and took a deep breath.

There was only one way out—bluff and hope she would not burn him. This only worked one-in-a-hundred times, but it was his only way to save any shred of his dignity.

With a grand flourish, he pulled out a card.

Two of Diamonds.

His expression was like a guilty puppy. Pleading.

She clapped her hands and hopped from foot to foot.

"Ooh, how did you do that? That's fantabulous."

The relief that washed across his face was laughable.

He did the hoary cups and balls trick, but was inept. She had no trouble watching the ball as it was palmed and shunted back and forth. The Sheltons were delighted, but Fiona was bored. Scanning the backyard, she made eye-contact with the magician's auntie hidden in the shadow of their old oak tree. He'd introduced her as his assistant, but she did nothing but sit and watch—when she was awake. Clearly, he was her caretaker and there was no room in his budget for a day nurse, so she came with.

With a bony finger, the old woman gestured.

A thought formed in Fiona's mind.

Come hither.

She was vague about what *hither* meant, but the request was clear. Looking around, she considered. Her mother was fussing with the cake and the twins were enthralled by Doctor Wonder's silk scarf pulled from a plastic wand.

What's the harm in seeing what the old woman wants?

Casually kicking a balloon, she worked her way over. The wheelchair was a hardwood relic. The woman's face peered out of a pile of dusty blankets. Deep in wrinkles, her eyes gleamed. Her voice was dry, barely a whisper, but every sarcastic word was clear in Fiona's head.

"You are a special girl, a golden girl with a perfect life."

Fiona lifted the sides of her skirt.

"Do you like my dress? Hand-stitched."

Laughter. It started with a phlegmy rattle deep in the old woman's lungs, then changed to a sour cackle.

"This is your last perfect day for a long, long time. I almost feel sorry for you."

As the old woman studied Fiona's face, a wave of confusion crossed her ancient face. Whether she spoke to herself or to Fiona was impossible to tell.

"I should have died last week. Thursday, a few hours after midnight. I'm ready. I've been ready for the next step for a long time. But, here I am. Now I wonder." She reached out with her skeletal hands and placed them on the sides of Fiona's face. "This cannot be."

Like autumn leaves from a tree, her hands drifted back to her lap.

She continued, "It doesn't seem possible, but am I here to talk to you. Why? Are you something or just a spoiled girl standing on the edge of darkness? Come closer, young lady."

Fiona leaned in. The old woman's wattled skin smelled like old mushrooms. Her sparse mustache was composed of long, black hairs.

"By the soul of Nabi Khadra, I'm sorry, child, but you have a long path in front of you—and not an easy one. I can't believe this. There are a billion youngsters in the world, but the long fingers of Dhul-Qarnayn touched *you* and I'm here. But, why?"

The woman's unconscious fingers drifted to a leather pouch hanging around her neck by a string. Inside, things clinked like glass.

"What's in the bag?" Fiona said.

"Ah, a curious girl, eh? Very well, I will show you."

Onto a brown palm with skin like old bark, she poured out gleaming orbs. They were bright-blue, so blue they hurt Fiona's eyes. She could not take her eyes off them.

"It's my birthday," Fiona said.

"So?"

She made her cutest expression.

"Those marbles would be a wonderful gift."

"Marbles?" The old woman laughed. "To you, these precious gems are a child's marbles?" She considered. "You have a tough stretch coming, so why not?"

She held out the sack and poured the stones into Fiona's cupped palms.

"Thank you, thank you, thank you," Fiona said.

In a flash she turned on her heels and dashed into the house.

The old woman mumbled, "For what is coming, no one will blame you for being a coward. But, young lady, when the time comes, you'll have to stand tall and risk everything. I hope you find it in yourself to do what needs to be done."

Fiona was long gone.

In the house on feet as light as air, she climbed the stairs and darted into her room. The room was pink. Pink carpet. Pink wallpaper. Pink bedspread. She rolled the marbles onto the floor then pushed them around with her little finger. They caught sunlight and amplified it. Each sparkled like a little blue sun, each the same, but different. For a minute, she was lost in them, but her mother called and broke the spell.

"Cake, Fiona. Cake."

She gathered the stones and dropped them one-by-one into frilly, mate-less sock. After tucking the bundle in the back of the bottom drawer of her wardrobe, she stood.

"I'm coming," she whispered.

While tip-toeing down the stairs, she noticed her father's whiskey bottle was empty and he was gone. She felt nothing but relief. For now, there was no need to creep. Heedless of the racket, she bounded down the rest of the stairs.

The cake tasted good and the marbles were soon forgotten.

However, her father was truly gone. Gone-gone.

He never came back.

In a month, her mother left too—permanently taken by pills and vodka. Also gone were the huge house, the pink bedroom and her perfect life. The marbles went into a moving carton—a forgotten one lost somewhere along the way.

Foster homes were not—they weren't homes at all. Slowly, Fiona's special sparkle faded and she learned to be afraid of every little thing.

At 18, scarred and wary, she worked and built a modest, but independent life. In her cottage, night after night over a steaming cup of tea, she slowly let magic come back in.

Inside, there would always be a little girl with a perfect life—along side the broken teenager who learned to trust nothing and no one. Inside, everyone has contradictions. Fiona's were vivid and stark.

Life is a Dream within a Dream

FIONA KNEW SHE was dreaming because the colors assaulting her eyes were unreal: lurid and cartoonish. The bright light pouring through the toy shop windows was devoid of heat and the pull of gravity on her molecules was weak—she knew she must tread carefully because any extra bounce to her step would make her fly into the air and bang her head on the ceiling.

She was sure she'd never seen this shop before, but felt calm—after all, being safely asleep in her bed, there was nothing here that could hurt her. Besides, for Fiona, the barrier between the dreaming and waking worlds was tenuous—she was accustomed to life feeling like a hallucination and dreams feeling real.

Outside the shop, it was a beautiful sunny day; pedestrians strolled on the sidewalk as if there was nowhere to go—except for the little girl who, giggling with glee, raced by like a gazelle.

Gazelle?

Fiona wondered where the *gazelle* image came from. This toyshop was not in Africa. She was glad to be dreaming because in slumberland, images need not make literal sense.

The shop was an odd, abandoned place. Where were the clerk, the cashier and the people who answered questions and stocked the shelves? Why was she wandering around unsupervised?

A large puzzle was spread across the floor—baby's first puzzle—with hopscotch numbers, green frogs and lily pads.

Were there people in the world who would actually buy such a thing?

Bright sunlight. A stuffed giraffe. She felt as if she was going mad. What was the expression? *Toys in the attic.* The image brought a smile to her sleeping lips.

With an aimless amble, she drifted through the store admiring toys that could not really exist—like balls decorated with bizarre beady-eyed frogs grinning with lurid red mouths.

Any child who saw such a sight would surely run away screaming. What must the Chinese factory workers who make these things think of us?

There was an absurd striped elephant in lollypop colors—it made her think of the stuffed elephants her father brought home after a business trip. She still had them, somewhere, packed in a trunk. The elephant called to her—it wanted to be taken home—but she ignored its pleas.

On a shelf, a precious sliced plastic apple.

A miniature stove and sink.

A toy pizza cutter.

She was alone; there was no one else in the whole universe. Or was she? There was giggling, but from where? The walls? There was no one to be seen.

Except...

Except for a fleeting glimpse of a small figure running through a doorway. But, no one was there; the backroom was quiet and empty. Then, behind her, running feet on a stairway and more giggling. Someone teasing her.

Hesitantly, she followed the trail up a creaky staircase. And there, in a colorful dress echoing the psychedelic elephant: a happy, carefree wisp of girl ran like the wind. Fiona picked up the pace and followed through a forest of colorful children's books where the girl, humming a vaguely familiar tune, spun like a top and disappeared behind a shelf.

"Hello?" Fiona said.

The floor was clear before, but now there was a picture. Fiona bent down to pick it up. A Tinkerbelle faerie surrounded by flowers—bluebells and brown-eyed Susans. In a blink of an eye, the giggling girl appeared behind the picture—with the grinning elephant clasped in her arms. Fiona studied her and searched for something appropriate to say. In her hair, the girl had a lovely blue ribbon that matched her dress.

"That's a pretty ribbon," Fiona said. "I'd call it blue—ocean blue. Do you know ocean blue?"

"Cerulean," the little girl said.

Fiona laughed. This clever girl was older and more clever than she first appeared.

"Right, of course. Cerulean." The girl got up and spun the elephant in joyful circles. "What's your name?"

"My name? My name is…"

At that instant a hand appeared on the girl's shoulder and she quickly turned, but there was no one to be seen.

"Are you all right?" Fiona said.

From downstairs came a tremulous voice.

"What have I told you about wandering off and talking to strangers?"

The girl dropped the elephant and walked to the stairs.

At the bottom, a crone dressed all in black broadcasted an imperious attitude, like a Queen whose will was never to be challenged. Fiona picked up the elephant and followed.

She addressed the woman. "She's a cutie. Small for her age, but she's about to bloom, I can feel it. She'll grow six inches in a year and burst out of everything in her closet."

Fiona handed the little girl the elephant. The sick, tired woman was unimpressed. She gestured.

"Come along, Minnie."

9

The girl placed the elephant back into Fiona's arms and tromped down the stairs and toward the front of the store. The woman gave Fiona a sour look and trailed after her daughter. Mystified, Fiona dashed down the stairs and followed them to the front door.

"You take care of your mommy, Minnie," Fiona quietly said.

Her mother tugged Minnie's arm and they walked though the doorway. From outside, Minnie turned and looked into Fiona's eyes before giving a small wave and running away. Fiona followed through the mishmash-maze of odd toys and stood looking out at the scene on the street. There she saw younger Minnie in a red dress and sweater laughing and talking to a healthier-looking version of her mother. They were happy. With a grand flourish from behind her back, Minnie's mother produced the elephant. Minnie took it, embraced it and twirled in joyous circles before running out of sight down the street.

Minnie's mother turned to Fiona and said one simple word: "Happy." Then she turned and walked away.

The elephant was in Fiona's hand. She raised it and looked into its eyes. Without speaking, she projected the question as strongly as she could.

"What are you trying to tell me?"

But, imaginary elephants don't bother to answer questions. In the morning—other than vaguely formed images—she remembered almost nothing of the dream.

The Beginning—Echoes

FIONA RUBBED HER temples while working through the numbers in her head—adding again to see if the total would come out differently with a fresh calculation.

She had twelve tattered dollars stuffed in her pocketbook, twenty lonely dollars in her checking account and not-quite one-hundred dollars in credit available on her emotionally scarred and domestically abused Visa card. So, should she buy a package of three socks for $9.99 or what she came to Wal-Mart for—one inexpensive pair to replace falling-apart socks with heels repaired twice too often?

Crap. Decisions. Endless decisions.

There was a mirror on a display of reading glasses. After a glance, she tucked untamable, silver-streaked auburn hair behind her ears and pulled her wool watch cap down her forehead. Her hand was in her mouth before she remembered she was trying to stop biting her nails.

Stop, Fiona, just stop.

A little face appeared from behind a display of fleecy Spiderman pajamas. Spiderman's eyes were disturbing, so Fiona tried not to look directly into them. She kneeled and reached for

11

the little girl. Pink cheeks. Thin. Sad eyes. At first glance, the girl seemed to be about six, but Fiona quickly realized her error. The girl was small, but she was at least ten. There was something about the girl—had they met before?

Fiona searched for something to say; she felt like the words coming to mind were from somewhere else, from a forgotten movie or novel.

"That's a pretty ribbon," Fiona said. "I'd call it blue, ocean-blue. Do you know what I mean?"

"Cerulean," the little girl said.

Fiona laughed. "Right. Of course—cerulean. What's your name?"

A bony hand appeared and pulled the little girl backward.

The little girl's mom spoke with a hoarse voice. "What have I told you about wandering off and talking to strangers?"

Fiona stood. The mother wore smudged eyeglasses—to her, the world must look greasy and out of focus.

"She's a cutie," Fiona said. "Small for her age, but she's about to bloom, I can feel it—she'll grow six inches in a year and burst the seams of everything in her closet."

The mother's mouth twisted downward so the right side matched the droopy left side.

Oh. minor-stroke? That must be hard.

"Come along, Minnie," the tired woman said.

Turning, Minnie stumbled as her mother tugged her hand. While walking away, the girl looked over her shoulder.

Fiona waved and didn't speak out loud—mouthing the words. "You take care of your mommy, Minnie."

Returning to the task at hand, Fiona studied a $3.99 pair of low-cut athletic socks, then realized—one week earlier, she'd stood at exactly the same spot and made exactly the same decision.

Socks can wait.

Outside, a rowdy nor'easter made its gusty presence known.

12

Howling winds accompanied driving rain coming from all directions except straight down from the heavens—weather designed to keep good folks safely tucked away indoors, not running around town to not buy socks. Walking to her car, Fiona tried to keep her hood up so rain wouldn't splatter her glasses. Weaving through the menagerie of Wal-Martian cars, she glanced over a few rows.

There was Minnie, bent over and searching the wet pavement. Those passing by glanced down, adjusted their rain gear and kept walking. As Fiona drew closer she saw Minnie and her mom picking up loose change.

"Here, let me help with that."

Minnie beamed. Her mother smiled, but insincerely—the expression didn't survive the long journey between lips and eyes.

Such sad distrust—her pain ran deep.

After fumbling and chasing runaway rollers, they got all they could. After one final scan, Fiona nabbed an errant, rain-soaked penny.

Gotcha.

These two needed help and it wouldn't take much to get them through the day. Fiona could invite them to her house and stoke the fireplace to warm their bones and chase away the clammy cold. She could heat up a pot of milk for hot chocolate and serve it in steaming mugs with sacrificial marshmallows that would melt into a creamy froth.

Her fingers twitched as she imagined healing and soothing spices that could be sprinkled and mixed. Ayurvedic herbs and organic Gotu Kola leaf. Fresh-ground Bourbon vanilla bean. Black Sumerian poppy seeds. The anticipated taste was vivid on her tongue.

Fiona deduced several truths about Minnie and her mom. For example, death hovered around Minnie's mom's shoulders—the next stage of her journey was imminent and this fact weighed on both mother and daughter. Fiona wished she could reach out and *touch* them and let them know the transition from pain to peace should not frighten them so—the body is a package and for its time, the package holds the soul. It was logical to be sad about the end of the fleeting time in one package, but there was no need to let terror kill transient instances of joy. While the flower is in bloom, it should enjoy the kiss of the sun, regardless of tomorrow's inevitable wilt and decay.

In a flash, Fiona knew Minnie's mother's name. *Vivian.* How did she know—and why? Over her years on Earth, these insights were things she learned to accept without question.

Fiona felt the pull; she longed to reach out to Minnie's mother with a helping hand, but Vivian's wounds were deep—she was unprepared to accept warm comfort from the universe. Spooked by things she couldn't understand, she would run and run and never stop. It was one thing to transmit, but the receiver had to be turned on and tuned in.

Don't press it, Fiona. Now is not the time. You've already pushed the boundaries with this woman.

"Thanks," uttered the mother—this time with a faint suggestion of sincere warmth in her smile. Clutching her money, she could relax a little.

"Get home safely," Fiona said. "Seems like a good one coming in."

While Minnie waved and grinned like a jack-o-lantern, her mom discovered another smile and it was like a stranger on her face—a transient foreigner bearing gifts.

That's all that can be done for now.

Their rusted-out Ford eventually started. After a final wave, they drove off and Fiona finished her sloshy journey across the parking lot to her faded purple VW Bug, where she shed her wet jacket. She was drenched and sodden.

Part of her craved music—she reached out to turn on the radio, but a quiet voice spoke from within.

Take a minute of quiet. What just happened?

Over time, she'd learned that every random act of kindness was a minuscule mustard seed that could sprout and take root—who knew how, why or when? Do what you can and hope for the best.

After putting the key in the ignition, she willed the old Bug to start. It did—another minor miracle.

She lovingly patted the dashboard and said, "Good girl. Stick with me a bit longer and we'll make it through the winter together."

While driving through the maze of shoppers and escaping cars, she thought about Minnie and her mom. Was it simply too much trouble to lend a helping hand in the rain when the storm devil dances and capers? How could people walk by and do nothing?

It was hard to know why people did things even when they were nice things. Someone holds a door open for you—was it simple kindness or did they do it for appearance sake? What floated through people's minds when they decided whether or not to help a stranger? The purest compassion would be unconscious, not even thinking it through—not feeling sorry for the poor wretch, just experiencing the quick intuition that there's a soul in the rain picking up spilled change with a child and we should brave the torrent and gale with them if only for a moment. For a brief span of time, we should share their burden. Simple acts, easily done. Why weren't they more common?

What would the Earth look like if the world woke one day to witness seeds of kindness sprouting in the sun? With these thoughts marinating, Fiona imagined the approaching comfort of home and the tea she would brew.

Tea, hot tea steeped with magical, exotic herbs, was an indulgence. Lost in thoughts about Minnie, her mom, compassion and tea, she suddenly remembered—she was running low on lavender and cardamom. After making the lane change to go to the herb shoppe, she passed a man standing on the side of the road—a very wet man holding a soggy cardboard sign. In a fraction of a second, she raced by, but was able to read the scrawl.

...will take a ride to anywhere...

She looked in her rear-view mirror—he'd turned his head to stare after her. Through her. Into her. How could that be? She shook her head to dispel the unwelcome thoughts. There was insolence in his eyes, so she resisted the compassionate impulse to stop.

Enjoy the cold rain a while longer, brash young man.

At the herb shoppe, she inhaled the warmth and aroma on offer. Sanctuary. The shopkeeper was an older woman radiating warmth like smoldering logs in a fire—steady and strong, warm and inviting. She had a cheerful, ever-present twinkle in her eyes and her face was careworn by time, but unstressed; she was truly a beautiful human being.

"What are you after today, love?"

"I'm out of lavender and cardamom. Cold season is here and I need to make a strong tea to ward off the booger bugs."

"Is that all?"

"Yes."

"Hmm—I'm not so sure."

She sees inside me—sees my churning whirlpool of emotions. Good thing she's harmless.

"I think," the woman said, "you need a touch of Malaysian nutmeg oil for your afternoon tea. Just a drop—no more or you'll have nightmares. No charge, take it and be happy."

The woman put a paper-wrapped bundle in Fiona's shopping bag. Fiona shrugged and paid for the rest. There was no arguing— the shopkeeper was always right.

After sharing a companionable hug, Fiona picked up her parcel. Back out in the wet world, twilight came on; it was her favorite time of day. Dusk. The between-time when the veil between the worlds was thinnest and magic swirled. It was the

16

border between beginning and end where possibilities were endless and potentiated convergence existed without earthly bound.

She slipped into her old Bug, rubbed the dashboard for luck and once again, the car purred to life.

"Let's head home, girl, it's been a day."

As she buzzed and rattled back onto the main road, she approached the spot where the man had been, but didn't immediately see him. Inexplicably, he intrigued her and she realized her unconscious hope that he'd still be there. Drawing closer, his misty outline drifted into focus. There he was—no longer standing, but crouched on the gravel shoulder like a gargoyle atop a cathedral. He had covered himself with a scrap of tarp against the driving rain. Still holding up his sign, his head was bowed.

Compassion had to be tempered by logic; she *knew* it was generally unsafe to pick up strangers on the highway, but an inner voice told her told it was all right this one time—she couldn't leave him there. Besides, what's was worst he could do?

Unbidden images of rape, murder and body parts in plastic bags flooded her mind.

Stop it, Fiona.

As the internal debate raged, her car, as if having a mind of its own, pulled up beside him. He lifted his head and smiled an unsurprised smile—a smug, infuriating and self-confident grin.

She didn't know him, but she was already annoyed. Regardless, her hand was on the crank and down rolled the window.

"Do you need help?"

"Not particularly. But perhaps you do."

"I'm not the one freezing in the driving rain under a tarp at twilight."

Oh, Fiona, was this smart-ass sarcasm necessary?

"I'm sorry," he said, "was I being impolite?"

"It's okay, I expect nothing less."

It felt odd—as if they were in the middle of a long conversation—not at the beginning of a fresh, new one. She felt as if she knew him, but from where?

"It's a small car, but hop in."

She moved the aromatic herbs and random papers to the back.

Would the clutter bother him?

Lordy, Fiona. The man is a road bum. He would thank providence to have a warm, dry place to hide from the rain, no matter how messy.

"I suppose I could fit a ride with you into my busy schedule," he said.

She could already tell dealing with him would be impossible. Her foot twitched with the impulse to floor the gas pedal and race away as fast as the lazy little Bug could manage, but then he was in—backpack, folded tarp, wool hat—and toothy, vexing smirk.

Getting to Know You

THE WET STRANGER settled in.

"Good thing you're not huge or you'd never fit."

Oh, geesh, when will that censor in my head ever kick in? No man appreciates the implication he's small. Why not just call him a little person? A dwarf? A midget. And ladies need to be careful about double-entendres. Will the man fit? Fit? Nice, Fiona, good job.

"You can stop second-guessing and wishing you could take back your words—I'm not offended. My name is Sean. Pleasure to meet you and thanks for picking me up."

Fiona was dumbstruck.

What have I gotten myself into? What can I say that's safe? I shouldn't give him my name—that will give him the beginning of power over me.

"I'm Fiona."

They shook hands. He tossed his backpack into her back seat. As it flew by her head she felt energy from it; something old and mysterious. Magnetic. Electrostatic. Sean watched as it passed by her head and smiled. He reached out and started fiddling with the heat control. She batted at his hand, but he evaded her and then

19

turned on the car stereo—her music played softly, faintly—nearly inaudible.

"Cute car, it suits you. I like the flowers and the 'Om' bumpersticker. Whatcha listening to?"

Okay, who is this cat?

"Um, Trevor Hall. Most people haven't heard of..."

"Oh, he's one of my favorites. For a young kid he's got his shit together, pretty impressive if you ask me. I saw him and Michael Franti on a Rombello cruise over the summer—awesome show."

Unbidden, a melody formed in her head.

Stuck in the storm, but there's no need to mourn
You're my roof, you're my shelter,
Your love keeps me warm
We sail away, you and I...[1]

A fellow music hound stepping from a half-formed dream into my car? I'm forty and I've lived a life. There should be few surprises left for me.

While watching the road, she flicked her eyes toward the stranger until she had a sense of him.

Medium build, height-weight proportionate with broad shoulders. Curly salt-and-pepper hair worn to mid-back. Normally she wasn't a 'beard girl', but his shaggy goatee suited him. When he looked in her direction it was his eyes that got her. Piercing and black like a raven. He could see through her—into her. She knew him. *Knew* him. She felt comfortable. Was he hypnotizing her? Nah—she wasn't that easy. He had well-fitting jeans, black motorcycle boots and a black leather jacket. He smelled like a wet dog.

"Where're you headed?" she said.

---

[1] *All I Ever Know*, David Lichens and Trevor Hall, © EMI Music Publishing

the daydreaming Vivian the chance to venture into wonderful, high-end homes. It wasn't in her to be jealous. At the expense of relationships and peace of mind, these people worked hard for what they had.

She would envision her and Minnie living in one of these grand palaces with high ceilings, crown moldings, granite countertops and hardwood floors where the cold Maine climate was held off by radiant heating in the floors, good insulation, triple-paned windows and powerful, forced-air furnaces. These were homes where shiny cars lived in garages nicer than their apartment. The wealth of others did not damage them—Vivian and Minnie were as warm and satisfied as they could be considering Vivian's illness.

She wanted more for her daughter and sensed in Minnie a grand purpose and destiny. Minnie was extraordinarily clever and—regal. That was a good, descriptive word for her: regal, she overflowed with dignity and grace. She glowed. Was this just motherly pride and wishful thinking? Isn't this what every mother sees when looking at her child?

No, Minnie was special. She had a connection to the Earth. She spoke to animals and oft times seemed to know the thoughts of others before they were spoken—she had an eerie sense of things before they happened.

Someday her ship will come in, perhaps long after I am gone.

Craig, Minnie's father, abandoned them less than a year after Minnie was born. He was a wanderer—a lovely, charming and handsome man—eloquent, dashing and quick-witted with a thick mane of auburn hair, a twinkle in his eye and a hearty laugh. His people were Irish Travelers and constitutionally unsuited for the daily routine of regular work. He worked when he needed money for drink and drank when he had money. He was not a mean drunk—when inebriated and sufficiently lubricated he was cheerful—a soulful folksinger, story-teller and jokester. Great company in the pub, but not so good at holding onto the rent money to pay the bill by the fifth day of the month.

"Minnie," he said, "was a mistake." He did not mean this in a cruel way, he simply meant she was unplanned, but Vivian corrected him. "No," she would say. "Minerva was a surprise— there's a big difference."

To her, Minnie was a wonderful blessing completing her in ways she never knew was possible. Minnie didn't remember much about her father—he was a vague shadow cast across her memories. Vivien kept a picture of him next to her bed, and kissed her fingers and then the picture every night before slipping into fitful sleep. She didn't love him as he was, she loved the man it was in him to be.

She found no solace when her eyes were closed. When she dreamt, it was always of dark places and dark times. Deep inside, she knew her time in this life was short and the thought of leaving Minnie behind haunted and tormented her. She tried her best to keep these thoughts from taking over and polluting their daily life, but it was written in the lines in her face and clearly painted in her eyes. Clever Minnie knew as well; she could smell the lurking miasma of death emanating from her mother's skin.

Today, however, was a day when Vivian was still here and walking the Earth. It was not to be wasted—she would live it for dear little Minnie. She walked to the kitchen cabinet and looked over what was available.

"Whatcha want for dinner, Minnie? We have great options if you're in the mood for either spaghetti or grilled cheese."

Vivian never thought about it, but even many years prior, she never used baby talk with the quick-witted, scary-smart Minnie. Others commented that Minnie might be eleven, but she could pass for a small, eloquent teenager.

"What's easier for you to make, mom?"

She was such a sweet child. Vivian knew Minnie's favorite was grilled cheese but canned spaghetti was easier.

"How's grilled cheese and bologna sound? I'll make it extra

cheesy for you."

Minnie squealed with delight; she ran over to hug her mom.

Grilled cheese it is.

Vivien worked on carving slices from a big block of cheddar while Minnie flopped on the floor—pulling out her treasured bag of marbles—rolling them around and flicking them off each other.

She'd always loved marbles. One day a small blue satchel bag of them mysteriously appeared outside their front door. Neither she nor her mom could explain where they came from—Minnie thought her mom secretly bought them from the dollar store and Vivian thought they came from a friend taking pity on their no-budget for toys. They humored each other by pretending they had magically appeared from nowhere.

They were Minnie's favorite things to play with. She had other toys, mainly garish plastic figurines from Burger King and McDonalds. For cost and nutrition reasons, they never ate at these places, but people collected the toys and brought them around, but they stayed in a drawer in Minnie's room while she played with her marbles. For some reason, the clicking of the gleaming, glossy orbs soothed and enchanted her.

She sat for hours rolling them around in her hands or making geometric constellations with them on the carpet. Sometimes she would get her drawing book and sketch them in patterns and formations—seeing things in them only she could see. Whenever she told her mom they were magic marbles, Vivien said nary a word about it, she simply smiled.

Who am I to say they were or weren't magic?

All Vivien knew was that one day they appeared and they brought her daughter great joy; so in that sense, they *were* magical.

Close enough.

Soon, the smell of grilled cheese and melted butter filled the small apartment. While Minnie's mouth watered, she caught the sound of her mom humming—her mom was seldom happy, so when she hummed it was beautiful music to Minnie's ears.

"Time for dinner," Vivian said.

Minnie was real good with the marbles; she always picked them up and never left any underfoot. She shepherded them into their satchel bag, then scooted out the dining set chair and clambered up. At her place at the table, Vivien placed a hot sandwich with accompanying heap of steamed snow peas.

"Here ya go, kiddo. Hope it pleases the princess."

Minnie smiled up at her mom.

Princess.

Minnie loved the sound of that word.

"Looks yummy, Mommy, thank you."

Her mom sat down and joined her. She had only half a sandwich and two pea pods.

"Not hungry, mom?"

"You eat, Minnie, go ahead. My stomach bothers me a bit."

Of late, Vivien's health had gone steadily downhill. She'd been coughing a lot—bringing up phlegm splotchy with blood. Every time she coughed she scolded herself for taking up smoking in high school and she wondered how things would be different if she'd never discovered the love of nicotine—smoking with Craig under a tree near a far corner of an isolated stretch of chain link fence. But, that was neither here nor there—she now had to live with the consequences of her youthful foolishness.

She watched Minnie eat the grilled cheese sandwich. Despite everything—no father, a modest home and few frills in her young life, this was a happy child. Vivian marveled at the fire burning in her, a soulful glow emanating from a deep-seated zest for life. She had a fighter's spirit and never let anything get her down, at least not for long. She'd learned so much from Minnie over the few years since she'd been blessed enough to have birthed her into this life. Her Minnie—such a wonderful child.

They finished their dinner and Minnie picked up the plates.

"Tonight I'll wash them," she said.

Vivien smiled. She knew that meant doing a second wash after little Minnie but that was okay. Minnie did her best and she was always so proud to help.

After the dish chores, Minnie snuggled with her mom on the couch. Vivien pulled up a soft blanket up to cover them while they settled in to watch a spot of TV—a PBS show about dragons suited them both fine.

"Do you think dragons were ever for real, mom?"

"I don't know for sure, Minnie. You can't believe everything you see on the television, but this show makes a reasonable case. After it's over, we'll see what *you* think."

Under the blanket, they burrowed deeply into the couch cushions as the winds outside howled and the cold rain spattered against the windows.

Vivien hugged her daughter closer.

Bad weather, bad omens.

Home Suite Home

FIONA LIVED IN a small farmhouse at the edge of the Falmouth Town Forest. When she first saw the old house she knew it was home—when she walked into the house it spoke to her. A young house at two-hundred years of age, it needed work but had character. It had warmth. It held promise. So it became hers. A modest, simple house at the edge of the forest, with just enough land to keep her busy keeping up with the seasonal changes and challenges living in Maine bestows upon those hearty enough to call home this harsh, beautiful land.

She had neighbors on either side—the best kind of neighbors to have; they kept to themselves but were always there to help if needed. No forced conversations, no uncomfortable social gatherings, just a quiet, peaceful co-existence.

Fiona had had plenty of loves in her life—they came in many shapes and sizes and ways of being, but they never overstayed their welcome. Fiona's simplicity was complex. Always in her head, her feet were rarely on the ground and she preferred flying with the wind, playing among the stars and calling the Moon her mother. The loves in her life lingered as long as they should, enchanted by her ways, but when it became too much and they wanted to

Lady in Waiting

TO MAKE A perfect hard-cooked egg, put it in cold water, heat it on the stove until the water reaches a rolling boil, turn off the heat, cover the pan for fifteen minutes, then gently introduce the hot egg to cold water. While waiting for the water to boil, Vivian leaned against the kitchen counter and looked around.

I used to be a great housekeeper.

That was before Craig left her and Minnie—and before her incident. *Incident.* A soft, spongy word for what the ER doctor described as a minor blood clot stroke. It was not such a serious *incident*, but was a foreshadowing of the big one coming—coming along as surely as night follows day. As surely as the end follows the beginning. As surely as death follows life. These things happen, no one knows how or when or why, the doctor had said with sad resignation, but Vivian knew better. Through his factotum, The Thinn Man, The Black Prince had reached out and touched her.

She thought back to the events of the previous six long months.

According to the doctor, she should be taking blood-thinners, but they were expensive—even at Wal-Mart they were more than she could afford when the choice was between a tin of tuna for Minnie's dinner or a pill. Besides, this medical technology was helpless against the blood magick of the Black Faerie King.

The University of South Portland hosted a gleaning program set up in a rundown storefront near the waterfront on Franklin Street. It was an old brick building with cracked windows—cold in the winter and hot in the summer. On a whitewashed wall, someone had painted a giant mural of a cartoon family—mom, dad, two sons and a daughter—wearing toothy grins and patched clothing. The caption said, "Glean—gather the grain left behind by reapers."

Patiently, with Minnie in tow, Vivian waited in line for a look at a beleaguered bushel basket of smallish oranges. A shaggy-haired student with a scraggly beard and coils of Rastafarian hair topped off with a colorful Bob Marley knitted slouch hat guarded the fruit—the brownish bananas, the bruised pears and the midget oranges. The Rastafarian handed Minnie a silver-dollar-sized oatmeal-raisin cookie.

"It's one per person," he said, with a gentle tone.

"Of course," Vivian said. For one of the few times since Craig left, she felt good—even halfway cheerful. There was no reason except the sun peeking through the clouds, the small check arriving from the Labor and Industries insurance fund and the small, perfect oranges looking heaven-sent and delicious. As she reached for one, she felt a hand on her left shoulder. She looked down to see a silver ring on a man's finger—with a stone as ruby-red as blood and as big as a maraschino cherry.

She looked back. The man was tall, taller than tall, well over six-feet. He wore a long, black rain jacket with a wide belt pulled tightly around his skinny waist. The belt's buckle was a shiny silver moon.

Her innocent eyes traveled up his body, then froze on his face. In the dappled sunlight, she was sure she imagined it, but his face seemed to crawl with geometric scars. He wore sunglasses with round, tiny amber lenses. Thin lips. Big teeth in his grin like yellow slats in the picket fence around a down east graveyard.

Still no fear.

"Hello?" Minnie's mother said. "You're probably tired of people asking if you play basketball, but goodness me, you have the build for it."

The man's voice was a deep, resonant rumble—if basketball didn't work out for him, he could try singing blues in a Crossroads bar.

"You look happy," the man said. "Having a good day?"

"Yes," Vivian said. Thinking about it for an instant, she was surprised. After Craig left, she was sure there was no joy left in the world. "I guess I am."

"Mom," Minnie said.

The man had not let go—he squeezed her shoulder. Hard.

Vivian felt a first faint brush stroke of unease.

"Not now, little Minnie, I'm talking."

Minnie persisted.

"Mom?"

"Excuse me," Vivian said to the man. He lifted his hand and held it up, palm out. It was an odd gesture, but she thought nothing of it. She bent over to talk to Minnie. With a thumb, she brushed cookie crumbs from Minnie's mouth. "Polite little girls do not interrupt when adults are talking. What is it?"

"He's a bad man, Mommy."

"No, it's okay, Minnie." She stood and watched the man walk off and disappear out the front door. "Besides, see? He's gone."

She turned and held out her green shopping bag and the suburban Rastafarian dropped in two oranges. Shuffling the bag so she could free up a hand, Vivian pulled one out and studied it. It was perfectly round—mottled with brown and green patches.

"The simple things can be the most beautiful."

The Rastafarian laughed.

"Once you figure that out," he said, "the rest of life is easy."

Vivian, carefree for the last time, shared his laugh.

"Come on, Minnie," she said while tugging the youngster's hand. Halfway across the room, while walking toward the exit, she felt a tingling on her left side. It didn't hurt; it was as if her shoulder had been resting at an odd angle on the couch and fell asleep. The tingle turned into numbness. The next thing she knew, she was on the floor surrounded by scattered cucumbers and a bundle of carrots.

The Rastafarian rushed over.

"Did you slip?" he said.

She tried to tell him, but her mind was foggy and shredded like...

Like what?

The images in her mind were irrational and stupid.

She was shredded like wheat. Shredded like a fence post. Shredded like a hot air balloon falling from the sky. Shredded like a laughing King holding a leather whip and a wedding ring.

I'm in trouble.

"I'll call an ambulance," the Rastafarian said.

Good idea, Vivian thought.

Regaining her senses, Vivian picked up the sauce pan's lid to cover the egg and found herself on the floor again. The lid hit the floor with a *spang* and rolled across the kitchen. Before, there was no pain, but not this time; her left side felt shredded—ripped to pieces by one of Stephen King's voracious industrial machines.

No, no, not now. At the least, I need to turn that burner off. Minnie won't know what to do.

Minnie ran up and slid across the floor on her knees.

You'll ruin your tights, girl.

"Mom," Minnie said.

"I love you like a cloud loves a rainbow," Vivian tried to say, but couldn't. "Ngghh," is what came from her mouth.

Everyone gets their quota of days of walking the Earth—their days to live and cry and be over-filled with bliss and struggle and strife and sleep and holding your child and feeling your man give you everything and bleeding and sneezing and helplessly hoping for a bad day to end. Then, soon enough, it's over.

For Minnie's mom, that day was this one.

Minnie held her mother's hand as tightly as she could—as if this grip could hold something back from the dark, mysterious frontier. It didn't work. It never does.

Kneeling Minnie released her mother's hand and gently patted her mother's fine, silvery hair. With her other hand, she slowly reached up and turned off the stove burner.

The Echoes of History

ONCE FIONA FINISHED pouring the tea, she wandered into the big room where the fireplace lived. Surprised, she nearly dropped the mugs.

Sean had the room alight with a million candles of all shapes, sizes and colors. Where did they all come from? It looked like a billion stars had landed in the room. Incense smoldered atop the fireplace mantel. He had plugged his iPod into a miniature wooden speaker.

Was that Blackmore's Night playing, or was it Woodland?

With her mind swirling, she couldn't tell, but the music spoke to something deep within her.

"Where did you—how did you—I was only in the kitchen for a few moments, how did you. . .?"

Her voice trailed off in a whisper and her eyes were as wide as a child's when seeing a faerie for the first time.

With an innocent, *who-me* expression, Sean sat in his chair and smiled.

"What?" he said.

"Don't *what* me, Sean, you know what I'm talking about. An hour ago there were seventeen candles in this house and that's counting a stub with maybe a minute left in it, tops."

"I just thought it was time someone enchanted *you* for a change."

Fiona felt color flood to her cheeks. She was not a woman prone to embarrassment but suddenly she felt shy and vulnerable.

What in the world was happening?

She looked at Sean's feet where his backpack rested.

"What else are you carrying in that magic bag?"

"In time, I will show you everything. For now, have a seat—drink tea with me and we'll talk."

Did her feet move? It was as if she floated to the couch—which felt warm and squishy as it enfolded her. Sean walked over and sat beside her. Thigh to thigh, they comfortably gazed into the cozy, creaky-crackling fire. Flames jumped and danced. By turning her eyes to the side—peripherally in flickers and gauzy waves—the fire dragon could be seen.

Glancing at Sean, she sipped tea and felt the magic elixir swim inside her. Leaning back and craning his neck, he looked at her and smiled. No words were exchanged while a comfortable, magnetic longing grew and surrounded them like a warm, fuzzy blanket.

"How's your hearing?"

"What do you mean?"

"Oh, come on, Fiona. I know you're losing your hearing and I know you suffer. I was just wondering how that was going for you."

"I don't recall mentioning anything about my hearing to you or anyone else."

"No, you didn't. But I know you, Fiona, more than you think, perhaps even more than you know yourself. Here's another mystery to try on for size. That mermaid tattoo on the top of your left foot—she's smiling but her eyes are full of sorrow. Your tattoo artist gave her your body and face, down to the sad eyes. How do you suppose I know about that?"

"You *don't* know about it because I've had socks on all day—

unless you've been creeping around peeping in windows or you know my ink artist. You know nothing about my mermaid or any of my other tattoos. Period. Topic closed."

Fiona's heart beat faster and faster, yet, despite the banter, she was strangely comfortable. The facts before her said he was a creepy stranger, but her heart was at ease.

Odd. At the sight of the candles, I should have run away screaming, but here I sit. Clearly, Sean is a stalker of the worst sort, but my hands are steady and my thoughts are calm.

She took a sip of tea, then another and then another.

Get a grip, Fiona. He's not dangerous. Why you know that or why you think you know—that's the mystery.

Think, Fiona. What the heck is going on?

Sean got up from the couch and from his magic bag, pulled a wooden recorder. From head to toe, she felt a zing of electricity. She *knew* that instrument.

"Do you recognize this, Fiona? I made it for you a long time ago."

He started playing along with the music coming from his iPod. Or was it his own song? The sounds melded together perfectly; she couldn't tell where the recording began and Sean's playing ended.

Was it the tea?

No, she had made it herself and there was nothing extraordinarily hallucinogenic in this batch.

Was it the fire? The candles? The incense?

Ah, the incense. She felt smoky tendrils like warm fingers on the back of her neck.

She sank further into the couch's embrace and let her eyes drift closed. As he sang, his hypnotic voice was smooth and carefully modulated. She knew the tricks for drawing the subconscious into the hard-edged physical world and felt like she should be immune, but clearly, not. Not at all.

"Yes, Fiona. Close your eyes and go back in time. You'll

understand on the other side. I'll keep watch over your body. No harm will come to you, I promise."

Soft, calm words that captured her heart like a dove held in toddler's hands—protecting and gently holding.

She gave herself permission to relax and surrender to what this night might offer.

When Fiona opened her eyes, she wasn't in her house. She stood in front of a round house, almost like a yurt, but not; it was something more ancient and magical. It was a round house bearing a thatched, mossy roof. There were small windows, but no glass.

She looked down at her hands; they were hers but they weren't. She looked down at her clothes. Barefoot and wearing a smock type dress for lack of a better word, taupe in color with a woven rope cinched around her waist. Her hair was the same, only not. It was longer, down to her waist, and silvery in a color reminiscent of the shimmery colorescence of tinsel.

A white owl flew down and perched on her shoulder.

Ahh, this I recognize.

It was Selene, a large owl, her guide. Selene is why she had a white owl tattooed on her right forearm. Selene had been with her through several lifetimes.

"Ohhhhhhh—I'm in one of my past lives—I get it now."

A red-furred fox wandered near. He glanced at her and then lay down in a basket lined with an old flannel shirt.

Ahhh, my other guide.

She had him tattooed on her right hip.

No sooner did that thought flash through did it fade away. She lived this life for this moment.

Out of the hut came Sean, only it was not Sean. He was dressed similarly in handmade, taupe trousers covering his knees and a loose cotton shirt with a notched collar exposing the bones of his upper chest. His skin was darker, like he worked in the sun. His hair was longer, though with the same curly mass, but without the grey. He wore a full beard, but his raven-black eyes, they were the same.

So this is how I know him.

"I promise to haul more wood when I get back. I won't be gone long; I just need some space, okay? Seekers have been in and out of her for days and I can't breathe, Ceara. I'll be back before the sun reaches the top of magnum tree, okay? Don't be mad."

"Fine."

"You're angry."

"No. Yes. I don't know. I just know when you say you won't be gone long, you lose track of time and it will be a cold night and I can't carry wood right now with my foot like this but go and find your air and please don't be gone so long."

"Sometimes you treat me like your servant, Ceara. Is it any wonder why I need space sometimes?"

"Faolan, that's not fair. You are my love, not my servant. The spirits have been agitated lately and the Earth speaks and cries. Am I to ignore that and play with you in the woods all day?"

"Always with the responsibilities and answers. Fine. Do as you will and I'll be back soon, I promise."

He held her and kissed her and skipped on his way.

"Ah, so I was a sage of old," thought Fiona.

That would explain her uncanny knowledge of herbs and alchemy and her connection to the Earth and moon.

Ceara—fire in Celtic.

Maybe that's why I'm so enamored with fire.

In an odd dichotomy, she inhabited her alternate self, but, as well, watched with Fiona's objective eyes.

Ceara puttered and assisted the souls who found their way to her cottage; sitting and counseling them and offering remedies and tinctures as needed and reading stones and sticks for signs of this, that and the other. Always Selene was on her shoulder or nearby, protecting and watching.

At one point Ceara looked at the sun hovering over the

massive tree that stood by their house.

Faolan wasn't back yet.

She muttered and shook her head.

Typical.

More time passed. Suddenly Selene rose and flew into the air, as if something called to her, then flew back to perch on Ceara's shoulder. Her attitude that meant one thing: trouble. Ceara grabbed her walking staff.

"Show me, Selene," she said.

Selene took off. Respecting Ceara's foot injury, she waited on a branch when necessary to adjust to Ceara's pace. Their path led through the forest along the path Faolan would have taken—the trail leading to the lake. Once there, Ceara looked around and saw Faolan's clothes strewn across a rock.

"Guess he needed water along with his *space.*"

Selene flew out over the water and came back. Ceara followed her with her eyes. She could barely make out a figure in the water.

"Faolan," she called out.

Hobbling as fast as she could, she found their raft hidden among the reeds. Faolan had made the raft earlier in the spring—it was sturdy, steady and beautiful. After untying its rope, she settled in and paddled as fast as she could out to the figure.

It *was* Faolan.

He wasn't moving. She managed to pull him onto the raft and there he lay, nearly lifeless.

"Don't you leave me, Faolan. Now is not your time to go."

With that Faolan opened his eyes. His lips did not move, but still, he spoke.

"My love, you know a lot and you're a wise, sage healer, but even you cannot hold off death's hands when they reach out and grasp one's soul."

She knew this was all too true—she'd saved many during her years and yet knew death's reach could not be stopped once it settled in with serious intent.

She put Faolan's head into her lap and pushed wet hair away from his face. She needed to see his eyes to ease his passing.

"Why go swimming anyway? You were too tired to swim."

"I wanted to play with the turtles."

"If you die, who will gather wood for my fire?" she said, half scolding and half with laughter.

"I tried calling out for you…" He took her hand. With his dying breath he looked up into her eyes. "I will always be with you, you know that. Now is my time, but it is not yours. I will find you again, Ceara, I swear I will."

With that, he was gone.

Ceara let out a wail as deep and mournful as a lonely wind from the deepest abyss—it came from the depths of her soul. Darkness and sorrow filled her and she no longer wanted to live. If she could not save him or turn back the hands of time, what use was she? She felt helpless and alone.

Selene, with claws clamped on the raft's lamppost, perched next to her and wept with a wail that could be heard for miles. Ceara paddled back to shore. She had no strength nor the will to drag him back up to her beloved enchanted cottage, their cottage.

No, they would stay here.

She couldn't leave him; she knew his spirit had left his flesh, but she couldn't leave his body to the animals. No, the Earth would not claim him, not yet. She lit a fire and lay on the raft next to him. As night came and the fire blazed, magic filled her body and her spirit.

She whispered to Selene.

"If playing with the turtles is what he wanted to do, then play with them forevermore is what he will do. But I will watch over him so we're never apart."

She gave instructions to Selene—told her what herbs to gather from the woods and the cottage. Selene flew away.

In an hour or a minute, Selene returned.

"Selene, I go now to the world of water. Your physical form is the white owl and it's up to you to choose between the water and the sky."

With claws clenched on the perch and ears perked, Selene stared at the stars and into the dark forest while Ceara created a magic brew. Ceara's grief and sadness was profound and all-consuming. Once the tea was set, she looked to the infinite wisdom written in Selene's moony eyes. Selene knew this is what Ceara had to do and Ceara knew Selene would stay in the air and not follow.

"Selene, you have been my dearest and most trusted friend and you will travel with me through all our lifetimes. At times, I will come back to the surface to get the news and chat with you."

With that, Selene stirred and fluffed her feathers.

Whooo...

It was settled. Ceara drank shape-shifting tea, said the incantations and lay back on the raft to wait for the magic to settle over her. Throughout the night, the transformation worked. First her feet fused, melding together like raindrops mixing with lake water. Then her legs. Her fingers webbed and scales formed on her skin. Gills sprouted and grew on her neck and pumped with the night air.

She was becoming.

Becoming a mermaid.

She would take to the water with her love and live a life with the fish and water spirits and forever guard Faolan and keep him safe—something she couldn't do when she was on land.

Come dawn, the transformation was complete.

She turned fishy eyes to Selene.

Could they still communicate?

"Do I look like a creature worthy of the water?" she said, caressing her new body. Selene looked on with great approval.

Whooo...

With webbed fingers, Ceara leaned over to pat Selene's finely feathered body. There were many things she would miss when giving up walking on the Earth, but her heart no longer belonged to land, it belonged to the water.

Selene understood and would lead those seeking Ceara's aid to the lakeside bank. Ceara slipped into the water and gently pulled cold Faolan after her. There were dark places in the deep water which would be their new home.

Selene flapped her massive wings and soared into the night sky—she was a drifting shadow cast against the Milky Way.

Whooo...

Fiona woke with a start. She was still on the couch, but now lying atop lumpy Sean, who had pulled a quilt over them. Her hand rested on his chest. She lifted her head and looked up at him. He rubbed his hand along her head and wiped away her tears.

"Now you know, Fiona. I told you I'd find you and I have. Shall I go into the woods and fetch wood for *this* fire?" he said with a smirky mouth and a twinkle in his eye.

Fiona laughed and stretched up to kiss him—a sweet kiss echoing from historic lifetimes. She remembered everything about him with that kiss. Pulling away and putting her head back on his chest, her head was filled with an infinite number of swirling thoughts and none at all.

"Forgive yourself for not rescuing me, Fiona. I went too far out and drowned. That was not your fault."

"I'm so sorry, Sean, I should have..."

"Stop, Fiona. I forgave all your sins that very day—let it all go."

With that, an unknown weight lifted from Fiona's shoulders. She emitted a huge cleansing sigh.

Her clothes were restricting her, so she worked them off. All of them. In the candlelight, her skin glowed and her tattoos came to life and moved freely on her skin. Still fully dressed, Sean's eyes wandered over her with hunger.

"Must I do all the work?" she said while loosening his belt.

"I don't want to be accused of taking advantage..."

His comment would have seemed more sincere if he did not need to lift his mouth from her breast to speak. She pressed his head back down to its work. Their bodies were designed to fit together like a lock and a key. In the afterglow, she left a trailing hand on his hairy stomach and drifted away.

"There ya go love," he said. "Sleep now—just sleep."

Fiona slipped away into blissful slumber, knowing a deep peace she'd never known before. She felt whole, though never before remembering feeling incomplete.

Funny how life works.

The next days, weeks and months flew by but it felt as if no time passed at all. The vivid memories of her ancient life faded and her feelings about Sean and how he integrated into her life grew complex and mysterious. It was a bubble, an iridescent bubble and inside it, Fiona and Sean were inseparable. They loved often, sensually and passionately with souls mixing and combining in a perfect recipe. They cooked, drank, sang, lit campfires, played with fireflies and danced under the stars. The moon caressed and blessed them with holy grace and crystalline light. They took hikes and watched the sun rise and set from the tops of mountains, beaches and the forest.

They were blissful days filled with love.

Eventually, she remembered nothing from the old world other than vague, faded images drifting in her peripheral vision when an owl hooted in the woods.

Something always happens; it's just the way of things.

Fiona buried that thought deep within her, but it reared its ugly head every now and again.

One day, he will leave me alone to cry bitter tears on the lakeside under the trees. But now, they danced under the stars, swaying and singing along with a portable stereo.

"I don't want this to end, Sean."

"It will end when it has to, Fiona. Every bubble shines in the sun during its time, then pops and disappears into nothing. You know this, so we must enjoy every morsel we can hold in our grasp because there is a storm on the horizon. Flow, Fiona, flow. Flow as you only you know how…"

"Storm? What storm? What are you talking about?"

"I'm sorry," Sean said. "I can't talk to you about this. You're not ready. For now, build your strength and enjoy what we have before the Queen comes."

Fiona pulled back and pushed him away.

"Queen? What are you talking about? I'm your Queen. There is no other Queen."

"Oh, forget I said anything."

Blarney.

That was her grandfather's word. Blarney. Sean was an undisputed master of it.

Queen?

The word irritated her, but she could not hold onto the thought or emotion.

"I have a surprise for you," he said.

"I don't want a surprise, I want to talk about—wait, what were we talking about? My mind, it slips and slides when I'm with you."

"We were talking about the surprise I have for you."

"What surprise?"

He pulled his rucksack across the ground in front of their fire and loosened the drawstrings. He pulled out something small and hid it from her. She reached for it.

"What is that?"

"Hold on," he said while pushing her away. He held up a loop and blew soap bubbles.

"Mr. Bubble."

The bubbles, wafted by the circulating air of the fire, danced and shimmered in the moonlight. They had their time in the cold air—then popped. It was a simpleminded pleasure, but it was perfect for the moment. Fiona giggled like a schoolgirl.

"Give me that," she said. "You know nothing about making perfect bubbles."

The child's toy amused them for an hour, then they put it aside and let the moonlight soak into their naked, intertwined bodies.

Time passed as it always does, and Fiona grew twitchy. Now and again, Sean would disappear, sometimes for days.

He's entitled to a life of his own; it's not like we're bound to each other; it is in his nature to wander. But where does he go, and what does he do?

When he returned, her discomfort was forgotten.

One day she came in from strolling in the woods and heard Sean talking. He was gone on one of his adventures, wasn't he?

He must have come back while I was outside.

She snuck into the house and planned to surprise him with a welcome-home hug and sloppy kiss when something made her stop.

He was talking, but to whom and about what?

And, what was he using for communication? She didn't have a landline phone and there was still no cell phone coverage in her rural area. Feeling guilty, she crept toward the corner and listened.

"No, she really does not know. She has no idea."

Who? Me?

She felt a surge of lava-hot anger start in her core and spread through her body. Ugly, acidic, unwelcome anger.

Uncomfortable at being a complacent victim of cruel jokes or games, she stomped around the corner.

"Who are you talking to? Who are you talking about?"

He fumbled with something at his ear. It was not a phone; it looked like a small, red, glowing crystal. He palmed it and slipped it into the pocket of his jeans.

He grinned like a politician, a new expression from him—something she'd never seen on his face before.

"Ah, Fiona, I thought you were still outside. Did you dig up some carrots? I'm ready to start my famous barley stew for you."

"Don't charm me with greasy-smooth Sean-patter. I have a right to know what's going on in my house."

"Oh, Fiona, this is not the right time for this conversation. After dinner, I promise, I'll tell you everything, and if not tonight, then later in the week. It's nothing bad, I promise on my mamma's soul. You're not quite ready, that's all. Pearl onions? I hope you didn't forget them, they are vital—essential—to my granny Emma's recipe. Gotta have 'em—they make all the difference."

There was something stirring in the air, she could feel it. There was a tug toward thinking about the fire, the wine, the corded muscles of Sean's body and the taste—already on her tongue—of his handed-down recipe for barley stew with pearl onions. A velvety fog covered the real issue. She hardened her mind against the pull.

"I want you to leave. I'm retracting your welcome in my house."

He pulled produce from the shopping bag and her fridge.

Celery. Tofu. Pearl onions.

"Oh, these will do just fine, Fiona. Perfect. Let's start cooking and make our kitchen magic. What music would you like to cook to tonight?"

He's not leaving. He's never going to leave.

She stared at him. From outside, a ray of sunlight pierced the room and reflected in his eyes while he projected a playful, mischievous, intoxicating innocence.

Forget it, Fiona. It's nothing and all will be explained sooner than soon. All is well. Just be.

Blarney.

"Damn you, Sean, if you won't leave, then I will."

She walked to the door and out to the gravel driveway. He stood on the porch and watched.

She turned the ignition key and the car turned over, but would not catch. Grinding, grinding, it would not start.

Her anger blossomed—she pounded the steering wheel with frustration.

A thousand times in a row, the car starts, but not now?

Guess the car thinks it knows what I need more than I do.

Sean walked to her window and motioned for her to lower it.

"Leave me alone," she said.

"I'm going to help with your car, Fiona. Roll down the window."

She hit the steering wheel with the heels of her hands one more time, then relented and turned the window crank.

"Look at me, Fiona."

She pursed her lips and took a deep breath.

"Fine," she said, "what do you want?"

"I want you to relax. You have the same angry, stubborn streak you had so long ago. I loved it then and I love it now, so calm down. Let your anger go—let it float away on the wind."

She closed her eyes and let her mind drift to a quiet place. Sunlight through trees. Burbling brook. The crisp, cold smell of winter. She held her hands in front of her face and let them relax.

"There are things you already know, Fiona, and things you sense that are not yet in focus—and other things which will be revealed over time. Not long, but not now. Please."

"Okay, I'm calm. Now what?"

Sean smiled.

"Try the car again."

Fiona frowned. She gently placed her hand on the dash and stroked it gently.

"Once again, for me?" she whispered.

She turned the key and the car started instantly. The motor

purred.

"You can go if you like, Fiona, but I'd prefer to open a bottle of wine, turn up the music and fill your house with the irresistible scent of my gran's secret stew. With you, Fiona. With you."

Breathe in. Breathe out. All is one.

"Okay," she said. "Okay."

She reached out to turn off the car's ignition.

The Routine

WITH EVEN THE most dramatic changes, routine settles in quickly—even after life transforms in a space and place on the wild frontier of the unknown.

How many days or weeks or months passed is unknown—Fiona was happy and she didn't care. Besides, time is only an illusion; an artificial construct invented by Mother Nature to prevent the biological machine from confronting unanswerable questions and uncomfortable contradictions. The past is framed by elusive memory while the future is a mass-cloud of endless possibilities and probabilities. The only thing that *really* exists is the current instantaneous moment, but what is that? Chimera, fantasy—a transient wisp of smoke in the wind.

Though, like autumn evolves into winter, transition loomed, but transition to what? Toward what? Was this transition another illusion and instead of making forward progress, was she rotating in pointless circles?

On the kitchen stereo, Antje Duvekot sang; her straightforward voicings and simple, plain instrumentation filled Fiona's heart with boundless joy. She hummed along to *Dandelion* while stirring herbs in her dream tea.

But I am the fourth of July
I'm throwing you a fire in the sky
You could go blind in my light
But you were looking for an orchid
And I will always be a dandelion.[4]

Sean walked up from behind her and wrapped his hands around her waist—reaching under her blouse to cup and caress. He twirled her around and hip-to-hip, they swayed and danced while a cool breeze slipped through the window and tossed her curls. An errant strand fell into her mouth—she poofed it out.

"This unruly hair of mine," she muttered.

"I love it. It's you. Untamed and unkempt. The silver shows more and more—like snail-trails of quicksilver moonlight."

She smiled up at him with a mischievous grin. "Snail slime? You are an eloquent, silver-tongued rogue. A girl must watch herself when she's around you because you could talk the knickers off a Botticelli angel."

He spun her back to her teapot of magic and drifted to the main room. While leaving, he spoke over his shoulder.

"Don't scorch the tea," he said.

Like a mantel picture of a bucolic picnic on a summer day, life was good. Yet, underneath the easy love and food and tea and sweet music and dancing and wine—something was off kilter. Something small and nearly imperceptible, but there nonetheless.

Fiona was sensitive to the subtleties of life, energy and spirit, so she waited for the other shoe to drop, for the butcher's axe to fall. She saw the future in snippets and images both vague and infinitely detailed. Immediate or far into the mists of time, she always had some sense of the span and scope of potential future events—like a wave washing over her head. It could be so vivid

---

[4] *Dandelion*, Antje Duvekot, © 2008 Antje Duvekot, from the album *Boys, Flowers, Miles*, Pantjebear Publishing

that it would take her breath away—like diving in the ocean so deep the surface recedes and disappears. You crave that first gasp of sweet fresh air to dissipate the stale air of your lungs and chase away the oppressive claustrophobia of the water and the pressure and the murky darkness—the cleansing breath that takes you back into the world of the air and sky—the breath that puts you back in sync.

That's what she felt: like impending change was in the air. She waited for the breath of fresh, clean air that changes everything.

Mermaid. Why does the image of a mermaid drift in my mind? What do I know of mermaids?

She finished stirring the teapot and watched herbs swim in a golden-brown whirlpool. Glancing backward to make sure Sean's attention was elsewhere, she waved her fingertips and whispered a few words of incantation.

The eternal prayer: may all good things last forever.

Feeling tingly and alive, her fingers danced and played in the steam. She loved the damp, airy warmth enveloping each finger. She finished playing with the steam and wandered into the other room to find Sean lying on the couch in front of the bay windows with angular sunbeams streaming in and bathing him in soft light.

Nap time?

His eyes were closed and he looked peaceful and comfortable.

Fiona sat on the floor and leaned back against the couch, sipping tea while her fingertips idly traced patterns in the warp and woof of the old carpet—outlining the rug's runes, moving in and around the lumpy levels of the intertwined braids.

Peace is a joy that never overstays its welcome.

Enter the Queen

FIONA WAS UP to her elbows chopping romaine lettuce for a salad when there came a vigorous knocking at the front door.

"Sean, babe, would you see who is pounding? It must be a stranger—all the neighbors know it's unlocked and come right in."

Sean leaned against the doorsill. She couldn't read his expression.

Somber? That's a new one. Resigned? He looks like a customer with a toothache in the waiting room of an oral surgeon.

"Did you hear me?" she said. "Please get the door—I'm in the middle of our salad and the radishes are being unruly."

As if having a will of its own, a fat radish rolled to the edge of the counter, but she grabbed it before it went over the edge.

"No you don't."

With brisk strokes, she hacked it in quarters and tossed the pieces in the big bowl.

"I'll take over," he said.

"What? I got this. You haven't even washed your hands yet. I'll finish here. Invite in whoever is molesting my door to join us for lunch, there's plenty to share."

"It has to be you," he said.

"Oh, my Lord," she said. "What are you talking about? Once again, a simple thing I ask becomes complicated."

"Go ahead," he said.

She rinsed her hands in the sink and dried them with a kitchen towel. When she was done, she threw the towel in his face.

"Fine," she said. "I like lots of cilantro. Don't skimp." The beating on the door had become almost continuous.

"I'm coming," she said crossly.

She threw open the door and the small man almost hit her in the chest with the bulbous brass end of the walking stick he was knocking with. He wore a wool suit, a paisley cravat and a size-too-big bowler hat pressing down on his ears and making them splay.

"Stop it with this unholy racket. What do you want?"

"The Queen would like your leave to enter your home."

"The Queen? What Queen?"

"She's unaccustomed to waiting."

"Well, tell her to show herself, and come in."

The little man took a deep breath.

"You have to formally say the words. The queen has your permission to enter your home?"

"Yes, of course, I don't care. The Queen has my permission—she can enter."

He turned to leave.

"Thank you, m'lady," the man said.

"Aren't you coming in? You can if you like."

"I shall wait in the carriage."

She peered into the driveway where a 1950's Ford station wagon waited. With wood panels along the side, it looked like a prop from a B-grade surfer movie.

Carriage?

"Where is this Queen?" she called out to the man's receding backside.

"You already invited her in," he said over his shoulder.

59

Queer.

She shut the door.

"You won't believe this," she called out to Sean.

There came a voice previously unknown to this house.

"I'll have herbal tea with cinnamon and—anise. You have some, I can smell it. Upper shelf behind the nutmeg, I believe."

Fiona stopped. A tall, thin, gray-haired woman sat in Fiona's rocking chair with woolen blankets draped over her legs. The candles were back—hundreds flickering with tendrils of smoke wafting in the big room's draft.

"What? How?"

"You invited me in, so here I am."

"Who are you?"

"Is she always so clueless and dense, Sean? Her vacant expression is quite unattractive." She turned her head toward Fiona. "I'm the Queen, of course. Throw another log on the fire— the Queen is prone to catching a chill."

The Queen Doesn't Quite get to her Business

SEAN KNEELED AND bowed his head. After long, uncomfortable seconds that stretched like old rubber, the Queen nodded.

"You may rise and address me."

"Madame Queen, she's not ready."

"Ready for what?" Fiona said.

"Try to focus, young lady," the Queen said. "Right now you should be attending to my tea. Go."

Fiona looked to Sean for help. He grimaced and made a shooing motion toward the kitchen.

I'm being 'shoo'd in my own house?

The Queen spoke to Sean as Fiona left the room.

"I can quite readily see she's not ready, you fool. You failed."

"With another month..."

"You're not getting another second. You are dismissed."

"No, my Queen."

"Must I repeat myself? How am I ever supposed to get anything done if I have to walk around all day repeating myself? You are dismissed. Log. Fire. Then go."

"You haven't walked anywhere in a hundred years," Sean

61

muttered while loading splits into the fireplace.

The Queen produced a gnarled hand from beneath the heap of blankets and pointed it at Sean. Her shaky fingers were twisted like old twigs.

"What was that, boy? I didn't quite hear you."

"Nothing, my Queen." He swept his hand around in a grand gesture. "By your command, I shall depart. Good night."

Fiona watched the stove's blue flames lap the bottom of her glass teapot when she heard the front door close. It was a vigorous close, though not quite a slam. She couldn't squelch the instant thought.

Are we rid of that wretched Queen?

But she knew it wasn't true. The Queen remained—it was Sean who left. Her Sean. Gone.

Anise for the tea? Who took anise in their tea?

The idea sounded revolting to Fiona, but the Queen was right, a forgotten packet of powdered aniseed lay on the top shelf behind a bundle of waxed-paper-wrapped cinnamon sticks. She looked over her spice collection.

The Queen likes strong tea.

I can make her something especially disturbing.

She smiled when she saw a green-glass bottle tucked away in a dusty corner. Coriander seed powder. After working off the rusty metal cap, she cautiously sniffed it from afar and recoiled from the bitter, mossy stink. She tapped in a smidgen and after considering, tapped in another.

Enough to wake the dead.

Now, which cup?

She looked over the collection of misfits in her cupboard. There was a giant mug—a hideous, luridly decorated give-away cup from a giant, soul-less and long-defunct semiconductor company.

Perfect. It will grate on her aesthetic senses like a cockroach on a buffet table. She will hate this. She must.

This minor defiance buoyed Fiona's spirits, so she was cheerful when proffering the aromatically steaming mug. She stood and watched as the Queen blew on the tea's surface before taking a gulp.

"Ah, very nice, Fiona," the Queen said. "The coriander is a lovely touch. Thank you."

Fiona scrunched her face like an old mitt.

"You're welcome," she said grudgingly.

"Sit. We shall talk." Fiona turned and flopped backward onto her couch. It was an undignified maneuver, but Fiona did not care. After another generous sip, the Queen continued, "It's been a lovely party—dancing in the woods and enjoying the slippery curves and creases of your young bodies. Wonderful for you, but it does not prepare you for what comes your way. It's time to get serious—no more lollygagging."

"Did you send Sean to the market for something? When will he be back?"

The Queen snorted with disapproval.

"The passions of youth and the illusion of ample time—time enough to waste. That's a luxury we cannot afford. Live long enough and you'll see Sean again in this thread, don't worry about that. Worry about yourself and poor, sad Minerva. She's what we must focus on."

"Who the wretched hell is Minerva?"

The Queen sighed—a long exhalation that seemed as if it would never end.

"This will not be easy, but in an energy cell in the Sonoran Desert at high noon at the summer solstice, Princess Minerva must murder the Black Faerie King. Minerva is not just in danger of losing her life, but worse, she might lose her soul. We can't let that happen, and may the Gods curse the twisted humor of Brighid, you are the only one. Dagda save us, *you*."

"I don't know any Minerva and can't think of half a reason I should care two whits and a shingle."

The Queen drained her cup and held it out for Fiona to take. After an insolent moment, Fiona rose to take it.

"Lovely tea," the Queen said. "If you live long enough, perhaps you'll share the recipe."

Fiona walked to the kitchen to put the ugly mug in the sink.

"I made a huge mistake inviting you into my home," she muttered. "Huge."

When she returned to the living room, she already knew. It was empty—the Queen was gone—leaving only the rank smell of bad tea and old-woman skin. Fiona sat on her couch and watched the flames of the fire. She felt empty. Poured out. Abandoned. She wrapped herself in the quilt and breathed deep of Sean's lingering earthy scent. Wrapping her arms around her legs, she hugged her knees and chewed her bottom lip.

She made a solemn vow.

No one named Minerva will ever be any friend of mine.

Goodbye, Mommy

MINNIE WAS UNAWARE of time; she never noticed it and it was doubtful she ever would. The clock said she'd been sitting for a long spell—holding her mom's hand and talking to her. The deepest part of her, the place closest to her soul, knew her mom had moved on—to the beyond where she now walked with the angels in a place beyond pain.

She spoke the words to guide her mother over the dead river and into the peaceful place where she could be finally happy. The outer part of Minnie was still an eleven-year-old little girl, but the inner part was six and painfully alone in the rough-edged world. Her mom taught her to call 9-1-1 in an emergency and she thought this surely an emergency, but something in her told her to wait before making that call.

So, in the kitchen she sat, humming tune after tune while salty tears streamed down her cheeks. She covered her mommy with a blanket and put a pillow under her head. She even brought her favorite stuffie to tuck into the crook of her mom's other arm. Vivien grew cold and stiff as her life spirit left her body.

"I'll get a warm hat for you, Mommy, you're starting to get chilly."

She stood and tucked the blanket around Mommy a bit more, then scampered off to get a hat. When she reached the other room she found a man sitting on the couch. She emitted a small shriek. Perhaps it should have been a full-out scream, but she was startled, not afraid. Shuffling her feet and twisting her hands around each other, she stood and stared at the man.

The man stared back and then spoke.

"Hello, Minnie. My name is Sean and I won't hurt you."

He smiled sweetly and sadly all at the same time with brimming tears in his eyes as he looked at Minnie and then past her to the kitchen where lifeless Vivien lay.

"My name is Minnie, but you just said that. How do you know me? Why are you here? Are you here to help me?"

Sean studied her.

Such a wonder is this child. Most would scream and run away, but not this one. Here she stands before me, strong and solid. Mystified as to who I am and where I came from but not at all shocked that I'm here.

Sean unleashed an infectious grin with dimples like apostrophes. His eyes sparkled and radiated infinite kindness. Giggling, Minnie ran up to him to climb onto his lap. He wrapped a blanket around her.

"Yes, I'm here to help you and take you away."

She was no longer eleven going on twelve—a much younger version of herself inhabited her body.

"My mommy just died—her body couldn't hold up any longer. I know she loved me and didn't want to leave me but it was her time. A bad man touched her and she was never right from then on. My mommy said he wasn't a bad man that day but I knew he was. I think he infected her with a poison. Not like from a bottle with Mr. Yuk on it. A bad-magic poison."

Sean took it all in. His heart was full of sorrow.

Such a wise child. So young to have experienced all of this already.

"Yes, Minnie, he was a bad man. But let's not worry about him for now. Before we take our leave, do you need to spend more time with your mommy before we release her? She needs to become a part of the world."

"Mommy always wanted to play with the stars and the moon, can you send her there?"

"Consider it done," said Sean.

Minnie twinkle-toed to her mother where she smoothed the fly-away hair and tucked the blanket around her shoulders—crying as she spoke.

"I love you, Mommy. Sean is going to send you to the stars—I know it's where you always wanted to be. Stuffie will keep you safe. I know you'll be watching me. You were the bestest mommy ever and you will be a part of me beyond forever."

Minnie flopped onto Vivien's body, hoping she would magically get back a hug, but her mother's body remained cold and motionless.

Unconsciously Sean hummed a simple melody. It took an instant to realize where the haunting notes came from. He took a moment to grab all the words, then began singing.

> *In this fair land, I'll stay no more, here labor is in vain*
> *I'll seek the mountains far away and leave the fertile plain*
> *Where waves of grass in oceans roll into infinity*
> *I stand ready on the shore to cross the inland sea*
> *I am going to the West*
>
> *You say you will not go with me*
> *You turn your eyes away, you say you will not follow me*
> *No matter what I say, I am going to the West.*[5]

---

[5] *I am Going to the West*, from the CD *The Border of Heaven* by Connie Dover, © 2000 Taylor Park Music/Connie Dover

While he sang, Minnie had visions of where she'd been and where she would be. Her heart began to sing—her soul understood.

When Sean had finished, she sat up, kissed her tiny fingers and put them to Vivien's lips. Sean walked over and sat pretzel-style beside them on the floor. Minnie crawled onto his lap. He said a spell in a language both known and unknown to Minnie. She stared wide eyed at her mom, whose body began to glow.

Minnie gasped.

The light became so bright and pure that Sean had to shield Minnie's young eyes. Then, in an instant, there was a sound like a thousand crystal goblets breaking. Minnie moved Sean's hand as Vivien's body turned into a million tiny stars twinkling and glowing and rising to disperse in the air. One cold spark landed on Minnie's nose—she giggled. Cupping her hands, she held them out and another landed and burned brightly before floating upward. For that one moment, it was as if the entire universe inhabited the tiny apartment. Minnie jumped up and twirled and danced and repeated over and over...

"I love you Mommy—you're free now."

"Quick, Minnie, let's run outside so we can watch," said Sean.

He scooped her into his arms and they raced outside. It was a clear night. They watched the tiny stars race heavenward—it was a glorious sight. Vivien was now free from pain and sorrow and loss. She didn't have to run or hide anymore. She was home.

Sean looked at Minnie and pointed to her heart.

"Your mommy will always be right there," he said.

Minnie hugged Sean as one who hugs someone they'd searched for their entire life. Like Fiona, Minnie felt instantly at home with this strange man.

"Where to now, Sean?"

"I know a place for us, but it means leaving here. Are you ready?"

Minnie looked at him, wide-eyed and full of wonder. She nodded yes as quickly as her little head could nod.

"Oh, wait, I need to go get something. Can we go back inside for a minute?"

Sean put her down and let Minnie pull him back into the apartment. A fresh scent, like wild beach roses, filled the apartment. Minnie smiled.

"My mommy is happy—wild beach roses were her favorite."

Sean watched the little girl with wonder.

Fitting. Beautiful, yet wild. Fragile, but with thorns. Rest in peace, Vivien, I'll protect Minnie with my life.

He bowed his head in reverence. He knew Vivien heard his vow.

Minnie picked up her satchel of magic marbles and her drawing pad and pencil. She put them in her Hello Kitty backpack. She grabbed her favorite black cat beanie baby named Luna. She looked at him and spoke quietly.

"We're going on an adventure, Luna."

Luna was stuffed in the backpack. She picked up her few books, the ones about faeries, pixies and gnomes, and the other one about dragons. She grabbed the one picture she had of her mom when she looked younger and happier—carefree and not so worry worn. She picked up her many pairs of multi-colored striped tights and her few skirts and looked at Sean with a questioning look.

"Yes, yes, some clothes would be good. There will be plenty where we are going but by all means bring what you like."

She finished filling her pack and grabbed her small, well-worn blanket as well—it still smelled like her mom.

"Every night, we snuggled under this. Is it okay if I bring it too?"

Sean smiled and nodded his head.

Such a gentle, unselfish soul. Her whole life can fit inside one pack.

Minnie did one more sweep throughout the apartment and finished by standing next to Sean.

"I think that's it. What now?"

Sean bent down and picked her up. He arranged her pack around her shoulders and wrapped the blanket over top.

"Close your eyes and be open to all that will happen, Minnie. We're going to a faraway place, but it will be safe and you'll be happy. You'll never go hungry or thirsty and you'll be surrounded by those who will love you. I won't leave you. Does that all sound okay?"

Minnie smiled and nodded at her savior. She liked him. She yawned and rested her little head on his shoulder.

"Yes, child, close your eyes and sleep. When you wake, you'll be home."

He whispered again in an unknown tongue and Minnie thought she felt faerie kisses falling like snowflakes on her face. She fell into a deep sleep, knowing she was safe and sound in the arms of her protector.

It had been a while, but finally, she too could rest.

Thoughts

ONE OF FIONA'S pet peeves was people who said *I told you so* or *Seeeeee*, or people who point their finger at anyone other than themselves—refusing to look in the mirror to recognize they're part of the problem.

Fiona disliked it most of all when she did it to herself.

Looks like the other shoe dropped, Fiona—you knew the dream life was too good to be true. But noooo, you let yourself go into the deep end without any sort of floatation device. Nothing to save you—no branch or lifeboat or rope hanging down from heaven. Nothing. Nada. Now where are you, Fiona? Empty-handed, broken-hearted, lost and alone—utterly alone. You were used to a being alone with your cat enjoying a wonderfully simple life.

Then what happened?

Why did you let all this happen when you knew better? You could have driven by him on that rainy, stormy night but instead you had to stop and pick him up—you had to invite chaos into your tranquil realm. Really, Fiona, when will you ever learn?

She berated herself until her mind went numb—then her body followed suit and her brain shut down. How long did she sit on that couch, clutching her quilt like it was all she had in the entire world—her one last lonesome friend? Crying and drowning in self pity. She'd never know—was it days, weeks or months; minutes or hours? All she knew is that when the emotional storm passed, she was hardened. Hardened with resolve to find Sean. He found her after lifetimes, why couldn't she find him? At least she had a roadmap of sorts—a path from that wretched Queen, whoever the hell she was.

Who gave that old hag license to come here and destroy my world?

"Oh, yeah, I did when that odd little man urged me to say the magic words of invitation."

She shook her head at that one. The Queen must have counted on the fact that Fiona had no internal censor—when confused and caught off guard, she'd simply comply.

Where had that foul beast of a Queen gone to, anyway? She could still feel her.

"I feel you, wretched beast. You might not have feelings and you might completely disregard what Sean and I had, but I don't. If you want my help you'd better keep that in mind or your beloved Minerva and her world will fall. To hell with you all. You won't get my help."

In return, was there a faint echo of maniacal, mocking laughter?

"That's right, Fiona, put away your heart and summon anger; that evil seed has not sprouted in a long time—your unchecked temper becomes a beast all unto its own."

Fiona folded the quilt as carefully as one would a sacred shroud. She said a simple spell over it and for a moment it shimmered.

"It may be all I have left of Sean—it will have to hold me for now. Luna will keep it safe."

Fiona walked to the hallway desk to grab a writing tablet and pencil. Things kept slipping away; she had to record her thoughts before they dissolved into mist. Omens? Garbled messages from beyond? Half-formed memories? Thoughts swirled in her head—she needed to get them out and lock them into words before they evaporated—poof. She carefully made black dots on the paper—agonizing over their round perfection, like black graphite moons on the white paper.

Damn it, this is how it happens—obsessive compulsion distracting her from the issue at hand. The next thing she'd know, a month would have passed and her head would be empty like a wasp's nest in winter.

Focus, Fiona.

She concentrated on forming the letters on the paper.

Princess Minerva must kill the Black Faerie King and she might lose her soul or her life.

That's what she was told. That's what she knows.

To begin with, who are these people?

Fiona set her mind into gear to figure it out.

Presumably, Minerva must have a son to carry on the royal bloodline, that part makes sense. Losing her life implies less than ideal health conditions or no modern childbirth technology? Losing her soul, however? That's a tricky one. Does this Princess make some sort of sacred pact to bequeath her life to the devil so her son might live? Does this all happen in the future or the past?

She hoped it would make sense when written in black words on white paper—when captured on paper was when logic had the most power over the spirit world. That's why the plastic-robot people had such awesome power. Of course, she wanted to be a good person and didn't want to cause anyone to lose their soul, let alone an innocent girl. Princess Minerva. She let that name roll around in her head. Something about that name. Something vaguely familiar. But from where?

Fiona got up to make a mug of fresh tea. In the kitchen, she poured out the Queen's foul brew.

Coriander seed powder, ugh.

Nasty.

She washed the glass tea pot twice, then, because the odor seemed to linger, once more.

Careful, Fiona. Don't lose your mind to the routine.

Her focus was nibbled away—like piranha taking pieces from an unwary swimmer.

While the fresh batch of tea brewed she stepped out through her porch door. The air smelled fresh and clean—a welcome respite from what swirled in her safe haven, her enchanted home.

She looked up.

Overhead, a lone eagle soared. She loved living near the river in the eagles' flight path—they often flew so low that she could see their talons, their black, scanning pupils and hear their powerful wings beat the forest air. The experience was majestic and humbling. She watched him carve circles in the sky before flying off toward the river.

Fiona went back inside and turned the heat off her glass kettle. She let the herbs and steam share blissful communion and thought of Sean. Her cellular longing returned, but she pushed it away. Lonesome despair would not help her now. Sean was where he was meant to be and he could neither help nor save her—she was alone. She closed her eyes and let her fingers wriggle in the steam. A tendril of vapor reached up and wrapped around her finger. It spoke as it wrapped.

She opened her eyes with a start. She knew.

At this instant of realization, there came an angry pounding at her front door.

Whoever it is, I will not invite them in.

I will not.

Luna—One

LUNA SAT AND stared at the quilt-nest Fiona left on the couch. Like fat-Althea next door, Luna enjoyed lounging around—playing in sunbeams, chasing pixies and eating to his heart's content. But, he had duties...

Fiona did it again—left me behind to protect things. Are there no other cats in the world who could fill this role? But nooooo, Luna must thanklessly stay home to guard the house and yard against unwanted spirits.

Althea was what Fiona referred to as a "Dat"...her made-up term for a cat-dog. She stood on her hind legs and begged with her paws, chased her tail and was generally more doglike in character than catlike—until she decided to be more catlike, then Althea's calico finickiness would kick into high gear—here I ammmm, the multicolored princess in allllll of my splendid glory. Come and bestow boundless compliments upon me and I might graciously allow you to stroke my fine fur.

On the other hand, Luna was the mystical one—all-black and fluffy with eyes that changed from yellow to green. Though he and Althea were siblings, Luna was house-mistress-Fiona's communicator and interpreter. He was Fiona's familiar.

Now I'm charged with protecting this quilt, huh. How exactly am I to do that with all the unwanted ruckus and flitting spirits coming and going?

Luna jumped up on the couch and gave it a good once-over inspection. He pondered the spell Fiona left behind.

Comfrey and clover, and something else—ah, elecampane to banish the evil energy that wretched Queen brought in with her.

Hmmm—what can I add to this?

Luna left the house and meandered about the gardens. He clawed and collected bits of juniper and rosemary, myrrh and hazel, and last of all, a rose blossom (to protect himself). He carried them all into the house and dropped them into the center of the quilted nest. Immediately, a shimmering miasma bloomed and hummed with spirit-energy.

Seeing the result, Luna puffed up with pride.

Try doing that, Althea. That's a job well done.

Purring contentedly and feeling extraordinarily pleased with himself, he perched on the back of the couch to stand watch over his domain—while letting sunbeams pierce the window and terminate their arduous journey from the sun in his thick black fur. Then settling deeply into a well-deserved nap, Luna slept with one eye partly open to make sure nothing interesting happened without his notice. Outside, Althea prowled.

"Don't worry about a thing, sis, Luna is on watch. I'll give a call if I need your help. You're dismissed."

With measured insolence, Althea marched home.

With Luna on watch, Fiona reappeared and worked on her notes. The house seemed to hold its breath as if knowing something would happen soon—looming events hovered on the fringes of time and space.

A book hopped from off the bookshelf—startling Luna and Fiona and making them jump. Ray Bradbury—*Something Wicked This Way Comes*. The pages flopped open and Fiona glanced at the words glowing on the page.

"Which? Hold on. Wait." The salesman searched deep in their faces. "Some folks draw lightning, suck it like cats suck babies' breath. Some folks' polarities are negative, some positive. Some glow in the dark. Some snuff out. You now, the two of you...I—"[6]

"You're a little late, Ray," Fiona mumbled into the motey air.

---

[6] Bradbury, Ray, *Something Wicked This Way Comes*, HarperCollins, © 1962 Ray Bradbury.

Boot Camp—Lugus Arrives in his Carriage

LATELY, NOTHING GOOD came from someone rapping on the front door, so, without even being conscious of it, Fiona dreaded it happening again. With Luna on snoozy watch from the broken spine of the old couch and Francis Dunnery whispering about sunflowers[7] on the stereo, she painted vague floral shapes in her day room, nothing specific, just daydreaming and playing with aquarelle hues and washes using a sable brush on a scrap piece of Arches textured paper.

Her reverie was smashed to smithereens by an aggressive knocking on the front door. She knew the knock—it was the annoying little unwelcome man in the bowler hat.

Back again.

This won't work, but I have to try.

"No one's home," she called out. "Go away."

As if determined to break down the door with the brass head of his walking stick, the knocking increased in aggressive intensity.

Sighing, she rinsed the fine paintbrush and placed it carefully

---

[7] Light a candle and hold up my love to the sky, I would like to buy you sunflowers. *Sunflowers*, from *Lets Go Do What Happens* © 1998 Francis Dunnery.

on a blotting pad to dry. Tea leaves had settled in the bottom of her favorite mug—she looked into them for answers. Sometimes the universe spoke to her in this way—projecting meaning by aligning the leaves with flux lines of alternative energy from the spiritual world. Tea leaves can be a port hole, a window, a portal.

But today, it appeared the window was closed. The tea leaves were tea leaves—nothing stirred them and nothing was written in them.

Blah.

She got up and walked to the front door which shook in its jamb from the battering.

"I'm coming, hold your fire," she grumbled.

She stood for a moment with her hand on the knob.

Luna? What do you think? Shall we run out the back door into the woods and never come back? Or, should I hitch up my bloomers, take my medicine and open the door?

Luna's expression was blank. He was clearly disinclined to help. She pulled the door open.

"Whatever you're selling," she said, "I don't want any. Go away."

Bowler-man stepped back and stabbed his walking stick into the floorboards of the porch. Though short—barely five-feet-tall, he was solidly built and massive—like a bowling ball. Fiona towered over him.

"Lugus requests permission to enter your home."

Her tongue stumbled on the unfamiliar name.

"Who is this L-Lugus? You?"

"No, I'm Llwyd. Lugus waits in his carriage."

Fiona looked. This time the *carriage* looked very much like a mud-splattered, powder-blue 1965 Dodge Dart. She could see the man in the car; he stared straight ahead through the windshield. He wore a huge beard, tangled like an osprey's nest. There was no joy in his eyes—he looked as if he was perennially angry—as if he found the world a constant source of dismal disappointment. His expression was intense.

A friendly, nice man?

No.

"I do not grant my permission," Fiona said. "So, that's that, right? Have a good day, sir."

"Excuse me?"

"Are there more formal words I must say? No. Negative. Through my doorway he shall not pass. Unwelcome. Forbidden. No permission—I do not want Mr. Lugus Angry Sourpuss in my home."

"Fiona, I know this seems unpleasant—it *is* unpleasant, there's no getting around that fact, but it's necessary. Like medicine, no matter how terrible it tastes, sometimes you have to take it for your own good and for the good of those you love. There are dangers and Lugus will prepare you—prepare you better than any other man on Earth."

"No."

The expression on Llwyd's face was unvarnished anguish.

"Fiona, this is no game—lives hang in the balance. Your life. Minerva's life. This will seem unbelievable, but we're literally talking about the future of your fellow humankind."

"I don't know any Minerva and I hope I never do. I like peace and calm and friendly companions. Where's Sean? Go away. No."

"Please, Fiona."

"No, and that's final. No."

Llwyd turned toward the car and spread his hands in supplication.

"She said no," he said.

Lugus turned his fiery eyes toward them. If the sun's rays are focused with a magnifying glass, a fire can easily be started. Lugus' gaze was a thousand times more intense.

"There's nothing I can do," Llwyd plaintively said to the angry man.

Slowly, the man in the car raised a hairy forefinger and

pointed it at Llwyd.

"What?" Llwyd said.

Lugus didn't speak out loud, but his lips formed the word.

"You."

Llwyd stuttered like a neurotic parrot.

"What? You meaning me? What? No."

"I'll leave you two to your debate," Fiona said. "I have other things—useful things—to do."

She stepped back and started to shut the door. At the very last instant before it closed, Llwyd pushed back his walking stick to stop it.

"What's this?" Fiona said. "I don't want you in my house, either—you're no more welcome than him. Go away."

He turned.

Was he crying?

He was—robust tears dribbled down his cheeks. His hangdog expression was forlorn and his voice was a strangled whisper.

"You already invited me in and that cannot be revoked."

"What? No, I didn't."

"You did. Let me think. You said, 'tell her to show herself, and come in.' It was clear your invitation was directed at both of us."

"No, I just meant her."

"It's easy to test. Step aside. If you're right, I will turn to dust if I try to enter your home."

A sense of dread filled Fiona.

What had I intended with those words?

She couldn't recall. Standing aside, she pulled the door fully open.

"Okay, then, let's see," she said. "A little dust to sweep up and throw away never bothered me. My broom and dustpan stand ready."

Llwyd took a deep breath and closed his eyes before taking the big step. Inside, he opened his eyes and looked around the room. He pulled a handkerchief from his jacket pocket and mopped his face and forehead. Luna raised his head and looked at him with unveiled suspicion.

"You have a comfortable home," Llwyd said. "Unfortunately, there is no time to waste—we must get busy with your training."

With shoulders slumped and resignation to being out of control filling her body from head to toe, Fiona surrendered to that which appeared inevitable. She ran fingers through her unruly, silver-streaked hair.

"Do we have time for a cup of tea first?" she said.

Llwyd leaned his walking stick against the wall and sailed his hat toward a kitchen chair. Missing, the hat rolled on the floor. He shrugged off his waistcoat and tossed it on the couch.

"Yes," he said. "We can take time for that. Nothing bizarre for me, thank you, a nice, hot cup of Red Rose and honey will be fine if you have it."

She nearly protested—opening her mouth to suggest something more exotic, but realized...

Red Rose. The company was formed in the 1890s by Theodore Harding Rand Estabrooks and the tea, formulated in 1899, was a perfectly respectable blend of Sri Lankan and Indian tea leaves.

I have it, and it sounds perfect for where we are right now. Something simple and familiar.

"Good call," she said. "Coming right up."

Boot Camp—Day One, Luna

MADNESS ABOUNDED IN the house from nearly the first instant the man appeared. Luna could barely move fast enough to stay out of the way.

Where was Sean?

Sean was cat-approved for providing treats, plentiful petting and stimulating conversation. This new man seemed to think the proper attitude toward a cat was to ignore it. Neglect it. Break its long-suffering heart by walking by without a word. Stroll by the food bowl without making any welcome contribution. Luna liked fresh water in his dish—refreshed once or twice or three times a day was sufficient. Now, Luna's water could be afoul with fur and dust and the man wouldn't even notice.

And Fiona.

Where is her mind?

Not on Luna, that's for sure.

What were they doing? Regardless of hours of study from the pinnacle ridge of his couch-mountain, Luna could not figure it out.

There was exercise—lifting weights and walking on the horrid mechanical treadmill. The noise and fruitless activity of this was bad enough, but then there were the hours spent cross-legged

on the carpet chanting and droning on and on with eyes closed.
Ohhhhm—ohhhhhm.

Prior to the disruption, the ways of humans were pointless and mysterious enough. Now things were much worse. The boring, dreamy idleness was torture. The intermittent new bustle was intolerable. And the talk, the endless babble. Talk in the living room. Talk in the kitchen. Talk in the dayroom. Talk, talk, talk. The man talked and after a while, Fiona began to listen.

Luna was no fan of static electricity—it made his nose tingle and made his fur stand up like a porcupine. There was far too much static electricity being generated as the humans waved their arms and spoke to the big spirits they conjured.

Luna was no fan of bright lights—particularly when it was time for one of his twenty-three daily naps. So, the modulated beams emanating from the walls and the ceiling were very unwelcome.

Sparks were ugly things, what with the noise and shocking lights and the nasty smell of ozone left behind. What good were they and why did Fiona raise her walking stick over and over until the man was satisfied with the sparks created from thin air?

Luna was no fan of swamp gas and the ethereal emanations of spirits. Cats had a very sensitive sense of smell—as was proper for tracking a trespassing mouse or locating a fragment of treat hiding in a crack. So, the brews and mixtures and potions and poultices and garlands and sachets made from ginseng and ginger and goldenseal roots and skunk cabbage and garlic and balsam apple and lavender and mint and chaparral and neem bark and betel and malva seed—a pox on anyone bringing these obnoxious plants into Luna's house.

Peace—how Luna craved peace, but nowadays in this house, there was none to be found.

Luna—Two

ON A FRESH new day, Luna woke with the warmth of the morning sun shining on his ebony fur as he lay curled up amidst the down comforter atop Fiona's bed.

In sunshine, that's always the best way to wake up. Wonder what today will have in store for me.

He purred contentedly, rolling away and exposing his belly to the probing rays of the sun—he was feeling kittenish today. At the tender age of five he was anything but elderly—in human years he was in his thirties, but today, however, the sun must have given him extra energy—he felt all tingly from the tips of his whiskers to the end of his poufy black tail and everywhere in between.

Hmmm, today could turn out to be a rather interesting day. Though, truth be told, wasn't every day in this enchanted house something of a wonder?

Luna sat up and yawned a big cat yawn, licked his paws and did a quick shake and fluff until he felt presentable enough to venture forth to greet the day. He hopped off the bed and padded quietly down the stairs, wondering if Fiona had his breakfast ready. Of late, she'd been awfully distracted with the queer little visitor; Luna couldn't get a handle on all the activity. He'd resigned himself to the fact that he was on the back burner for now and he had to trust that Fiona was doing the right thing.

Luna wandered into the kitchen and noted Fiona making her morning tea.

Ahhh—calm before the chaos.

"Good morning, my beautiful Luna," his mistress said. "Did you sleep well?"

Luna mewed approval. He was a cat after all, and worship, admiration and adoration were expected, necessary and required.

Fiona walked across the room to change Luna's water and give him a morning splotch of wet food. On today's menu: lobster and chicken. Luna ate it all in a matter of moments, drank water to cleanse his palate and walked onto the porch where he gave himself a quick bath and proceeded to paw at the door.

"Out, please," he mewed.

As summoned, Fiona scuttled to the porch.

"Yes, your highness? Are you all set to go out for a while? If you wouldn't mind, if you would be so kind as to do a perimeter scout? I've heard scratchings and murmurings in the walls as of late. It's a bit too early for the gnomes to be venturing in and they usually don't bring digging tools in with them. It might be just a rogue squirrel but if you wouldn't mind checking?"

Luna's eyes lit up and sparkled. A mission. As master of the house, he loved missions. He sat up straighter and mewed again. Yes, this was a mission and duty he'd accept.

So out he went.

Hmmm, left or right. Nope, first things first; he needed to venture to the compost heap and do his business.

One his way back he saw something moving through the grass. He crouched low down—looking every bit the miniature jaguar he envisioned himself to be. Wiggling his tail end, he rose and made a flying leap toward the movement. Waiting wasn't one of his strengths—he preferred pouncing right away and asking questions later.

He landed on top of a gnome, Sebastian—who looked quite unamused.

"My goodness, man, must you enter the scene in such a dramatic fashion?"

"I'm sorry, Sebastian. Fiona said she'd been hearing things in the wall, and there have an abundance of oddities going on the house. When I saw rustlings in the grass my imagination took over and well, I pounced. I'm so sorry to have startled you—please forgive me?"

He bowed his head down to his front paws.

Sebastian was one of the oldest gnomes in this realm and thus was accorded great respect.

"Oh, stand up silly boy, of course I forgive you."

Sebastian took great care in looking after Fiona's gardens. He had a lovely home under the great maple tree on the end between the forest and the lawn. He and his family had grown and prospered here. He received many visitors—and all were in awe of how he lived so close to Fiona and how they worked and existed in such harmony. Sebastian had done much to dispel the human myths—that all humans were at war with nature, for example—and in doing so, had become quite the expert on human-gnome and animal-spirit relationships.

He and Luna sat for quite some time, going over the news of the day, the changing weather patterns, latest on the night skies and migrations, so on and so forth. Like Luna, Sebastian felt a new energy around the place which made him uneasy.

When Luna told him about his mission for the day, Sebastian's eyes widened.

"Yes, Fiona is right, Luna. There is something scuttling about. I am not sure what it is either, there are strange markings—like runes or logograms or petroglyphs along the side of the house in the smaller of the herb gardens—the one with the rock the Missus is fond of leaning on now and again. The marks are under the basil, next to the wild thyme. And, strange little holes, almost like tunnels—I noticed them just the other day. Subtle and hidden. I don't think they are faerie. They don't feel entirely evil so I didn't sound the alarm—they seem more mischievous in nature. If you're investigating, you might start over there."

Luna thanked Sebastian for his insight and meandered on his way to the herb garden.

As he approached the garden, he took a whiff of the air. Earthy. Healthy—good signs. He nosed about and found quills near the basil. The tracks Sebastian noticed looked like claw marks, as if something had dug there recently. Upon closer inspection, yes, that's exactly what it was—someone or something had dug into the house. He went back to the quills. There was short fur tufted onto one; they looked like they'd been shed in haste, or perhaps pulled off in a scuffle. This was a puzzle for the human.

Fiona should study this, he decided.

He left the herb garden and looked around the rest of the house. Nothing else was out of place; he could see where Sebastian and his family had been tending the gardens. The toads kept watch in their shallows and the dragonflies and mosquito-faeries flitted about. The birds sang and all seemed right with this part of the world. Back to the herb garden.

Near the cowslips he happened upon a small hat. Not a gnome-like hat, for it did not have a pointed peak and was not red. He took a sniff and sneezed.

Ah, he now knew.

"Pixie," he uttered.

Luna knew pixies often times took the form of hedgehogs which would explain the quills and tuft of fur. The hat was probably tossed off in haste. Hmmm, now that he had a pretty good idea as to what was in the house, the lingering question was why and where is it now? He decided to bring the hat to Fiona.

In trotted Luna, looking most pleased with himself and his *prey.*

He sauntered up to Fiona, let out a muffled meow, and

waited for acknowledgment.

Fiona looked down.

"What did you bring to me, dearest Luna. Let's take a look-see."

She took the hat from Luna's mouth and pulled close for examination. Like Luna, she took a whiff and wrinkled her nose. She looked down at Luna and Luna smiled.

Yes, Fiona knows that smell too.

"Well, my dear sweet Luna, it looks like we have a pixie in our midst. While the hat is rather cute, the smell leaves a bit to be desired, wouldn't you say? I suppose it's not entirely surprising that a pixie has found us given all the activity and different energies swirling about us at the moment; this would be the perfect place for a mischievous pixie, huh? Well, then, we can only hope it's a pixie on the friendly side of playful, and not of the gone-wrong, evil sort. All the same, would you root it out for a chat and find out its intentions?"

What—one mission a day wasn't good enough for this one anymore? Harrumph. Really, Fiona, I've had quite the morning already. I've already missed several of my naps as things stand.

As if Fiona could read Luna's mind, she bent down and picked him up. She realized she'd not been the most attentive human lately—her mind was elsewhere and Llwyd kept her busy with her training. She snuggled into Luna and cooed.

"Okay, Luna, go rest for a bit. Take the hat with you—perhaps it will coax the pixie out of hiding so it will be less work for you. Once you've rested, please be a good boy and seek out this new house guest, will you?"

Flattery and unconditional love will get you anywhere with a cat. Luna purred and nuzzled Fiona's chin. Fiona bent down and they rubbed their foreheads together.

Fiona put Luna and the hat onto the floor. She went back to whatever it was that she was doing while Luna picked up the hat and wandered out of the kitchen.

Luna pondered the situation.

If you were a pixie, where would you be hiding?

He decided to display himself and the hat in the fireplace room where Fiona stored a collection of old marbles from her youthful days—bunches of pretty glass orbs resting in their collection tray.

What pixie could resist that treasure?

After pulling the box from under an end table, he pawed the box and scattered the marbles on the carpet; then curled up near them with the little hat under his paw—and drifted into a well-deserved nap. Not knowing if he'd been asleep for a long or short time, he was annoyed to be awoken by a tugging at the hat. He was determined to ignore this violation of his tranquility when he realized this could be the very thing he was on watch for; the pixie. He cracked open an eye just enough to peek undetected. Lo and behold there was the imp trying to muscle the hat from under Luna's paw.

Is gentle delicacy unknown in the pixie realm?

In one swift movement, Luna lifted his paw and trapped the pixie. He could feel it squirming and making the most horrible racket.

"What a way to be awakened," said Luna. "Now, if you don't stop squirming, I will simply eat you and we'll be done with this whole silly business."

With that, there was instant stillness. Luna fully opened up his eyes and thought about his next move.

"I'm going to lift my paw from you and I expect you to stay put. Don't be alarmed, I simply want to have a chat with you. Do we have a deal?"

"Mwoerueoteoing teowteohygn."

"Excuse me? Are you speaking pixie gibberish? That's not a language we speak here."

"Weerweotueytoinhyoeitne."

"Oh, really, this will not do."

Luna moved his paw ever so slightly so the pixie's head popped out.

"Why thank you, my King. I was trying to say 'yes we have a deal' but your paw made it difficult to talk—you had my mouth covered."

"Oh, dreadfully sorry about that."

"I won't run."

Luna relaxed his paw and the pixie pulled himself the rest of the way free.

"May I seat my weary self on your plush paw?"

Luna nodded.

The pixie sat and wriggled to settle in.

"Let me begin. My name is Luna, master of this house and familiar and confidante to the human Fiona who also belongs in this house. And you, little one, who are you?"

"My name is Kailen, which means warrior, in case you care, and clearly I am a forest pixie. I am humbled by both you and your mistress. I come here to serve. I live in the forest with all of the other good creatures and live in peace and harmony and create mischief only now and again—and when we do, it's all good natured pranks and such. We never cause harm."

Luna licked his foreleg and cocked his head to urge Kailen to continue.

"Of late, we've noticed a different air about the place. A darkness. We're beginning to taste of it on the wind and see it from the corners of our eyes. A band of us trekked about and happened upon your abode. We've been watching for a while and the consensus is that the oddities are coming from here. So, we drew twigs and I was the one chosen to come and explore your realm. Thus, here I am—presenting myself for your service."

Luna took all of this in. He'd not met a pixie before. Gnomes, yes. Faeries, yes. Ghostlings and sprites aplenty. But pixies, not so much—they were uncommon in this corner of Maine.

Kailen and Luna sized each other up and down, left and right, inside and out. Clearly, Luna could eat him, but pixies were magic folk so he needed to be cautious.

"Would you like your hat back?"

"Oh, please, I feel most out of sorts without it. Not that a furry creature like you would know or care, but they are very useful for keeping one's head warm."

Kailen pulled his hat on his head.

He looks much more like a proper pixie with it on his little head.

"If it's all the same to you, I propose to present you to Mistress Fiona."

"Oh, that would be grand. I am tired from having to dig my way in—would it be too much to ask for a ride upon your back?"

Luna, not prone to being a pack horse, decided to be gracious just this once. If he was to join forces with this little one, then it wouldn't hurt to start out on the right foot.

"Don't be asking every day, but this time, I will allow you the privilege."

Kailen climbed aboard and Luna walked to the kitchen to find Fiona. She sat on the couch reading a book and waving her hands about.

"Look what I found, Fiona."

Fiona bent down and held out her hand. Kailen climbed into her palm and sat down. He told his story to Fiona who listened intently. Fiona pondered, but not for too long.

"Looks like we have a new house guest, Luna. You may stay for as long as you'd like, Kailen, but should things start going awry, you may want to leave. I trust you will do us no harm, for if you do, Luna has my permission to do with you as he sees fit. Do we have a deal?"

Kailen looked down at Luna who licked his lips and made a smacking sound.

"No problem, Mistress Fiona."

From that point on, Kailen and Luna were inseparable. Kailen rode atop Luna like a King atop his finest stallion. They made their morning and nightly rounds—securing the grounds and routing unwelcome pests. They gathered gossip and news from the whispering winds, and reported back to Sebastian, Fiona and Llwyd.

At the very least, Luna now had another friend to keep him company while Fiona was busy concocting and training and whatnot. At the very best, they had another ally for whatever was coming their way.

Pixie Princess

SEAN WAS BANISHED from Fiona's training and from her life, but he knew it was only temporary. Rather than sulk and pout about it, he prepared a house for her eventual arrival. Beyond having a way with animals and magical folk, he was handy with his hands, so rebuilding a house was a natural project for him. Beyond being practical, it would pass the time because who knew when she would show up—but show up she would, someday.

So, in his time away from Fiona, he set to clearing land and building an enchanted home. The house design was a puzzle—why did it have to be just so? Then he realized he was duplicating Fiona's house in Maine, everything about it. Layout, fixtures, everything.

So she won't feel out of place.

He had just barely finished the main structure when he got the call to gather Minnie. He had left the pixies and gnomes in charge of doing the finish work so he hoped it was done. When his newest charge awoke he wanted her to feel safe—he wanted her to feel like she was home. He didn't want her to forget her past life, but he didn't want her to dwell in sorrow. He just wanted her to *be.*

When Minnie woke she thought she was dreaming. The last thing she remembered, she was resting her head on Sean's shoulder. Now, she was sleeping in a princess bed.

'I'll never leave you,' echoed in her tender ears.

She sat up with a start and saw Sean rocking in a chair.

He had a book splayed his lap and was quietly reading.

When he saw Minnie stir he smiled and said, "Good morning, princess. I trust you are rested?"

Minnie nodded and rubbed her eyes in disbelief.

"Where am I?"

"You are here," responded Sean.

She smiled and said, "And that is where?"

"Oh, that would be in our new house. You're one of the first to see it. What do you think? One day, it will be our surprise for Fiona."

That name—Minnie knew that name. A twinkle came to her eyes as she blurted out, "I know her! I met her in a parking lot on a rainy day with my mommy. She drove off in a purple punch buggy."

With waving arms and stabs of her index finger for emphasis, Minnie weaved the story of their meeting for Sean, who wondered if this impish child ever stopped to take a breath. When Minnie was finished, her face bore a proud expression.

He smiled and said, "Yup, sounds like the Fiona I know. She'll join us when the time is right."

Minnie had a sudden thought.

"We're not dead, are we?"

Sean let out a laugh that jiggled his belly.

Such innocence this one has.

"No, no, my dear one, we're very much alive. Would you like to have a bite to eat and look around or laze around in bed a while longer?"

At the mention of food, Minnie's belly rumbled. She couldn't remember the last time she'd eaten.

"Ah, food it is. Come, let's venture downstairs."

Minnie climbed out from under a mountain of fluffy covers and hopped to the floor. Detecting the faint sounds of whispering and scuttling, she dropped to her knees and peered under the bed—then, wide-eyed and perplexed, popped back up like a Whack-A-Mole to look at Sean.

"Oh," he said, "heard something did you? Well, Minnie, I should confess to you now—this is an enchanted house; it was built with magic which infuses everything in it. There's the magic we see, like faeries, pixies, gnomes, dragons, unicorns and such—and the magic we feel with our core, our being. Does that make sense?"

She nodded and whispered.

"So they are real."

He smirked.

"As real as you or I."

He was hungry too, but apparently, food could wait.

So much for breakfast—now nothing will distract her from exploring her room.

Minnie looked at everything inside and out, front-ways and back-ways, left to right. She took it all in and absorbed every detail. She felt the rhythm and hum of the place and found the magic intoxicating.

Sean tried to remember what it felt like to see it all in a new way—his childhood seemed so long ago and far away. Like a touch of a feather, he felt it—that first moment when you realize how much magic surrounds you, how wonderful it all is and how much there is for the taking. While lost in his thoughts as he watched Minnie "ooh" and "ah", something scurried quickly across the floor.

"What was that?" said Minnie.

Whatever it was ran behind Sean and began climbing the back of the rocking chair. It got to the top and heaved itself over to plop down on Sean's shoulder.

"Oh, him? This is Flix, one of the house pixies. He's a

troublemaker, but harmless—he won't hurt you."

Minnie approached and did a curtsy. With a solemn expression, Flix inclined his head.

Off to a fine start.

Flix whispered in Sean's ear.

"Oh, yes, that's right. Minnie, do you have the marbles?"

She went over to her pack and pulled out the blue satchel. Flix squealed with delight. He slid down Sean's arm and took a flying leap onto the floor. Minnie seated herself on the floor and rolled the marbles from the bag. Much to Minnie's surprise, Flix scurried over to perch atop her knee where he sat dangling his long legs in the air, swinging and kicking and staring at the marbles.

"It's been *so* long since I've seen them and I'm so happy to have them back."

Minnie looked perplexed.

Flix looked up at her, then looked to Sean to see if it was okay to proceed. Sean shrugged.

"Well, Princess Minnie, the stars and the prophecy foretold your mother's journey. I hope you know she is now safe among the stars."

Minnie nodded. Flix patted her knee.

"So, knowing you would be alone and knowing you would need protection from..."

Sean cut him short by clearing his throat.

Now was not the time to overload this poor child.

"So, knowing you would be alone, we pixies crafted magic marbles and the blue, star-covered satchel. From the old Queen, we, uh, *borrowed* them and gave them to Selene to carry to you— she had trouble getting into your abode because the door was locked and no windows were open. So, she left them on your doorstep. She waited outside in the birch tree and blended into the bark. As soon as she was certain the stones were in your possession, she returned to us here. We then knew your whereabouts and could keep track of you through the magic marbles. We could watch and listen and monitor. When the time was right, Sean knew to go and get you. Does that all make sense?"

Minnie nodded.

"They've been my favorite since I found them—thank you so much for giving them to me."

Flix jumped off her knee, turned and glared up at her.

"Giving? No, dear Minnie, we *loaned* them to you and now I must have them back."

"Flix," Sean whispered.

"These are special and not for spoiled little girls."

"Flix," Sean said.

"I hoped they were mine forever," Minnie said with her eyes brimming with little tears, "but I understand."

"Flix!" Sean said loudly.

Flix turned. The expression on his face was cross.

"What?"

"Surely, she can hold them for you for a little while longer."

"No," Flix said. He turned to look at Minnie's face. "Oh, badger-scat, I see where this is going. Spider-juice. Crow-spit. Yes, she can hold them for a while longer."

Minnie picked up the little pixie and hugged him.

"Aaaack—you're squeezing a *bit* too hard."

"Oh, sorry," said Minnie.

She quickly put Flix back down.

"I hope you eat a bad cherry," Flix said. He turned and ran from the room like a silver streak. Sean took a deep breath and muttered an old-stone prayer.

That went better than I expected.

Minnie still felt like she was in a dream. A wonderful, glorious dream. Then suddenly, she realized she wasn't in a dream. Little girls don't have full bladders in a dream.

"Sean—I have to pee."

"Oh, right, me too. Let's go."

He led her to the bathroom, which was down a short hallway.

After a few moments she came out, much more refreshed. Her tummy rumbled. Sean grinned.

"My turn," he said.

When he came out, he said, "Weren't we going to find a bit of something to eat?"

Minnie nodded vigorously.

They went downstairs to the kitchen.

"Everyone, this is Princess Minnie. She's safe and sound."

A chorus of yelps and whelps and banging and clapping erupted. Minnie hid behind Sean's leg and looked around the room.

"It's okay, honey, you'll get used to it. Remember the magical folk I mentioned? Well, they're all here, always about. Sometimes you see them and sometimes you don't. They will borrow your pretties and tweak your ears, but won't ever really harm you and when it comes to it—they will protect you just as I will. Now, what suits that empty tummy? Would you like a snack or something hearty?"

Minnie hadn't ever been given that sort of choice before; her prior choices were between foods, not between quantities. She considered the options.

Hmmm, what do I feel like?

"Maybe, a snack?"

"Snack it is. Coming right up."

Sean sliced an apple and arranged the slices on a plate. He then cut thick slices of dark, hearty bread from a loaf, toasted the slices and topped them with fresh, flowery honey. Last of all, he put a mound of almonds and cashews next to the apple slices.

Minnie looked at the plate with wonder.

If this is a snack, I can't imagine a full meal.

She ate to her heart's content; food had never tasted so good. The water was as fresh as if it had been tapped from the heart of a mountain. Sean relished at seeing Minnie eat. Yes, she would thrive here, being nourished in body, mind and spirit.

When Minnie was done, Sean took her plate and dropped it in

the sink. Suddenly, weariness fell on him—he was tired from this adventure. He looked at Minnie—lost in thought, she seemed far away.

"Minnie, how's about snuggling up in the hammock outside and taking a rest? It's a beautiful afternoon, not too hot. I know you recently woke, but I think it may be best to sleep again and let some of this sink in. How's that sound?"

Sean's voice was soothing. Hypnotic.

She had to agree, she did feel sleepy.

"I think that sounds great, Sean."

Minnie followed Sean out to the front porch. She had much more to see of the house and the gardens and the forest, but all that could all wait; it would be there later.

She's been through a lot.

Sean climbed into the hammock and arranged its pillows and blanket. Minnie climbed in and after wiggling and writhing and negotiating with her sharp elbows, she found a place at Sean's side with her head resting on the back of his outstretched arm. They lay there, looking up at the sky and talking about what flew overhead, what they saw in the puffy white clouds drifting by and singing a simple song Sean improvised.

Cheeky girls and wind-swept rosy clouds
Touched by dragon fire from the sun
For every perfect day, dusk soon falls
For all of us, each and every one...

Peace, sleepy peace, catch it, hold it, sleep.

Before long they were both asleep. Flix came out and pulled the blanket over them. Some of the flower faeries flew around them singing a simple lullaby in faerie language and bell-like musical scales. Flix waved them away and worked the satchel-bag out from under Minnie's arm. He untied the silk ribbon closure and wormed his body into the opening—to come out with a glistening blue-sapphire marble as big as his head.

She doesn't need all of them.

With an insolent stride, he walked away with it.

There they rested. There they would restore their strength, the strength they would need for the coming trials. Sean would protect her with his life, though he hoped it wouldn't come to that.

But for now, they slept while the others kept watch.

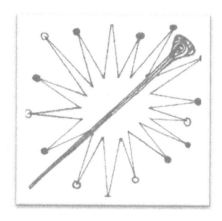

Boot Camp—Stickman

LLWYD TAPPED FIONA on her forearm to emphasize his point.

"Raise your stick a little higher or the spirit force could come around the top."

Fed up, Fiona turned around.

"If you touch me with that cane again I'll ram it down your throat."

Llwyd's face crumpled. He dropped the cane on the oak floor—it hit with a clatter stirring Luna and Kailen from sleep. Kailen, buried in the soft fur of Luna's belly, stretched and opened his eyes to exchange an exasperated look with Luna. Luna broadcast his thoughts into the room.

Keep it quiet, I've had a long day.

As usual, no one paid any attention.

Llwyd stumbled backwards onto the couch. He buried his face in his hands.

"I can't do this physical stuff. Lugus is tough—he knows what to do. *He* should be here."

Crying? Again with the crying?

Fiona felt a wave of sympathy wash through her body.

"I'm sorry," she said. "Perhaps we should return to the spells again."

Llwyd's face brightened.

"I'm better with the bookwork—the incantations. And maybe a spot of tea? A man works up a terrible thirst."

Works up a thirst crying all the time...

Fiona sighed. She loved tea as much as anyone, but ten or more cups a day? The man must really enjoy his quiet time in the bathroom.

She filled the glass pot with spring water and lit the blue flame with a wooden match.

Llwyd needs fortification. What can I do?

She studied the contents of her pantry and cupboards and considered her options. South African rooibos, of course, that's always a good start. Mix in a little 3-X maté de coca and Mandarin oolong, but that would not do a fraction of the job. She smiled. The maté de coca was the right idea, but she had a canister brought back by a friend—a special coca leaf tea from the Yanakona's region in Columbia. To add gravitas to the brew, she started an infusion of *Papaver somniferum* poppy.

A dollop of organic opium should stiffen his backbone.

Then, to be sure, she added a couple of ounces of Royal Navy Rum from a stone flagon hidden where no one would think to look—behind a tall, dusty stack of Spam tins.

This will put hair on his chest.

She had a wide selection of honeys from around the world, but this brew would require exceptional sweetness and body. It took a few seconds, but she found an ancient Mason jar of inky buckwheat honey. She mixed everything into a giant Lady Ga Ga-designed teacup she hoped was ugly enough to distract him from the taste of the noxious tea. There was plenty of tea left over, so she filled her cup too and carefully carried the steaming cups into the dining room.

"Here we are, Llwyd," she said.

"Lovely. I was admiring your figurines. Am I correct? You collected some from the Nigerian Noks? Big eyes? Fish lips? Reproductions, I assume."

"Reproductions, sure, just bric-a-brac, but made from the same clay and infused with proper Kapsiki sorcery."

"I admire your taste in decorations," he said. He sipped the tea. "Ugh. I don't so admire your taste in tea."

She took a sip.

"It's not so bad," she said.

Yes it is.

"I'm sorry, I can't drink this. I know my way around—don't trouble yourself, you drink my cup and I'll brew up a pot of Red Rose."

Fiona summoned everything she could think of to increase the weight her command.

"Drink," she said, using her subvocal speech.

He sat back down.

"I have to?" he said.

In toast, she tapped her cup against his.

"To your health," she said.

With one hand, he plugged his nose—with his other hand he lifted the giant teacup and drank. The effect didn't take long to kick in.

"I know nothing will ever come of it—we live in different worlds at different levels and you will be a high priestess and warrior Queen," he said, "but I already love you with all my soul, Fiona."

Horrified at what came out of his mouth, Llwyd dropped the cup and covered his mouth.

She tried to remember the ingredients of the tea—and the order they were mixed, which was sometimes important—and what incantations she'd spoken into the coiling tendrils of steam.

Did I accidentally create a powerful truth serum or love potion?

She too felt the warm infusion in her veins.

"You can speak freely, Llwyd, it's okay." She reached over and pulled his hands way from his mouth. "Tell me what you love about me."

"Oh, I love the smell of your skin early in the morning when sleep still clings. I love your unbound breasts under Sean's thin cotton shirt you wear when you're painting. I love your figure when the sun shines through your dress."

Hmmm, interesting.

"What *don't* you love about me?"

"Your stinky tea, for one thing. It tastes like mongoose bile."

"You really know what mongoose bile tastes like?"

The words seemed to be trapped in his throat.

"Y-y-e-s-s. Please don't ask why."

Hey, this is fun. Let's cut through some of the veil of mystery...

Veil of mystery? That was overheated and florid. She realized how much the tea was affecting her, too.

I hope he does not ask me any questions.

"Let's get down to it—why are you here?"

A puzzled expression washed over his face.

"To prepare you, of course. That should be obvious even to an unconscious person like you."

An unconscious person like me? What?

"Tell me more about my unconsciousness."

"Fiona, you have strength and power, but you're untrained, undisciplined and—well, like I said, unconscious. You have a vague sense of the spiritual overworld and a natural, organic power you wield on occasion, but you're using one-percent of your ability, if not less. You're soft and fuzzy, Fiona, when we need you to be tough and hard and disciplined."

"What if I don't harden? What if I like myself the way I am and I don't want to be a silly warrior-Queen?"

He looked forlorn.

"Then we'll die, you and me and the old Queen and Sean and Luna," he whispered, "and worse."

"What's worse than dying?"

"Minerva dying. Your soul in a dark place forever. The world dying. Those things are worse. Please don't ask me any more questions; I am not supposed to tell you anything. I'm here to train you, not educate you. You're not ready."

Right. Now that I'm finally learning something, I'm going to stop.

"What are we fighting?"

"It's not safe to even say it..."

Anger sprouted in her gut like a mushroom casserole gone horribly wrong.

"What are we fighting? Say it."

"The Black Faerie King—Custennyn. If his son, the Black Prince, marries Minerva and she bears his son..."

Luna stood on the ridge of the old couch—he arched his back and hissed. Fiona realized her skin was tingling and the fine hair on the back of her neck stood up like hackles. Three heavy books flew off her shelves and scattered across the floor.

What?

The windows rattled in their sills and the electric lights dimmed. Llwyd held out his hand and his brass-headed walking stick rose in the air and flew into his grip.

"Get behind me, Fiona. I will protect you if I can."

Aping the maneuver, Fiona reached out her hand and willed her walking stick to come. This had never occurred to her before, but her sturdy walking stick...

Staff.

An image flooded her mind—Moses standing on a hill raising the almighty staff of God high above his head—speaking to a rock, striking it twice and producing water for his people.

My walking stick is my staff.

It moved. She was shocked and surprised. Focusing, she called to it and it came to her—bouncing painfully off her head before dropping into her hands.

Shytte. Ouch.

Obeying instructions for a change, she took a position behind Llwyd and settled into a defensive stance. Underfoot, the floor rattled and rumbled like an existential earthquake. She reached around Llwyd and grabbed her teacup—draining it in one gulp. Instantly, her blood felt foamy and effervescent as her brain fluoresced and the top of her head threatened to fly off into space.

It occurred to her that maybe, just maybe, mixing Royal Navy Rum and the poppy infusion was not such a great idea.

On the opposite side of the room, Luna stood on the couch with Kailen riding high on his back. The humans were focused on the bay window facing the backyard, but there was action on the other side of the house—something ugly sneaking in. Luna hissed and tried to warn Fiona, but he could not get her attention. The shape was not large, but it was filled with malice.

"I guess this is our part of the battle," Kailen said.

Luna dropped to his belly and crept down the side of the couch.

Across the room behind them, from an inky shadow, a thin form took shape—its skin looked like thin, yellow-leather pulled tightly over dead bones. Fiona's knees were weak.

Teeth, oh my Lord, cannibal's teeth.

In slow motion, the thin figure swung a sword with a rusty blade.

Was it rust? Perhaps it was dried blood.

Llwyd raised his cane to block the sword and Fiona saw the man's stealthy maneuver. While the stickman distracted Llwyd with the larger, blood-crusted blade, in his other hand was a dagger and, like a darting lizard, it headed straight toward Llwyd's heart. Stepping around him, she slashed with her staff and the dagger fell to the floor while the stickman clutched his hand to his bony chest and howled. Emboldened, Fiona stabbed her staff into the thin man's eye socket and knocked him to the ground. Stepping onto his chest, she raised and lowered her staff over an over until the man's head was crushed into dust—slowly the dust flittered into the air as if blown away by an invisible wind.

Adrenaline and hallucinogenic tea flooded her body—she raised her staff and tilted her head back and howled like a she-wolf. Llwyd collapsed on an overstuffed chair and mopped his forehead with a lacey handkerchief produced from his vest pocket.

The battle was still fully engaged on the other side of the house where Luna bared his teeth and cornered a skeletal creature.

"Be careful, Luna," Kailen said. "I know these horrid monsters, they are Ankou pets—guardians of the graveyard. Soul collectors."

The creature carried a lantern made from a baby's skull. Inside, a black candle guttered and emitted greasy smoke. It carried a spear made of bone.

"Stand aside," the skeleton-beast said. "This house is ours."

"Never," Luna hissed.

He took a step forward while the creature raised his spear.

From the side, Kailen rolled one of Fiona's marbles. The creature shied away and then noticed his fellow fighter vanquished across the room. He dropped his spear and crawled back into the cleft of the wall from where he appeared. He tilted his head over his shoulder and spoke with evil malice.

"You haven't seen the last of us," he said.

Luna snorted.

"We'll be ready and the result will be the same." He turned to Kailen. "Marble?"

Kailen shrugged. "Fiona played with them when she was a child. They're filled with magic."

Filled with pride, Luna strutted across the room; prowling the walls and sniffing at the floor where the stickman had dissolved. He dropped the Ankou creature's spear on the floor at Fiona's feet.

Fiona looked down.

"Don't bring sticks in the house, Luna."

Without looking closely, she bent down, picked up the spear and dropped it in a wastebasket.

Disgusted, Luna walked across the room, climbed the couch to resume his nap.

"Humans know nothing," he said to Kailen.

"*We* know," Kailen said. "But, like them, we have our part to play in protecting this house. They need us."

Across the room, Fiona spoke with pride.

"I killed him. He came into my house and I killed him. If that's all we're up against, then what are we working so hard for?"

"That was nothing," Llwyd said.

He leaned over the dining room table and grabbed the lurid, over-large teacup and drained it in one large gulp. Fiona propped her stick against a chair and settled at the table.

"Where were we before being rudely interrupted? Oh, I want to hear more about this King Custennyn and his son."

Llwyd studied her face with frank intensity.

"No, the tea wore off and it won't work again, so don't bother. When you're ready, I will tell you everything I know about the King, but not today."

"I saved your life—that should buy me something," she said.

"Oh, it does," he said. "A sandwich." He held out his palm to stop her from moving an inch. "A tuna-salad sandwich. Don't trouble yourself—I'll make it."

Camp Minnie

WHEN SEAN WOKE on the porch, he was filled with a brief moment of sheer panic. The blanket beside him was cool—she'd been gone a while.

Where is she?

He listened for signs of danger, but all was peaceful. By stretching and exploring with his mind, he should be able to find her, but she was not in the first places he checked—the kitchen, the living room—ah, there she was, in the bedroom. But, something was wrong. He went in and climbed the stairs to the bedroom. There, in the middle of the floor, she sat with a woebegone expression. Sean kneeled.

"What's wrong, sweet-pie?" he said.

"Nuthin'," she said.

Sean tried not to laugh.

Nuthin'? It was clearly written on her face—she was very troubled and hurting.

"I can't help if you won't talk to me."

He let the silence stretch, and stretch it did, like sidewalk gum on a scorching-hot afternoon. He shrugged and turned away.

"If I can't help, then I've failed and I should jump out of the window."

He took a step. She didn't speak, but made a little squeak, like a dormouse. He turned. With a limp hand, she extended the blue satchel.

Empty.

"Where did your marbles get off to?" he said.

"I—I don't know," she replied.

"Don't worry, Minnie, I will take care of this. Flix! Get your thieving hands in here, now!"

There was a rustle and a scurry. After a leisurely minute, Flix sauntered in.

"You called?" he said with studied innocence. "Is there something loyal and honest Flix can do for you?

"Bring back Minnie's marbles."

"Marbles? Flix knows nothing about marbles. If you're searching for marbles, that's something Flix cannot help with. I would love to help, but here we are. I can offer nothing."

There was something about the way he said marbles...

"Oh, very well, then. I know you can't lie. Go ahead, go on, we'll find the marbles on our own."

Sean turned to look at Minnie's tear-streaked face. He winked. As if having no care in the world, Flix turned to walk away. Sean let him get all the way to the door.

"Oh, Flix?"

"Yes, Sean."

"What about one, single-solitary marble? Perhaps the cerulean sapphire?"

"Worm-dirt," Flix said.

"Bring it back."

"I only took the one."

"Yes, but you see what happened. You took one—then Joly took one, then Swin took one and the next thing you know, we have a poor, sad little girl holding an empty bag and that's not what we want. Go get it—and say you're sorry."

"I'll bring the marble back, but I won't apologize for taking what's mine, not in a thousand-big-zillion years."

He ran off. Sean turned to Minnie and whispered.

"Give him a little wiggle room to preserve his dignity."

When Flix came back, he was a colorful blur moving at the speed of light. Before Minnie could focus her eyes, the bag in her hand held a marble. She weighed it in her hands.

"He's fast," she said.

"That he is," agreed Sean. "Slippery and fast."

The air buzzed with pixies and soon Minnie's bag was refilled—weighing down the lap of her dress. She poured the marbles into the coiled rug and admired them. She couldn't help herself—she counted. There was an extra. A new one amongst all the blue—a ruby-red orb with streaks of gold.

"It's beautiful," Minnie said.

Sean reached out and nudged the red one with his finger.

"They like you," he said. "Can I see it?"

Instinctively, she wrapped it in her little fist.

"I'd rather you didn't," she said.

Sean tilted his head back, ran his hands thorough his longish hair and laughed.

"Fair enough," he said.

Minnie realized what she was doing and was embarrassed. She held out the gleaming stone marble in the palm of her hand.

"I'm sorry."

"It's okay, Minnie," Sean said. "I understand."

Boot Camp—Taking a Break

BATTERED, BRUISED AND bone-weary, Fiona opened the back door a crack to let Luna out. Like a furry rocket, he shot through the gap and ran into the tangled bramble at the back of the yard. She envied his freedom to run and run and not look back.

In the mud room, her coat hung on a hook and her boots were brushed clean and ready to go. She looked back at the living room where Llwyd reclined on the couch with his head buried in an ancient leather-bound tome—something he'd brought with him. She'd glanced at the title, but it was written in German and she didn't take the time to unravel it.

Der Verbrecher aus verlorener Ehre.

He sipped Red Rose high-grown black tea from a delicate china cup—the nearly full, gently steaming pot rested on the table in front of him. He would be okay for hours.

Hell, days, knowing this impossible little man.

Stepping out on the back stoop, she looked to the trees for guidance from Selene. It was afternoon, but the full disk of the washed-out moon floated like a ghost over the dark forest. There was a roost-spot high in Selene's favorite tree. And there, a splotch of dark against dark.

Okay? Will I be safe if I walk?

No warning of imminent danger came back, so she laced up the boots and slipped her arms into the heavy wool coat. There was a deer trail where she sometimes saw a shy, peeping bobcat from her kitchen window. Deer would come to nibble on the Summer Sweet apple tree—where they could get to it through the chicken wire fencing installed to discourage them. This time of year, the apples were just a blossom's dream—as she passed by; she ran her gloved hands over the barren branches to stir them. A random thought entered her head.

> *If you want to replicate a particular variety, say a McIntosh, you must graft a short piece of a one year old McIntosh twig, called a scion, onto another tree called a rootstock.*[8]

Her thoughts drifted. Life was cruel, but it was also beautiful. The coin of the world displayed indescribable beauty on one side and black-evil horror on the other. How did it all balance out? Which concept of God or Gods could take all the credit or all the blame? She shrugged off these philosophical thoughts when she stepped into the woods.

Living on the ragged edge of hundreds of acres of forest, she had many options for where to go—for example, she could follow innumerable streams toward the Piscataqua River or she could walk in the direction of civilization toward the boardwalks and mountain bike trails, but she wanted to be alone, so she idly followed the interlinked trails to the north.

Ahead was a well-known top-secret treehouse-fort built by pre-teen boys generations earlier—it was maintained by a current crop of pre-teens, including a girl, a lanky tomboy named Rochelle.

---

[8] From the Fedcoseeds.com website, Bunker, John, *Apples Originating in Maine*

Fiona knew them because she watched them ride skateboards and kick a soccer ball on a grassy field near the cove.

Enjoy it now, Roach. In a couple of short years, you'll enter mysterious territory—you'll inevitably pair up with a brooding troublemaker and shed these comrades like a snake sheds its skin. Sorry, girl, but that's the way of it.

The tree house was assembled from pallet slats and scavenged door panels. Someone had scavenged a leftover roll of tar paper, so, after nailing on flattened aluminum-can shingles, miraculously, the roof was waterproof. She watched for a few minutes to make sure the gang was gone—there was no need to violate their supposed secrecy.

All clear.

The trail weaved around a tree and under a huge white pine deadfall into a small patch of meadow. There, the fortress was fifteen feet above the ground and easy to reach with well-secured ladder slats leading up, up, upward. This time of year, the wildflowers of the meadow were downtrodden and brown. Frost aster, puttyroot orchid, slenderleaf foxglove and Dutchman's breeches all slept and waited for spring's cosmic alarm clock.

She climbed.

Inside, the treehouse was a large, square structure about seven feet on a side. Inside among the secret treasures, the kids had a pipe. Fiona sniffed it. Borkum Riff Black Cavendish. One day, the pipe would smell of pungent herb and that would be a signal that the boys (and girl) were growing up and would soon move on to other pleasures beyond the secret fort in the woods.

In a wooden box, there was a magazine—of course there was. A well-thumbed, two-year-old Penthouse filled with imaginary plastic creatures only vaguely similar to real women.

Don't let this twist you all out of shape about your perfectly functional body, Rochelle. Most men are smart enough to figure how to be happy with what they're going to get—and if they're not? That's not your problem. Dump the fool and move on.

There was a window of sorts—foggy Plexiglas looked to the west. She arranged a camp stool, settled in and watched the sun move through the sky. She'd never counted, but her coat had at least seven pockets. She explored them and found a small plastic bottle of organic apple cider and a Ziploc bag of home-assembled trail mix.

A feast.

In her kitchen, she had assembled the trail mix herself just the way she wanted it—with dried cranberries, carob chips and organic pecans. Fiona had a slender though womanly figure, and sometimes someone would ask her—'what's your secret for staying slim?'

Here's a good start, she'd say. Any foods you've ever seen advertised on TV? Stay far away from them.

The snarky wisdom made her smile while she munched. Simple answer, right, with a dollop of truth embedded in it. But, as usual, simple did not mean easy. Though it was far from quiet with the brisk wind in the trees, the rumble of far-away traffic on the highway and the birds chattering, she felt at peace.

Can others feel this?

Oneness. Unity. The flow of life and Earth and sun and air and water and the cycle of stars in the sky. The phantom moon was on the other side of the sky, so she couldn't see it, but she felt it move—felt its tidal pull in her blood. All this is always there, but can be easily blocked by noise. External noise. Internal noise. To tune into it, step away from the bustle and let nature's voice take over. Open the doors and make sure reality's welcome mat is prominently displayed.

She breathed in and out and chanted her secret seed mantra. It wasn't an English word, it was a spiritual word.

Shaabu.

She whispered it and drew out the long syllables.

What did *shaabu* mean? Nothing, it was just her personal key for unlocking the door to her soul to admit the divine. Far away,

Selene gave a mournful hoot.

Breathe in.

Breathe out.

The master painters dabbed a black beauty-spot on the creamy-skinned faces of their models because perfection was not of the human domain—perfection belonged to God and no one else. As Fiona's mind reached out toward unity with God, she could see a black, beauty spot off to the side growing like a cancer—an annoying flaw drawing her mind's eye away from focusing on perfection. Selene's faraway cries grew more intense and urgent. It was a warning.

Dammit. I was close.

Fiona stood and stretched her legs.

How long had she been sitting?

Her joints were stiff and her back was crooked like a comma. The sun had ratcheted across the sky. It would be dark soon—the winter woods were no place to be when the sun went down.

Okay. I'm coming.

There was light enough for now, but it wouldn't last. In the heavy boots she ran—tromping through the woods as if the devil was on her heels.

Minnie Learns to Sing

TIME IS SLIPPERY; sometimes it flows quickly and other times—like maple sap on a frigid day—it hardly seems to run at all. We can look over our shoulders at passages and life events with sorrow or elation; sometimes we can look forward with trepidation or excitement for the glorious unknown, but always when we're not looking, on its soft feet, time sneaks by.

In contrast, children have an innate understanding of time's illusion. Minutes turn into hours, into days, into weeks and eventually into years—and vice versa. Seasons come and go and blend together. So it was for Minnie.

Her world was constantly changing. Every time she twirled around something was different, but always, she felt safe and secure. She loved being with Sean in his enchanted house. As he predicted, she grew and blossomed on the path to becoming all she was destined to become. Often times, Minnie would catch Sean sitting and watching her; she basked in the love and pride emanating from his eyes. While she had not forgotten her mother or her prior life, this was her life now, her true life and her soul's purpose.

Every day brought a new adventure, a new lesson—a new *something* for Minnie to digest and take in. On this morning,

Minnie awoke to Sean singing a lovely tune. It wafted up the stairs to gently wake her.

> *Where dips the rocky highland*
> *Of Sleuth Wood in the lake*
> *There lies a leafy island*
> *Where flapping herons wake*
> *The drowsy water-rats*
> *There we've hid our fairy vats*
> *Full of berries*
> *And of reddest stolen cherries*
>
> *Come away, oh human child*
> *To the waters and the wild*
> *With a fairy hand in hand*
> *For the world's more full of weeping*
> *Than you can understand* [9]

Minnie loved Sean's songs—the music was haunting and mystical. Often, she giggled when he sang. Not because he sounded silly, but because the songs filled her with delight. Sean feigned offense at Minnie's laughing when he sang, but once she said he tickled her heart, all was forgiven. Fiona had once said something similar to him long, long ago. He understood. His music spoke to Minnie; it spoke to a deep part of her just beginning to awaken.

Minnie tippy-toed down the stairs to quietly sit and soak in the scene. Sean sat on his favorite rock. At first it seemed odd to Minnie that Sean would have a rock in the house, but it suited him. It was a rock worn from time; smooth from centuries of washing and wearing by a raging river. Granite, it was the softest shade of grey with flecks of black like freckles on a newborn harbor seal. Like freckles on a fawn.

---

[9] —Yeats, William Butler, *Stolen Child,* as sung by Loreena McKennitt

On the top was a well worn "seat" where Sean perched like a master surveying his kingdom—with one leg bent and the other reaching for the floor. So, there sat Sean, playing his beloved lute, with all sorts of magical beings dancing and cavorting about him. When Sean was done, Minnie couldn't contain herself—she clapped her dainty hands and giggled.

Sean and company looked up at her. Some of the faeries curtsied while some blushed; the younger faeries were embarrassed by an audience. Minnie bowed her head and spoke softly.

"Forgive me; it was just so beautiful I couldn't contain my joy."

That was all it took for the fairies and pixies to get over their shyness and fly and run to surround sweet Minnie. Sean let out a hearty belly laugh as Minnie sat and chuckled. He admired the scene.

Ahhhh, a child's laughter, how I love that sound. One day, before long, Fiona will hear it and fall in love with it as I have.

Once the revelries subsided, Minnie made her way the rest of the way down the stairs and ran to Sean for her morning hug.

"What shall we do today?" she said.

Sean put his fingers on his chin and tugged his beard like the evil genius Dr. Fu Manchu pondering a mysterious crime.

Lately, they'd been spending a lot of time studying— memorizing the patterns of the nighttime sky, poring over illustrations of medicinal plants, reading the lore of the magical forest folk and creatures and practicing simple spells; all the usual things a young mystical princess in training should know of.

"Is there anything in particular you'd like to learn about today, Princess Minnie?"

Nothing jumped into her mind.

She smiled and gave Sean a coy look.

"Maybe I could think better if I had a little something in my tummy."

She has settled into her new life.

When she first arrived, she wasn't much more than skin and bones—meek and worn to shreds. Now she was vibrant and alive and stretching for something just barely out of reach. She wanted to eat, wanted to learn, wanted to be. Sean shook his head and marveled at her.

"You are truly a wonder, Miss Minnie. I'm sure the cupboards are empty, but come along anyway, let's venture to the kitchen and see if we can find a few scraps and crumbs to break our night's fast."

Perhaps the kitchen was not so barren after all. Sean found Irish oats, fresh peaches, a crock of heavy cream and a string of plump sausages redolent with sage, sea salt, white wax onions and black peppercorns. These sausages soon found themselves sizzling in a cast iron skillet.

Once they ate (and ate and ate) and cleaned up, Sean and Minnie sat on the slate-paved patio to ponder their plan for the day.

There, Minnie let out a gasp and spoke breathlessly.

"Ooh, I know, I want to venture into *there*."

She pointed into the hills beyond the fringe of the sparse forest around the house. Sean choked on his tea when he looked up and noted where Minnie's index finger was pointed.

I knew this was coming, but what can I say or do? Why am I unprepared?

Wide-eyed with wonder, Minnie looked up at him. She had struck a nerve—she'd instinctively stumbled on something unready for unearthing and being examined in the sunlight. She sat patiently and watched as Sean framed his thoughts. As much as possible, he tried to keep nothing from her and answer her questions directly and honestly, but she was unprepared to face the harsh realities lurking outside the house's protected zone.

Now was the time for learning and building strength, not a time for overwhelming a young princess with skulking, nightmarish dangers.

The deep forest. Oh, the black forest.

It was a topic he hoped they could avoid for a while longer.

Please, not today.

He assembled his thoughts—marshaled and arranged them in tidy rows.

"Well, my sweet child, the forest on its own we should not fear because we are friends to all its animals and spirits. We are tree-keepers and treat the noble giants with the respect they deserve. The nearby forest around us is very old, indeed, ancient. The roots of those trees run deep and strong down to the very heart of the Earth itself. There is no evil there, but beyond the magic circle, there are memories and spirits—and monsters. It is no mistake I cleared *this* land and built the house where I did, child. This land is where I lived with Fiona years and years ago, long before the dawn of this age. It is protected by ancient spells. If we venture into the dark part of the forest, you will see and feel things from ages past. Dangerous things. When the time is right, I will tell you what to watch for and how to slip by the black ghosts and leave them sleeping. For now, I beg you. Stay away. The grass and the garden and the spring walk and the path to the lake are protected and safe, but you must not go into the deep forest. I promise to take you further when you're ready, but not now. Please."

Minnie looked momentarily scared, and then the spark came back to her eyes. If this was a test of her resolve, of her will—she felt ready to take it on.

She looked directly into Sean's eyes and said, "At least we can walk along the edge—it seems like a lovely day for an adventure."

Sean laughed.

"Oh, my dear sweet Minnie, how I love you and your boundless spirit. Yes, okay, a walk along the forest path—it's a perfect day for it and we'll go."

Loading a backpack and picnic basket, they prepared for the afternoon and soon found themselves strolling on a path lined with bracken ferns and daisies that wove through fruit trees and bunchberry bushes—accompanied by bumblebees, grasshoppers and hummingbirds.

Minnie Speaks to the Forest

DAYS LATER, THEY sat again on the front porch.

Was it time? Was she ready?

"Minnie, how about a walk through the woods to the lake?"

"Oh, yes," Minnie said, "I've been waiting since forever."

They scampered upstairs to dress for their forest adventure, then stuffed a backpack with supplies from the kitchen—hunks of black bread, combs of dripping honey, huge red apples almost as big as Minnie's head—and a flask of spring water. When all was said and done, they looked every bit the epitome of classic forest explorers, right down to wooden walking sticks—though Sean's was more like a staff with a glowing crystal fracturing sunlight with its glistening facets.

On the porch, Sean kneeled and solemnly looked into Minnie's eyes.

"We'll walk along the fringe," he said, "but will not take a single step into the wild. This is very important. Promise me."

She nodded.

"I understand," she said.

They set out. Sean could feel Minnie's excitement and bold curiosity. He squeezed her hand.

"It will be fun, honey, I promise."

Minnie squeezed his hand back but didn't say anything.

They walked along a path through a scattering of trees where critters flitted—birds and bees, butterflies and dragonflies. They stooped to say hello to a red salamander and help move it to a neighboring pool. They played leapfrog along the way and sang silly songs. Then Minnie noticed it had become quiet. Really quiet—the air was still as if hushed in awe. Dappled sunlight found its way through the leaves and branches, but only in scattered patches. She looked up to Sean and him down at her—as if reading her thoughts he spoke.

"We're going back in time. Put your hand on a tree and you'll hear a story or catch a glimpse of a memory it holds. Go ahead, try that one over there."

Minnie ran to a white birch tree with heart-shaped leaves and thin, paper-like bark peeling off like onionskin. She put her little hand on it to feel the stored warmth captured from the sun. She felt as if she traveled through a tunnel, then an eye opened and the tree spoke to her in a voice that was a low rumble, though clear as could be.

"My name is Fergus. It's a pleasure to meet you, Miss Minnie. I see you and you see me. We are one."

Minnie pulled her hand away, as if feeling something hot. She ran to Sean shaking her hand in front of her face like it was alien and unknown.

"He talks funny, but I understood. He said his name is Fergus."

Sean smiled.

"You're young, but I hoped you could commune with the trees. Understand, Minnie, trees transcend time and space. They are the keepers of all human and inhuman knowledge. They see and know everything and give their secrets to the breeze. They carry more wisdom than the oldest book and their roots run straight down to the Earth Mother. They have earned the greatest of respect. They will protect you when times get tough. You are one with them as they are one with you. Do you understand?"

Minnie nodded, though the look on her face showed she didn't follow everything he said.

They continued on their path, stopping now and again to commune with the trees. To Sean, it appeared she was truly in touch with the Earth—she could effortlessly speak to most of the trees, though there were always those who slept or were not in the mood for conversation. Her ability extended beyond the trees to dirt, rock, flower and moss; anything in her path with spirit. It was remarkable, but deep inside and hidden under his grin, he still felt unease.

She's strong, and growing stronger still, but will she be strong enough? Is there anyone on Earth strong enough?

He gathered her into his arms and squeezed until she wriggled like a mealworm.

"You are a very special little girl."

Eel-smooth, she slid through his arms, and laughing, ran down the trail.

"Ever the sparkling pixie princess," he muttered while watching her run.

He caught up with her at the steep bank of the lake. From the pack, Sean produced a thick blanket and they sat down for lunch. In mileage, it had not been a long walk, but it was a long distance for Minnie's little legs—she was tired. She plopped down to rest. Lost in memory, Sean took a sip of water and turned his gaze over the water. He longed for Fiona—this is where their golden time had ended so long ago.

Sean turned his eyes to Minnie. With a bellyful of bread and honey, she was drowsy. One of her hands slipped off the blanket to rest on bare earth—listening to the stories it told. Time passed and dreams faded into reality while reality faded into dreams.

She's thinking about her mother...

Sean yearned to reach for her—to still her twitch and

whimper, but instead, he let her emotions flow. There was no avoiding it; just as there were times for joy and satisfaction, there were times for sadness and remembering. In her dreams, she slowly passed into a happier place where her honeyed lips twitched upward in smile. In approval, the sun peeked from behind a fluffy cloud and the wind breathed a soft sigh of relief. While watching over her, Sean relaxed. All was well, it was safe. Joining her, his eyes drifted closed and he entered the kingdom of dreams.

He woke with a start. The sun hovered over the trees and Minnie was gone. In an act of will and discipline, he pushed back at his fear and quieted his mind. He reached out.

Where is she?

He was afraid that, in spite of his serious warning, she had headed toward the dark wood, so he searched in that direction first. There was no sign of her there—no trail she left behind. She did not go in that direction. He heaved a sigh of relief before spreading his inner eyes in the other directions.

Lake. Shore. Beach.

She had wandered along the shoreline and...

Oh, no.

Though not as dangerous as the woods, there were hazards from the water too. Among the creatures of the black-deep was *An t-Seileag,* a monster big enough to gobble little morsel Minnie with a flick of its head and flash of its dagger-like fangs. His hand flicked to his belt. What weapon did he have?

Only a dagger—which would do nothing against the giant eel-dragon.

Stumbling and sliding on the slippery rocks of the shore, he ran as fast as he could. After vaulting a fallen tree, he saw her— knee-deep in the lake's cold, still water. An t-Seileag floated on the crystalline water like a deadfall. There was no hope for Minnie, but Sean raised his dagger and prepared to make the serpent-creature pay the ultimate price. He splashed toward them.

Minnie turned her head and calmly opened her eyes to look at Sean—her beloved protector and heroic silver knight on a silver steed. Sean stopped and placed his dagger back in its sheath.

She spoke. Her words wove a story.

"You died here and Fiona turned into a mermaid. And Selene—I saw Selene." While An t-Seileag's tail roiled and riffled the lake's water, she went on to recount all she saw and heard and felt, telling tales of people of old and people of recent times. She went on and on and Sean wondered if she would *ever* stop. But, as she told her tales, Sean watched her. Not only was he impressed with her skills at articulation, but he knew her words were carried on the wind to others, good and bad, who would listen with interest. Sean's emotions were mixed: elated and fearful at the same time.

When Minnie finally finished, she was clearly thrilled by the stories she told. Energy coursed through her, energy she'd never felt before. She was becoming; becoming one with the Earth, one with her past, one with her present and soon, one with her future.

With one hand resting on An t-Seileag's knobbed head, she took Sean's hand with the other.

"I'm so sorry you drowned. But maybe it had to be so for you to be with me now."

Such wisdom, such insightful things these young eyes see.

A tear trickled down his cheek.

"Yes, Minnie, all things happen for a reason. Always remember that. We may not know the reason at the time and we may not ever *like* the reason, but all happens as it should, and all we can do is trust in the happening."

"An t-Seileag says he bears no grudge. You can put your hand on his head if you like."

Sean grimaced.

"I'd rather not, if it's all the same to you," he said.

She chortled.

"You're right, there's no reason to press your luck." She

turned to the lake-creature. "I am honored to make your acquaintance."

Where did this little girl get such a sophisticated vocabulary?

An t-Seileag swept into a wide turn then drenched Sean with a flick of its tail before disappearing into the black water of the deep. Sean sputtered and wiped his face.

"Still angry about the time you trapped him and his brother in a net," Minnie said.

"I suppose he would be," replied Sean. "Let's get back to our picnic."

Back at their blanket, He pulled out a miniature bodhrán drum and began playing a rhythmic tune.

> *I am the voice in the wind and the pouring rain*
> *I am the voice of your hunger and pain*
> *I am the voice that always is calling you*
> *I am the voice—I will remain*
>
> *I am the voice in the fields when the Summer's gone*
> *The dance of the leaves when the Autumn winds blow*
> *Ne'er do I sleep throughout all the cold Winter long*
> *I am the force that in Springtime will grow*[10]

"Minnie, please remember, when the Mother Earth sings, that's the song she sings to you. Hold it near, hold it dear; it will be a light and reminder when times are dark. But now, my minnow, darkness approaches and this is not a good place to be when the sun goes down. We should head back home. Are you ready?"

Minnie spoke with solemn intensity.

"A minnow is a fish. I'm not a fish."

Sean tickled her ribs.

---

[10] Celtic Woman, *The Voice*, from *A New Journey*, Brendan Graham © 1996 Peermusic Music Publishing

"Then you're a minotaur," he said, "a minx, a lost minty minute, a miniature mineralogist and a mincing monkey minion."

They lost track of time and when the playtime was over, the sun kissed the tops of the trees across the lake.

"Time to move," Sean said, while gathering their things.

Minnie gave him a tired nod of agreement. While fingers of darkness followed on their heels, the brisk walk back remained enchanting. With defenses in disarray, Minnie saw the forest through unshielded eyes for what it really was; not with the eyes of a mere mortal, but with those of an awakening pixie princess. She was aware and filled with respectful awe.

As they approached the house, Sean sensed something troubling. There was hustle and bustle, and not simply because Sean and Minnie had been in the forest for the better part of the day—leaving the house unsupervised. Flix approached and babbled faster than they could follow. To no avail, Sean urged the little pixie to slow down. Finally, Flix resorted to what he knew how to do best—singing.

The game is in their hands, calling out the color
Togetherness, their courage, recognize the power
Make a stand before them, old ways follows the beaten track
Against the wind, against the wind[11]

Sean thought for a minute and let the words roll around in his brain. He couldn't quite grasp it.

Minnie kneeled and listened to Flix sing.

"He says we'll have visitors," she said. "Two. One, then the other."

Flix looked at her and nodded, and then looked gravely at Sean. Unconsciously, Sean pressed his fist against his chest as if to still his thundering heart.

---

[11] *Against the Wind*, from *Máire*, ©1992 Máire Brennan and Tim Jarvis

"One, then the other," he said. "Okay."

He took a deep breath and whispered to himself. "Okay."

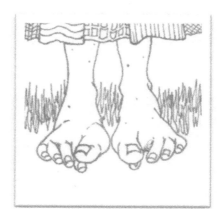

Camp Minnie—Once Again, the Queen Pays a Visit

SEAN FINISHED PEELING an orange and arranged the segments on Minnie's plate.

"I couldn't eat another bite," she said, while stuffing a segment into her mouth to join mashed-up remnants of a blueberry muffin.

"Then I will help you," Sean said while plucking a wedge from the plate and popping it in his mouth. He stood with his fists against his sides and examined the wreckage to the breakfast table. "By now," he wiped her chin with a napkin, "I should not be so surprised at how *big* a mess such a *little* girl can make."

She was giggling when there came a knock at the front door.

"Oh," he said. "One, then the other."

Minnie scratched her cheek and looked perplexed.

"Yes," she said.

Mentally, Sean reached out to touch the visitor.

Oh.

He finished washing Minnie's chin and dropped the napkin on the table.

It's the Queen.

He walked to the front door and stood for a moment gathering his courage. She rapped harder.

"I see you," she said, "so don't stand there like a buffoon, open up. To think, *I* have to knock on doors and announce myself. Tradition. Protocol. Words that mean nothing to the young and brash and ignorant."

He pulled the door open.

"My Queen. We are honored by your presence."

"Are you going to work your jaw all day or invite me in?"

"Of course, my Queen, please enter and consider our house your home."

"Took your time about it," she said as she brushed by him. She examined the living room. "Huh, I see what you're doing. This looks like Fiona's house. I don't know what you've heard elsewhere, but, to me, imitation is the sincerest form of stupidity."

"What brings you to our humble abode?"

"That should be obvious to even a dolt like you. Bring her—the Princess. I want to see how much you've been spoiling her."

Minnie was already in the room—hiding behind Sean. She peeped around his leg as the Queen settled on the couch and arranged her colorful, multilayered skirts. Cautiously, Minnie approached and offered her hand—palm up and bearing the new, little red jewel—to the Queen. The Queen sniffed.

"Ah, a bauble that fell off one of my gowns." She dismissed the offer with an imperious wave of her bony hand. "You may keep it." She studied Minnie from head to toe. "She's a pretty little thing, there's no arguing that. But, pretty does no good when an ice-wolf gnaws on your leg." She shifted and began lifting her patterned skirts. "Maybe that lesson would sink in if she saw the result."

Sean reached over and stopped her.

"I don't think that's appropriate right now—there's no need to traumatize the child with the scars of your war wounds."

The Queen grunted.

"Your house, your rules, no matter how idiotic. I'd change that rule in half a moth's breath if I could—it would reduce the gross ineptness I am forced to tolerate. Brew me tea—and don't skimp on coconut nectar to sweeten it, and thyme honey if you have it." She wrinkled her nose. "Which you do. Plenty."

Sean made an elaborate gesture followed by a deep bow.

"As the Queen so desires," he said. He stooped before Minnie. "Would you come to the kitchen to help me, please?"

"She'll just be underfoot—leave her with me. We'll make chitchat and talk about kittens and bluebirds."

Sean cast a skeptical eye on the Queen.

"Go," she said.

The old woman leaned over to make sure Sean was gone and not lingering by the doorway to eavesdrop. She waved her hand to draw Minnie near.

"Child," she whispered, "I have a notion. Why don't you go outside and play?"

Minnie shook her head.

"No, thank you—I'm supposed to stay inside."

"Go," the Queen commanded. "Go now and bring me the gall."

Boot Camp—Tough Lessons

FIONA SHRUGGED OFF the heavy coat and started unlacing her muddy boots. The house was quiet—bright lights from the kitchen radiated into the accumulating darkness. Llwyd was not reclining on his comfortable spot on the couch. The tipped-over teapot was on the floor leaking brown fluid into the coiled carpet. She raised her voice and called out.

"Llwyd?"

His response was weak.

"Here," he said.

With the incomplete boot-unlacing task put aside, she stood and peered into the shadows of the living room. There was a dark shadow in the corner.

Llwyd?

In haste, she kicked the teapot aside and stumbled across the room. Llwyd lay crumpled like a discarded blanket with blood streaming from a gash on his temple.

"I'm sorry, Fiona," he said.

"What happened? What is it?"

"Help me up."

"What? I need to call 9-1-1."

135

Llwyd chuckled, but the chuckle was accompanied by a dribble of blood that ran down his chin.

"9-1-1, that's a good one. Help me. I can't stand up by myself."

She tugged his arm and, leaning heavily against the wall, he was able to stand.

"Get my staff."

She looked around. The end of his stick peeped from under the couch. Propping him up, she extended a foot and worked the staff closer, then leaned down to grab it. He grabbed it with both hands.

"I'm sorry, Fiona, I did what I could, but this chapter is over. You need to run. Run now."

"What are you talking about? Let me get you to the sofa."

"There's no time, Fiona. Listen to me. Run. Run now."

"That's absurd. This is my house and I will defend it to death's door. You told me—we're strong here. Let's fight."

"I fought. We lost. You need to go, it's already too late. Run, dear, run for your life."

"I didn't pack a bag. All my stuff is here. You said we had more time." She looked around the house. It was quiet. "I don't understand. Have you taken leave of your senses?"

Weakly, he pressed her aside.

"I will stand as long as I can. Please, Fiona, on my Queen mother's lonely future grave, I swear it. You need to run now."

"Where will I go?"

"It doesn't matter and I don't want to—I can't know. If I know, I'll tell before he kills me."

"Is it the Black Faerie King?"

"No, he's still sleeping, thank the lonely spirit of Anextlomarus. Don't let me die so far from home for nothing, Fiona. Go. Go now."

She turned and raised her hands. Her staff flew across the room in into her fierce grasp.

"I'm not going anywhere. Where is this enemy? I will smash him to pieces myself. I'm not leaving my home. No one can defeat us if we stand together."

Llwyd moaned.

Across the room, a shadow coiled by the hallway wall. Three-feet-tall, it was short and stout, like a beer keg.

Gnome?

No, a troll.

Though solidly built, it did not look fearsome.

"Is this the thing?" Fiona said.

"Not just a troll. Áinfean. He's already eaten my soul, but I can fight for a while longer. Run, Fiona."

The small figure grew more substantial. At first, she felt amused; something so compact was comical, not fearsome. But, as he solidified, his teeth and claw-like hands became more visible. And his eyes—no mercy lived there. A tendril of fear stirred in her gut. She took a step forward and raised her staff.

"Don't let his sword touch you," Llwyd said through gritted teeth.

Sword? What sword?

In a flash, the creature tugged something from a leather sheath and slashed it toward her face. Llwyd pulled her backward and, in slow motion, she saw the crimson-stained razor-edge sweep in front of her eyes—it left behind a glimmering trail and the trail told a long, sad story of bloodshed and despair. Widows weeping. Mothers sobbing. Heaps of rocks in rows: cairns—sepulchral monuments. Death. Destruction. War. The edge wanted her flesh; she could feel its craving, its thirst. She felt its mad-hungry frustration at being denied and suddenly knew this could easily be it. Death was in the room. Fiona born. Fiona raised with unconscious magic at her fingertips. Youthful vigor. School. Boys, wine, tea, good food, sex, washing the dishes, sweeping the floor, sunlight on her bare shoulders, the taste of tears, the smell of roses in bloom. All ended in a fraction of an instant in her living room by a beyond-ugly three-foot-tall troll.

I'm not ready.

Spinning, she let herself be pulled around while Llwyd speared the troll's gut with his sturdy staff. The blade stopped and restarted in reverse, like film running backwards. Still spinning, she swept her staff around Llwyd and bounced it off the troll's skull. He opened his gapping maw and howled like a timber wolf. She kept her weight on the staff and followed through like a homerun hitter. The troll went down and his sword dropped the floor; it skittered like a cockroach. She raised her staff and pounded the troll's head.

"This is my house," she shouted.

Llwyd pulled at her arm and dragged her away.

"Run, Fiona."

"We got him," she said.

"Yes, but he's not alone." Fiona's shoulders slumped. He gripped her shoulder. "Seconds, not minutes. Go. I will hold them off as long as I can."

Shitte.

Splayed on the floor, the troll oozed like a slug—reaching for the hilt of his ugly sword. With a heavy, partially laced boot, Fiona stepped on his neck and put her weight on him until his throat collapsed with a satisfying crunch.

"For the love of—love, Fiona, I beg you. Run."

She stood for a long moment while shadows formed against the hallway wall. One, two, three, more. Absurdly, a song formed in her head.

One, two, three, four, tell me that you love me more
Sleepless, long nights, that is what my youth was for
Old teenage hopes are alive at your door, left you with nothing,

But they want some more...[12]

She put her hand on Llywd's cheek.

"There's more than one kind of love," she said.

"I know," he said. "Go."

She nodded. She strode toward the front door, then turned.

"Wait, did you say the Queen is your mother?"

"GO!" Llywd shouted.

He raised his staff as more trolls took shape in the hallway. As if in a daze, she walked through the front door, down the steps and onto the slate walkway in her front yard. While walking, she stopped to pick up Luna. On the street a hundred yards away, she stopped and turned back to her precious home. Flames licked at the windows where shadows capered and danced.

With tears in her eyes, she petted the black cat.

"I'm a coward, Luna," she said. "That man did not deserve to die alone."

In seconds the house was completely engulfed in black and red flames—then the screaming started as if the tortured Earth experienced existential anguish.

I will kill the Black Faerie King. If it's the last thing I do, he will pay.

With a heavy heart and million-pound boots, she turned to walk away.

I'll find him, wrap my fingers around his neck and choke the last evil breath from him. I swear it on my soul.

Camp Minnie—the Fringe

THE FRINGE OF forest around the house was familiar—like an old friend to Minnie because she'd played endless hours of hide-n-seek, Red Rover–Minnie Over and Ring around the Rosie with the pixies and sprites.

> *Ring a ring a rosie, a bottle full of posie*
> *All the girls in our town, ring for little Josie.*[13]

However, there was an abrupt demarcation where the bramble of blackberry bush, tangled holly and devil's ivy took over from the sparse fruit trees and friendly buffalo meadow grass. Sean warned her over and over to stay away, but the warning was superfluous— she sensed the lurking dangers and malevolent spirits reaching out and trying to *touch* her. Rational fear touched her heart. She loved her home and felt no compulsion to leave its confines.

However, there was no denying the Queen. Minnie didn't know what a *gall* was, but the mental image of how one might be found was vivid in her mind. She had to cross the forest's invisible

---

[13] Version from William Wells Newell's *Games and Songs of American Children*, 1883. Dated by Wells to 1790.

barrier and walk along a cobwebby trail deep into the dark woods to a giant, gnarled oak tree. There she would find galls by the hundreds. And among the hundreds, find the *one*.

With a black hole replacing her stomach, Minnie took deep, fortifying breaths and stood on the porch looking out into the gloomy woods. Wearing powder-blue ribbons in her hair, a navy-blue jumper, white blouse, black tights and a pair of brown leather moccasins, she could hardly be less prepared. She took a step down the stairs and realized something was missing. Turning back, she walked back through the house's front door. Under the critical eye of the Queen, she walked back into the house and grabbed her walking stick.

Clever girl, the Queen thought.

Passively, the Queen arched an eyebrow and raised an index finger a fraction of an inch to point toward the deep woods.

It took over half an hour for the tea to brew to Sean's satisfaction—he was proud of the thick, nearly black mix of steeped holly berries, millrose and hibiscus—sweetened by thick black honey and leavened with a dash of coconut milk.

This will curl her hair, he thought.

He poured the aromatic mixture into a giant clay mug and carefully carried it into the main room on a silver tray. The instant he entered the room, he felt the soulless vacuum.

Where is Minnie?

His knees loosened and he almost dropped the heavy tray.

"Oh, my Queen, what have you done?"

"You damned well took your time with the tea—so don't you dare drop it. My long journey left me with a considerable thirst. I can't drink it from there. Bring it over, Sean. Bring it now."

He dropped the tray on the table before her and ran to the bay window looking out over the forest.

No.

He turned back to the Queen.

"She's not ready."

The Queen shrugged.

"Who is ever ready for anything? I wasn't. You never will be. I know you think she is the one, but I'm unconvinced."

"She'll die out there."

She blew across the top of the steaming cup and then sipped her tea.

"And then we'll know, won't we?"

"I swear to you, Scathach, on the soul of Taliesin, if she does not come back—and, by the light of The White Lady, she can't, she won't, how could she? How could you?"

"I'm interested in your oath. What do you swear?"

Sean walked across the room and stood over her.

"I swear you will not leave this house. Ever."

The Queen laughed.

"You have considerable skill with brewing tea—this is worthy of Tephi herself. Though, perhaps a little more Sumac next time."

Minnie and the Dark Woods

MINNIE STOOD AT the fringe of the forest with one little hand on her hip and the other gripping her staff. She was torn between wanting to be the *good-little-girl* for Sean and the *I'll-show-her little girl* for the Queen. She gazed into the tall, dark trees as this internal psychological battle waged within. Finally, she spoke aloud.

"Well, if that cranky old crone of a Queen is trying to scare me well then, I'll show her—I can march right into that forest and get this *gall* she seems to so desperately need. Am I the only one who can get it? Is that why she's so insistent? And, what's its magic power? I, Pixie Princess Minnie, will take on this clearly important and noble task—retrieving the *gall* for the Queen. Yes, so be it, I will venture forth and face down every danger. Sean says I am a keeper of the trees and friend to all. What harm shall dare to come my way?"

She said these words with all the strength and will in her little body—with force and power and joy. Though saying the brave words, there was still a scared and frightened little girl inside her—an internal voice pressed down deep which she tried to ignore.

I was the chosen one?

If so, she would do her best to see the quest to its conclusion.

After a deep breath and taking final glance back at the cozy house, she crossed the threshold into the dark woods. A shiver crawled up her spine and she gripped her staff ever more tightly.

She was now *in* and there would be no going back empty-handed.

Back at the house, the Queen took a sip of tea with an arrogant curl at the corners of her lips. After licking her lips, she muttered, "Yes, child, go—and don't return until you have the gall in your sweet little hands."

Sean stood at the window with a craving gnawing at his bones.

Return to me, Minnie.

He glanced back at the Queen and imagined her scheming, manipulative thoughts.

Minnie was a strong child; a smart and resourceful child. She could commune with the trees and all the sentient creatures. She would be okay. She would. Keeping his back to the Queen so she would not see, he twisted his fingers into knots and whispered an incantation. When he was done, he held a small white energy ball between his hands.

He opened his cupped hands and whispered.

"Go. Keep watch over her."

With that, the ball arose and flew out into the forest. Sean was sure that the Queen saw it take flight, but he didn't care. It was all he could do for Minnie now and he prayed it would be enough.

"If you interfere..."

Exasperated, Sean interrupted.

"...then I'll face the consequences."

"You think there is time for training and building her strength, but time is a luxury in short supply. How do ordinaries talk? That account is overdrawn. Tapped out. The barrel's bottom has been thoroughly scraped."

She stopped to sip her tea. The slurpy silence was a relief to Sean—she couldn't blather on so much while drinking.

"My Queen, would you permit me to brew up more lovely tea for you?"

Minnie stood quietly to let her senses attune to this new land when she saw a ball of light rocket down from the sky. It made her giggle as it landed on the top of her staff. At once, she knew it was a gift from Sean and he was looking after her the best that he could.

The sooner this chore is done, the sooner I'll be back.

"If I were a magical oak tree bearing a gall, where would I be?" she muttered.

She was startled when a verbose and haughty response came from a thicket of brush.

"There are oak trees all over. Everywhere. There's a wonderful Water Oak right in front of your nose. This forest is filled with them: Northern Red Oak, Pin Oak, White Oak, Willow Oak, Cherrybark Oak, Swamp Chestnut Oak and many others you are not clever enough to name. If you move three feet to your right, you'll encounter a lovely patch of Poison Oak your creamy-soft skin will find memorable. So, regardless of the laxness of your vague query, let's assume you're looking for a special oak and acknowledge the fact that if your question was more specific, you'd have better luck getting a useful answer."

Minnie raised the light on her staff and studied the brush, but saw no one, though branches moved and leaves rustled.

"You don't scare me," said Minnie with a quavering voice. "Show yourself."

"Ahhh," the voice responded, "in addition to being an unwanted intruder in this forest, you're a liar. You deserve this—I *will* show myself."

With her staff grasped in both hands, she took an athletic

stance and prepared to do battle with whatever came forth.

Out from the brush came a Fachan. She recognized him immediately from a storybook Sean had read to her—Fachans were queer little creatures that hopped about on one leg—with a grotesque hairy hand growing from the middle of their body. He had a long mane of black hair and one eye in the middle of his face above a folded-over nose. His ears were long and pointy.

For a long collection of seconds, her heart stopped—frozen in her little chest like a cold, dead stone. Her head grew light and she nearly toppled over, but Sean had coached her—his voice echoed in her head.

"They are not so scary—if you imagine a floppy red bow tied on the long strand of hair poking from the top of their heads."

Her heart twisted left, then right, then expanded like a balloon. It was not beating. Seconds stretched. Then, after a wrenching boom-boom tickle, the muscle-metronome restarted. With the image of the red bow in her head, she stayed still—holding her ground—trying not to laugh and provoke the creature. The spell was broken; she desperately choked back an attack of giggles in response to his hopping up and down like a pogo stick—and his ineffective attempt at being fearsome and scary.

Minnie wouldn't underestimate him; she knew Fachan antics—the mere sight of them could provoke a heart attack in the unguarded. In fact, that was their usual strategy: scare the unwary into heart seizure, then dine on the cooling corpse at their leisure. Claws. Ragged teeth. Horned toes.

Absurd, yes, but harmless?

No.

By no means, no.

She racked her brain for additional details from Sean's storybook.

What had Sean said?

Fachans were susceptible to formal politeness and flattery.

"Hello there, kind sir. I see you are a Fachan of the most

splendid sort. I thank you for emerging from the brush to show yourself. I am most honored by your presence."

With that, the Fachan stopped jumping and stood stock still. Most humans he encountered simply dropped dead at the sight of him. This little one though, said he was splendid and that she was honored to be in his presence. How could he attack and eat her now?

"I would bow to you, child, but clearly I would fall over and after hopping around all morning looking for a morsel of something to eat, I am too tired for formalities. You two-fers don't care, but life on one leg is horribly unfair and difficult. And to catch a tasty crumb with only one arm protruding from the middle of your body—well, you try it and see how you like it. So, I wonder—might you happen to have a little something you'd be willing to share? If not, I'm afraid I will have to disregard my misgivings and gobble you up."

Understanding flooded Minnie's body. At the heart of things, this Fachan was lonely and tired—and insatiably hungry. Her heart swelled with love for the bizarre creature. How tough it must be to make it in the world while being such an oddity. Shifting the staff to one hand, she reached into the pocket of her jumper. Though she didn't remember putting it in there, she found a ginger scone sprinkled with coarse-ground cane sugar. Her mouth watered at the sight of it. For an instant, the selfish desire to keep it for herself inundated her body, but she fought off the impulse.

How did that get in there? No matter, there's enough to share and other pockets to explore later.

"My dear little fellow, I'm afraid I don't have much to offer other than this freshly baked ginger scone. If you've never had one I beckon you to try it—they're quite lovely. Come, sit beside me on this rock and let's see what you think of it."

"Ah, I see what you're doing. You think being polite will protect you, but those children's stories are nonsense. If I want, you will be my breakfast. A snack, really, because there's not much red meat on your dry bones."

He exposed his mossy teeth and her heart twitched.

Red bow.

She found a boulder and sat down—smoothing her dress.

"Come, kind sir, sit and join me for breakfast."

The Fachan raised his solitary eyebrow—what an odd day this was becoming. He had every intention of eating this small child but here she was, asking him to join her on a rock where he could eat her *scone*, whatever that was.

Harrumph, he muttered under his breath.

I could still eat her now, but perhaps she'd taste better if I wait.

He made his way over and sat on the rock where he looked at her and she at him.

Now what?

"Is it easier for me to put the scone in your hand or would it please you more if I break it up and feed it to you in pieces?"

If she fed him directly, it was possible he would choose to bite her hand, but she pushed the bloody image back.

Red bow.

"If you wouldn't mind, I prefer you to place pieces in my mouth," said the Fachan with a glittery twinkle in his eye.

Gathering her courage, she broke off a chunk and tossed it into his gaping mouth. He chewed, stopped, then chewed some more. He'd never tasted anything quite like this before. Dry, crunchy and tasty. Tangy. Sweet. He grinned and his face appeared a little less contorted.

"That is very nice. You call it a *scone*, eh? If you allow me to eat the rest of this *scone*, then I will not eat you today. Tomorrow, we shall see, but for today you'll be safe, I so solemnly promise."

"I think that's a fair deal," said Minnie, who proceeded to break off pieces and feed them to the Fachan.

After a short time, the scone was done and the creature hopped up to his foot.

"I thank you very much for the conversation and food, my young one. Now, I must be on my way. If it's an oak tree you're looking for, a certain, special one, stay on this path to the middle of the forest. There, by a bog you'll want to stay clear of, you will find a grove of ash, oak and thorn. It's a magical place—what you are looking for should be there. Good luck with your quest and beware because not all the creatures in this dark wood are as friendly and nice and splendid as I am. Fare-thee-well."

With that, the Fachan hopped back into the brush and Minnie was left alone on the rock—not knowing what to make of the experience. She survived her first encounter in the dark woods and couldn't wait to tell Sean about it.

I won't find any gall while sitting on this rock all day, so guess I should get up and carry on.

The dark forest smelled old and ancient. Not a musty, moldy smell but the dusty smell of times long past. The trees whispered secrets to the air. No nice fluffy creatures roamed here, but there were plenty of normal crows and ravens, snakes and frogs, dragonflies and moths among the varied creatures: bizarre, improbable and magical. It was not everywhere a sad place or a completely evil place—it was a place locked in time and infused with history. This dark wood held its secrets and its magic close.

She walked and walked.

Suddenly the air was filled with odd toady creatures with long tails and bat-like wings. Water leapers.

There must be water nearby.

From her studies with Sean, she knew the dangling stinger held a flesh-eating poison, so she ducked her head when a flapping creature flew up from behind. Teeth. Small, sharp, yellow teeth. She tried not to imagine what they ate, but the image intruded in her head. They ate everything. Anything. All taut skin and hollow bones; they were nothing really, and if one came near, she'd knock it for a loop with her staff—they seemed to know this and kept their distance.

One hovered ten feet away and stared at her.

"You're ugly," she said.

Their croak was like a rude little boy's endless burp—it spoke with a deep, growling voice.

"Not half so ugly as you," the creature responded. "You're nearly too ugly to eat.

With her staff at the ready, she held her head high.

"Come get a bite if you dare," she said.

The creature grunted, then darted toward a giant, brown fluttering Polyphemus Moth which soon crunched in its jaws.

"Why would we bother with something hideous like you then there are so many other delicious things to eat?"

B-B-Burp.

She pursed her lips and, flapping her lips, made a rude sound back—and pushed on.

The Fachan said the grove of trees was near a bog and these water leapers were a sure indication of nearby water.

Was this the right bog?

One could only hope.

As she trekked onward, she sensed something watching her. Whatever it was stayed out of her sight, but she felt it nonetheless. Was it best to ignore or confront it? Minnie opted for confrontation. She put aside her fear and stopped dead in her tracks.

"Okay, I know you're there and I know you're watching. I'm a nasty little girl, so I wouldn't be tasty to eat—if you wouldn't mind coming out of the shadows and showing yourself, I'd be most grateful. I'm on my way to the grove of trees near the bog and I have no time to tarry."

With that she held her breath. Was she foolish or smart to summon forth the unknown beast from the shadows? She stood still and was just about to move along when something came forth. Minnie gasped.

It was a Fir Darrig.

Thank goodness, it was a known creature—another denizen of the faerie realm picture books Sean read to her. This one however, was far more grotesque than in the book. To make matters worse, he smelled rank. He wore a red top coat, which was customary for his sort, and had a long beard—he stood not much taller than Minnie herself. He had a long scraggly tail and it appeared that he had a few too many arms emerging from his oval body. He carried a grand walking stick with a knob on the end and wore an odd sort of top hat.

Fir Darrig—notorious pranksters.

I must be careful and keep my wits about me.

He spoke while circling her.

"You are a brave little one calling me out of the shadows like that. And what, may I ask, are you doing venturing out all alone in these dark woods?"

Minnie tried to follow him with her eyes but found herself getting dizzy, so she opted for looking straight ahead along the path.

Perhaps circling is part of one of his tricks.

"I'm looking for the grove near the bog."

"Ahhhh, the magical grove is what you seek. It must be some important quest for you to be out here all on your own. You *are* on your own, are you not?"

"Yes, yes I am, kind sir. Now, if you've nothing more to say and if you're not going to help me, I'd like to be on my way."

"Oh, my, yes, you should be on your way. But wouldn't you like to dance with the faeries first? They've a lovely ball going on over there—just off the path in a patch of fennel. Their music is lovely and you'd be a beautiful sight dancing with them in that pretty dress. Wouldn't you like to join them?"

Oh, how Minnie loved to dance with the faeries. However, she knew of many a story where a human stumbled upon a faerie ring and remained dancing with them for many long human years—dancing, dancing until their friends and families grew old and died. As much as she felt the tug to go with the Fir Darrig, she came to her senses and spoke firmly.

"No thank you, kind sir. I must be on my way. Perhaps another day?"

"Very well then, another day perhaps. Be on your way then."

Off he scampered, back into the dark fringes running alongside the path.

Minnie knew that was too easy—it was safe to assume he still lurked nearby. She kept walking, but her little legs grew weary—she wanted to be done with this quest. While occasionally exhilarating, over all, this adventure was more dull and tedious and exhausting than adventurous. She just wanted to find the mysterious gall and go back to Sean.

At long last she came upon a bog. Not an overly stinky, smelly marsh, but a swampy-bog nonetheless with brown, brackish water. Now and again a toad or frog would sound an alarm and plop-splash into the deep. As Minnie stood staring at the fenland, she again felt like something watched her. She tried to tune into the what-and-where and got the impression something spied on her from underwater. She kneeled and peered into the murky depths, but did not get too close. The water was too dark to see anything clearly, so she gave up looking. She turned her back to the bog and began scanning the area for the mystical grove.

Minnie started to step away from the bog when something grabbed her ankle. Startled, her staff flew from her hands. She looked down to see a green hand wrapped around her leg. It dragged her toward the bog.

She recognized the form of this monster.

"Let me go, Jenny Greenteeth," screamed Minnie. "You will not pull me under and eat me today."

She kicked with her other foot but Jenny grabbed that one as well.

"Someone help me please? I'm Princess Minnie and I'm on a quest. Please help me."

While desperately holding onto an errant root, she felt the cold, soulless water of the quagmire soak through her shoes and then touch her ankles. She'd come so far and struggled so much—she didn't want to die like this; ripped to shreds and eaten by Jenny Greenteeth in the depths of this horrid bog.

Minnie thought she heard the Queen laughing on the breeze. She thought of Sean and their life and the Fiona of her dreams and wondered if she'd ever see them again. Her grip loosened on the root. Bog water rose up to her calves.

Is there no one to help me? Is this how it all ends?

While losing her grip and becoming immersed more and more in the frigid water of the murky quagmire, she suddenly felt a hand wrap around hers. She looked up and there saw an odd little creature. He wasn't the most pleasant thing to look upon but he had kind eyes. Minnie met those eyes without fear or judgment and spoke quietly.

"Help me, please."

The creature wrapped both hands around Minnie's arm and began to pull.

"Not today, Jenny Greenteeth," he said. "Not this one."

Jenny let out a screeching howl that made Minnie's heart stop—her little body shook with fear.

"She's mine, Urisk. Go find your own."

"I said no, Jenny, she's *chosen*. Not Minnie, not today and not ever. Release her or else."

Jenny grunted with effort.

"Or else what?" she said.

"Or I'll give Minnie her staff."

That's exactly what he did. Releasing Minnie with one hand just for an instant, he reached out bony fingers and tugged the staff near and dropped it in Minnie's flailing hand. She rotated her body.

Bap. On the head, bap again with the lightning ball at the end of her staff. Sparks flew.

Jenny muttered curses before relenting and releasing Minnie.

"May you never have a hearth to call your own and die raging like a fecking Doran's butt-ass."

The Urisk pulled Minnie to safety on the muddy bank as Jenny Greenteeth hissed in dismay. With bale fire in her eyes, Jenny drifted in the scummy water.

Minnie sat shaking upon the shore. The Urisk looked at her, now a bit meeker. He flicked his downcast eyes at her; he was accustomed to young people (the only ones who could see him) screaming and running away, yet here sat this waif.

Minnie looked him over. The Urisk looked like a bald, aging man with an extraordinarily long face and droopy nose, a wispy, billygoat beard and wrinkly skin with dirt worked in deep. His arms and legs were long and thin and he was unusually skinny. He had large pointed ears, a drawn, gaunt face and the legs of a goat. He wore a tattered shirt made of filthy linen. They sat staring at each other.

Finally Minnie found her voice.

"Thank you. You saved my life. As you know, I'm Minnie. How did you know my name?"

The Urisk looked down and cleared his throat.

"I bumped into the Fachan—he told me of your kindness and your quest. I thought anyone who could find kindness for a wretched Fachan might extend some to me as well; because of my eyesore hideousness, I live in solitude. No one ever visits me—they all run away. My hope was that if I found you that maybe we could be—friends?"

He looked down at the ground as he said that. Minnie smiled—a smile that drove the forest gloom back a few feet.

"What a world we live in," she said, "one so dependent on appearances. I would be honored to call you my friend." She grinned. "Besides, it's the least I can do for the kind soul who saved my life."

Shifting her staff to the opposite hand, she laid her free hand on his. He looked up at her and smiled for the first time in his life.

He stood quickly and spoke in a formal tone.

"With that, may I properly introduce myself? My name is Fenwick and I am an Urisk."

He bowed to Minnie, who promptly got to her feet and curtsied in reply. Feeling overwhelmed from her ordeal, she sat back down and while Fenwick listened intently, told him all about her adventure in the dark forest. He was most impressed—not only with her storytelling ability, but also with Minnie herself. Once she finally finished her account, Fenwick asked one simple question.

"Would you like me to take you to the grove?"

"Oh, my, could you?"

Fenwick nodded. Minnie hopped up to her feet, grabbed her staff and they walked along a wisp of trail side-by-side.

"Lead on, my dear Sir Fenwick."

Off down the trail they walked—through groves and meadows and skipping over streaming rivulets of crisp, clear water. In ten minutes, across a clearing stood the enchanted grove. It was reverently quiet in this copse. Shafts of beamy sunlight shone brightly down into it. Bounded by ash, vine maple and thorn trees was a massive tree and a centrally located rock upon which to perch. Fenwick bowed before entering and so did Minnie. She heard whispers, both ancient and near.

"She's here—she's finally come."

"Look at the Princess."

"Fenwick brought her to us."

"There's hope yet."

Minnie looked up to Fenwick and took his hand.

"Are they talking about me?"

Fenwick looked down at her and nodded.

"I don't understand, Fenwick. I mean, I know I can touch the souls of the trees, but I don't think I'm anything extraordinarily special."

"And that's what makes you so unique, Minnie. You will learn in time, as we all do, this adventure is just one more step on your path. You are here to gather the gall and bring it back to the Queen. What do you see, Minnie?"

In the center of the clearing was what must be the world's largest oak tree. It was broad and tall—more like a living mountain than a tree. It was not static—it appeared to swell while she watched, though it seemed as if it grew another fraction of an inch, the Earth would be unable to support it.

"That must be the tree."

"Let's sit for a moment and rest," Fenwick suggested.

As they approached the rock, the tree towered over them more and more. After a few minutes of soaking in the windy silence, she spoke quietly.

"Can I tell you something?"

His response was equally hushed.

"Of course."

She leaned her head close to his.

"I don't exactly know what a *gall* is."

Fenwick titled his head back and laughed. The trees around the clearing laughed. Crows perched on high branches laughed. The sun laughed.

"There's no shame in innocent ignorance as long as you don't pretend to know what you don't," he said. "A gall is an oak apple." He held his skinny hands three-inches apart. "This particular gall is a big one. Reddish-brown. Normally, they are created by gall wasps to protect their larvae, but not the one you're looking for."

He gestured and Minnie leaned closer.

"The one you are looking for was created by a chort—a forest ogre."

Minnie looked puzzled.

"Horns," Fenwick said. "Hooves. Sharp teeth. Smart gilrs stay away."

Minnie looked up and saw a bright light under the leaves of the massive tree. Fenwick let go of her hand and she gingerly walked closer to the base of the oak monster. In a cleft of the lowest branch, there was something that looked like a gall. Her belly churned.

There was something wrong, but she couldn't stop herself. As if in a hypnotic trance, she hesitantly reached for it. From across the clearing, a voice broke the spell.

"Excuse me, Miss Minnie."

She stopped reaching and turned to watch the Fachan hop across the clearing. Soon he stood before her.

"Might you allow me to get that for you?"

Something broke loose in her stomach. She knew. There was something wrong with this gall.

She gritted her teeth and waved her staff around the clearing. The glowing bulb throbbed with faint fiery colors, red, green and blue.

The Fachan bounded like a spring and grabbed the gall with his outreaching hand. The cleft of the tree opened like a gaping maw and in a fraction of a second closed around the Fachan and he was gone. For an endless few seconds, there was dead silence, then the innards of the tree rumbled like a grossly fat man who'd eaten a bushel of green apples, followed by a wafer-thin mint. The tree groaned with extreme discomfort.

The maw creaked open just a crack. There was a gassy explosion and a figure streaked into the sky like a rocket. Rotating her head, she watched it arc into the air and fall beyond the edge of the clearing's fringe of trees.

Angry, Minnie turned back to the big tree. Suddenly it was not so big—it shrank and collapsed into itself. Soon it was still a big tree, but not extraordinary. She banged on its trunk with her staff.

"You're a bad tree," she said.

"All God's creatures have to eat."

"Well, you're not going to eat me, not today and not ever."

She rapped the tree again.

"I'm only being what I am—please stop hitting me."

She struck again before turning and walking back to the rock. Fenwick would not meet her eyes.

"You could have warned me," she said.

Fenwick's strangled voice was awash in shame.

"I wanted to, I really did, but it was not permitted."

"If my one and only friend in this forest is hurt..."

She looked in the direction the Fachan had flown and began running through a grove of cottonwood trees and around a bayberry bush. She splashed across a creek and crawled over a massive Douglas fir deadfall. She saw something move under a pile of brown, dry leaves. She gathered armfuls and tossed them aside; underneath there were bones. Thousands of white bones.

The tree's voice echoed in her ears.

All God's creature have to eat.

She gently put the bones down.

How many souls?

Under the leaves, something moved. Something lived.

The Fachan spoke.

"A little help would be welcome," he said.

She rustled around near where the leaves were moving, then grasped his hand and hauled him out.

"You're alive," she said.

The Fachan shrugged.

"The tree does not like the taste of me."

"You helped me when everyone else just watched."

"The Queen will punish me, but I don't care." He gestured with his hand so she'd move closer. He whispered, "Between you and me, the Cailleach smells like a moldy rug and should be hung on a clothesline so the dust can be beat out of her. Shall we find the *right* gall?"

Minnie laughed.

"Yes," she said. She stood and brushed bits of dried leaves from her jumper. "Where is this thing? Perhaps a clue?"

The Fachan hung his head.

"That's not allowed." He looked left and right, then whispered, "however, if I were you—"

Minnie held out her hand.

"It's okay," she said, "you've done plenty, more than enough. There's no reason to irritate the Queen when it's unnecessary. I'll find it."

She walked back to the clearing. There, in the middle, the oak tree had shrunk to a nearly unremarkable size.

Minnie scoffed.

"Stupid tree," she muttered.

She slowly turned on her heels and studied the surrounding vegetation. There were many stately oaks but none of them called to her. However, there was a dark figure high on a branch in a droopy-leaved weeping willow on the bank of a scummy marsh.

Selene?

The owl hooted and took wing—in seconds it was gone. Minnie walked toward the willow. The ground was squishy and wet; as she approached, it appeared the willow was truly weeping; water dripped from its leaves in sad cascades. The splintered trunk was blackened as if struck by lightning. She ducked under the branches and saw a black seed pod the size of a tennis ball growing on a branch. It throbbed like a heart and spoke with a hiss like a little dragon.

"Don't touch me," it said.

Minnie looked to the Fachan for guidance, but he shrugged and would not speak.

With the tip of her index finger, she tested the thing—it was warm and soft. Minnie put her hand on the Willow's bark and spoke with reverence.

"Might I take this gall? I don't want to take something you own if you don't want me to."

The willow spoke with a clotted, teary voice filled with despair. It surprised Minnie, but this tree was a female.

"Please, oh please, take the intolerable creature away," the tree said.

Minnie slowly reached out and wrapped her hands around the throbbing heart. It was slippery and, as if glued in, would not budge. She handed her staff to the Fachan and grasped the warm, bulbous growth with both hands.

"Take your Danu-damned claws off me," the growth said.

She didn't know what a cancerous growth was, but that's the image that stirred in her mind.

Cancer.

Gritting her teeth in determination, she worked her fingers in deep and pulled. It did not shift, so she pulled harder. In an instant, it came loose and she stumbled backwards to land on her rear end in a mucky patch of brackish water.

"Put me back," the gall demanded.

She examined the ugly thing leaking brown fluid into her dress. From it's skin, wriggling albino tubers sniffed the air like blind worms.

"I am not the gall you are looking for."

This stirred an absurd image in Minnie's mind—some silly old movie set on an alien planet.

"Shut up," she said.

She stood and looked down on herself.

I'm a mess.

Muck dripped from her dress—there wasn't a clean spot to be seen. The still air stirred with breeze and water rained from the tree in intense torrents.

Minnie laughed and stepped into the shower—soon she was cold and wet, but clean. The rain stopped. The wind turned warm and in a minute she was dry. The cozy feeling was glorious.

The tree's long, green leaves were no longer sodden and drooping—they stirred on coils of swirling air like fluffy feathers. The breeze grew stronger bringing a reverent chant slowly increasing in volume until she could pick out the individual overlapping words.

Thank you, thank you, thank you.

Minnie bowed her head in reverence.

"You're welcome," she said to the tree.

She turned to walk away. After stepping from under the willow's branches, she looked around the enchanted grove and let the magic infuse into her. She felt alive and energized and wanted nothing more than to scamper back home and jump into Sean's arms.

"You'll be sorry if you don't put me back," the gall said.

She walked to the rock and dropped the gall on it. She held out her hand and the Fachan handed her the staff. She waved it at the throbbing heart.

"*You'll* be sorry if you don't shut up," Minnie said. Then she turned to speak to the Fachan. "Does this thing bother you? Would you mind carrying it?"

The Fachan grinned.

"Its magic has no effect on me."

He picked it up and stuffed it in his rucksack where it wriggled and grumbled. Feeling as if she walked on air, she strode back to Fenwick. He smiled at her and she smiled sweetly back.

"No offense," he said. "I was not permitted to help."

"Ah," she said, "so you say. That's why you lied and led a little girl to her certain death."

"Well..." Fenwick said. "Let's forgive and forget. I'll walk you home and protect you from the many other dangers."

"The Fachan and I will be fine on our own. But, I will leave you a gift."

She reached in the apron pocket of her jumper and pulled out a marble—it was solid blue except for a wavelet of green ink in its center.

"No, thank you," Fenwick said.

"Oh, I insist," Minnie said while pressing it in his hand. "If you tell another lie with that marble in your pocket, you'll dry up and blow away like powder in the wind."

"How will I talk a tree out of an apple? How will I convince a hen to give up an egg? How will I convince a frog it belongs on a skewer in my fire? I'll starve."

Minnie grinned.

"Yes, maybe you will," she said before turning to walk away.

"Please," Fenwick implored.

She took the Fachan's hand. They turned and oriented themselves with the setting sun. With the staff, she pointed.

"That way," she said. She and the Fachan walked to the edge of the clearing. Just before entering the brush, the Fachan spoke.

"I guess this is as good a place as any to say goodbye."

She turned and took his hand.

"You saved me and showed me the way; I don't think we should part just yet." The Fachan looked confused and taken aback. "Besides, you have the gall and I'll need it to throw in the Queen's face. Walk with me to the forest's border and if it pleases you, I'd love for you to live with Sean and me."

The Fachan's leg collapsed and he fell to the ground. He'd been on his own for a long time and never had any real friends.

Minnie plopped down next to him.

Exploring a hidden pocket, she produced a giant chocolate chip cookie. She broke it in half and gave half to her new-found friend. The Fachan's eyes glistened and twinkled. She really *was* his friend. He couldn't refuse a gift from this little one.

They ate in silence, taking in all the grove had to offer. When they were done, they brushed themselves off and stood, preparing for the long walk home.

As they strolled along the path and darkness fell, she felt fear growing in the pit of her stomach, but the light on her staff flickered and brightened. The Fachan seemed completely unconcerned, so she fought back her terror. She felt like she understood some of the dark wood's magic—she'd have to remember all she could to relay it to Sean; he really must learn to be less afraid of this place.

At the house, Sean paced as the sun dived below the tree line. He stopped in front of the Queen and watched her read a leather-clad book while pointedly ignoring him. Little eyes peeked around the corners of the walls from nooks and crannies.

"She had a slim chance during the day," he said.

The Queen sighed and closed her book on her finger to hold her place. She reached out and picked up her cup to sip the dregs.

"Cold tea," she said. "I don't suppose——"

"Forget your tea; we're talking about life and death. She was young and innocent and you sacrificed her for nothing."

"It would be nice to take all the time in the world and prepare for everything, but we don't have that luxury. We have to deal with events as they unfold, not at our convenience. We needed to know."

"Needed to know what? She's tiny and young, but she was amazing. Every day she grew and her power expanded. There was still time, there was no need to kill her. Her blood is on your hands."

"If hers was the only blood on my hands, I'd be a lot happier and I'd have many fewer sins to answer for on my final judgment day. Consider this, Sean, there're many reasons I rule and you don't. I bear the weight of the world on my shoulders—I make tough decisions and see them to their end and through tough times I learned to rule with my intellect, not my heart. We know Minnie is lovable and sweet, but what good does that do when facing the soulless Black Faerie King? We need more than little-girl sweetness and idle words on the wind. We needed to know the depth of her resourcefulness. We needed to know if she could face unknown dangers and conquer them. We needed to know if she's slippery and clever and capable of being—wise. She's not the only candidate and it's stupid to waste time and energy on her if she's not our best hope. There's a charming little girl in France and another in Malaysia."

"If you really thought they were better candidates, you'd be there and not here driving me crazy and breaking my heart. I meant what I said. If she does not come back..."

"Right," she interrupted. "I heard you. You'll lock me in this house like a prison. That would be productive, wouldn't it? Might as well offer the world to the Black King on a silver platter—all the souls of the Earth in flames forever. It's dark and I agree, Minnie is surely lost, so what are you waiting for?" She spread her arms and leaned back on the couch. "Work your magic and kill the innocent souls in the world. Go ahead. I'm tired of this thankless job. Is your head filled with visions of trolls tearing us limb from limb and gnawing the flesh from our bones? I see one route through the final confrontation with King Custennyn and it doesn't end well for me. So, is she up to the challenge? For all I will sacrifice, you begrudge me wanting to know for sure? Lock me in this pretty, doll-house dungeon forever and see if I care."

Sean's body vibrated with anger from head to toe, but he did not say the words and he did not spin the spell. He did not summon the dark mountain spirits. His shoulders slumped.

"I hate you," he said, "I really do."

"That's fine, Sean, you hate me, but the list of people who despise me is long and yours just another meaningless entry on an imaginary ledger. You're not going to trap me in this gaol, so why not make yourself useful in the kitchen? I'm easy to please, a bit of baked mutton, a hunk of roast beef or a nice cured ham with, oh, I don't care, mashed turnips and Burgundy Dream garlic and Blue Spencer sweet peas. And a pie for dessert, perhaps made with the Flordaking peaches you've been saving for a special occasion that's never going to come."

"I curse your cast-iron heart," Sean said.

"Curse it in the kitchen over the stove—and while the meat is baking, uncrock that small beer Sarsaparilla cooling in the root cellar. You sweetened it with maple syrup—that was a clever idea, boy."

While he shook in helpless anger, a tear worked its way down his face. She settled on the sofa and opened her book.

"Cry over the mutton, boy," she said, "it can use the salt."

At long last, in complete starless darkness, Minnie and the Fachan reached the forest's border. All that remained was for the Fachan to take one last step into Minnie's world. Minnie stepped over the heather hedgerow first.

Ahhh, the sweet smell of fresh familiar air.

She looked toward the house. Light through the windows fought brightly against the inky night. She giggled with glee—the adventure seemed to have been weeks, not the better part of a day, but she was home. She looked back to the Fachan and held out her hand.

"I became your friend in the dark forest and that won't change here. I live with Sean in this enchanted house—it's full of love and laughs and yummy food. Oh, yes, and music and dancing and all sorts of creatures, pixies and gnomes, sprites and faeries. All are welcome here. Are you willing to give it a try?"

As is so often the case in life, we cling to sorrows and pains like an old, comfortable blanket. To let go and cast malaise aside can be scary and unsettling. When we hold onto fear, it becomes a part of us and we begin to believe it *is* us. What would we be without it? What would it be like to live without sorrow and pain and loneliness? What would it be like to be free of the heavy shroud insulating us from joy?

Such is what the Fachan felt when he looked back into the dark forest. What was left there for him? Loneliness and cold—no laughter or delight. Besides, he could always go back if he wanted. He looked up at the house and down at Minnie and then squeezed her hand.

"As long as I won't be a bother."

"You'll be about as much of a bother to Sean as *I* am—he'll like you as much as I do. And if you don't want to stay in the big house we can build an outbuilding to call your own. We could build it here by the dark forest or over in a corner of the yard under a tree or anywhere you like."

The Fachan decided to take the plunge and make this change. He was loyal to Minnie and knew she would need all the help she could get. As he stepped over the hedgerow, he felt the air change. This air had lightness—it was fresh and clean. It was wholly different and he liked it.

Minnie couldn't contain herself. She and the Fachan hopped-ran to the house and as soon as Sean saw them in the window he sprinted out to meet them.

He picked up Minnie and swirled her around and around.

"I thought you'd perished," he said over and over. "I knew you were lost." When she was thoroughly dizzy, he stopped and spoke to the Fachan. "Thank you for bringing her home."

"Sir," the Fachan said, "*she* brought me home."

Sean tilted his head back and laughed.

"You, my friend, are welcome here for as long as you like. Our home is your home, or we'll build you a new one."

Minnie smiled.

"I told him that same thing."

Sean laughed and laughed.

They sat in the grass and in the manner of her word-soup-torrent, Minnie recounted her tale while Sean listened intently to every word. Once it was finished the Queen magically appeared next to them, cleared her throat and spoke in a harsh tone.

"Where's my gall?"

The Fachan rustled in his knapsack and produced it. Worse for the wear, it was squishy and limp. He handed it to Minnie.

Minnie stood with defiance in her eyes and said, "Here you go," while placing it in the Queen's outstretched, wrinkled hands.

The Queen inspected it. The corners of her mouth curled upward like the infamous Cheshire cat looking down upon Alice.

"You've never tasted a tea so delicious as a cup with a smidgen of heart-gall."

"Hey," the gall said.

"Just a smidgen," the Queen said. "You'll never miss it." To Sean, she said, "I'll put this in the kitchen—"

"I don't want to be in the kitchen," the gall said.

"—next to the grater," the Queen continued.

The gall spoke with a voice dripping with ichor.

"May the curse of Mary Malone and her nine blind, illegitimate children chase you so far over the Hills of Damnation that the Black Lord himself can't find you with a telescope."

"We'll grate your mouth off first," the Queen said.

Sean, Minnie and the Fachan watched the Queen walk away with the gall.

"Minnie," Sean said, "were there any lessons you learned in the woods?"

Minnie sat back down.

"I'm not sure," she said. "Maybe."

"Tell us."

Minnie considered.

"For one thing, you can't judge anyone by how they look."

Sean nodded.

"What else?" he said.

"Just because someone appears to be your friend doesn't mean they really, truly are—and the enemy of your enemy might not be your friend."

"Any more?"

Minnie stuffed her hand in her mouth as if to try keep from speaking.

Sean grinned.

"What is it? Say it."

Minnie had an attack of shyness, but she took a deep breath and spoke quietly.

"Uh, sometimes, to get something done, you have to get dirty and break the rules."

Sean burst out with uncontrollable laughter. He stood and gathered the little girl and her friend the Fachan in his arms and twirled with wild abandon.

"I love-love-love you so very much," he said.

Inside the house, the Queen stood before the bay window and drank from her oily-black mug of root beer. Her stern expression was neutral, but there could have been a slight, nearly imperceptible twitch to her lips.

Upward.

She sighed, drained the last dregs from the mug and set it down on the window sill. After standing in silence with her head hung low for a moment, she said the words and was gone.

The Comfort of Friends

WITH LEGS THAT would carry them no further, Fiona and Luna plopped down on the bare Earth outside their house. How long they sat there was unknown, but it could not have been long—seconds or minutes—before her friends David and Elizabeth pulled up in their minivan. David arranged a soft blanket around Fiona's shoulders and Elizabeth produced a mug of steaming tea in an insulated mug.

"We already called 9-1-1, Fiona. As soon as we sensed the first flame, we called."

Fiona looked at them blankly with the word *sensed* stuck in her mind.

Sensed.

"Thank you," she whispered.

David and Elizabeth; they were such good souls—fixtures in the tight-knit community. On Fiona's very first day in her new house, they appeared on her porch—David with a twinkle in his eyes and Elizabeth holding a basket of her internationally famous homemade salsa adorned with crispy pita chips. Elizabeth spoke with an infectious grin on her face.

"We didn't know what you liked to eat, but no one can resist

169

this salsa. Everything is fresh from the farmer's market down the road. It's just our way of saying *welcome.*"

Fiona instantly liked them. She sensed David had been blessed by a pixie when he was born; whereas, Elizabeth's paranormality was more complex—perhaps there was a smidgen of the mixed blood of Sucellus and Sirona flowing in her veins. David had an inner darkness he battled—historic demons not yet fully put behind him. In his own time and in his own way, one day, he would banish these evil spirits and then be fully at peace. Over the following days, weeks, months and years, Fiona shared his quest by studying yoga with him; she was consistently impressed at the way his aging body moved.

When I'm equally advanced in my years, I can only hope to be partially as limber as David.

As an eternal child at heart, Elizabeth had a fondness for younglings and stray animals.

Fiona watched David and Elizabeth move through time, so in love to even this day. Their love was a beacon even on this sad day when Fiona was deflated by a battle lost and a home eaten by the all-consuming fire—defeated in body and spirit.

Fire truck sirens wailed in the distance; this time their tolling bells were for her—to help her and save what they could. Up they came, with lights blazing and sirens blaring. Burly men, young and old, hopped off the trucks in perfect formation. While they did a quick assessment of the situation, the chief approached Fiona.

"Miss, is this your house?"

Fiona nodded.

"Is there anyone inside?"

Fiona's eyes welled with tears. What should she say? She did not want to lie, but this situation among the common folk was a time for subterfuge and secrecy, not for raw honesty. Regardless, the words were trapped in her throat like dry bones and it was a struggle to get them out.

"No," she said, "I was alone."

"Miss, do you know how this happened?"

What could she say that would make sense? Dark magic did this? The trolls set everything alight?

"I don't know. I came home and was putting things away and when all of the sudden my cat ran from the front room into the kitchen. I looked down at him and smelled smoke. I went to the front room and it was ablaze. I don't know how it started. No candles were burning in that room and a fire hadn't been lit in the fireplace for quite some time. I don't know, I honestly don't know."

The chief put his hand on her shoulder.

"We'll figure it out, miss. Not to worry now, okay?"

Speechless, Fiona nodded.

"Okay, Miss, we'll do our best to save what we can, but it does not look good."

Does not look good was an understatement. The house was fully engulfed and not in half-hearted, tentative flames, but in voracious, blood-red dragon tongues of plasma.

The chief walked back to the trucks and the operation commenced and the three friends watched like spectators— watched and wondered while lost in their private thoughts. After a few minutes with the fire's radiation searing their faces, David spoke.

"We have to get you away from here."

"Key?" Elizabeth said.

"What?" Fiona said.

"It's great that your Bug is in the driveway instead of its usual burrow in the garage," David said, "but it isn't far enough away to be safe where it is—we need to get it out of here. To do that, we'll need the key."

Thinking the key was surely in the house and lost, Fiona searched her pockets anyway. Deep in a front pocket of her jeans, miracle of miracles, she found it, though she was completely at a loss for knowing how it got there. With a shaky hand, she offered it to Elizabeth.

"You'll stay with us tonight, okay?" Elizabeth said. "You and Luna. I'll draw you a hot bath; you can take a good, long soak and snuggle down in our guestroom."

In the same way a sick child looks at a loving parent, Fiona looked up at Elizabeth. She fought the urge to run and run and never stop. She wanted to go back in time and forward in time all at once. She could barely speak. She nodded.

"Good and hot, that's the key. I still have some of those bath salts you made for me when I lost my mind over the death of our cat."

Ahhh, vestiges and echoes of times past.

"That would be lovely, thank you," said Fiona.

While Elizabeth made a beeline for the Bug—pretending not to hear the fire fighters warning her off, David tugged Fiona's arm and steered her toward their minivan. Inside, he strapped on her seatbelt as if she was a helpless child while Luna climbed on her lap and looked up at her, and she down at him. No words were exchanged while they shared the swirling emotions of loss and love and confusion. Fiona petted Luna's damp fur.

She had never been overly attached to material objects, but this had been her home, her sanctuary. This had been her place of peace where she loved and flourished, where she'd cried and been angry, where she'd been both blissfully happy and dreadfully alone. In a void where time stood still, she didn't know what to feel and she didn't know what to do—she was darkness and light merged into one; neither here nor there, neither hot nor cold, neither hungry nor full. She was uncomfortably numb.

After a spell she lifted Luna and looked into his eyes.

"David and Elizabeth are being kind enough to keep us safe for tonight. In the morning you and I will figure out what to do. Does that sound okay?"

Luna mewed and looked back towards the rubble. Fiona followed his gaze.

"Yeah, I know. What's to become of us?"

David patted her shoulder and started the vehicle. They drove across the little town in silence. Once parked, they looked at David and Elizabeth's house. Under a giant tree, its brave lights fought a minor battle with the encroaching darkness. Soon, Elizabeth parked the Bug along side.

Fiona sighed, then unstrapped herself and carried Luna into the house. David and Elizabeth showed her around and helped her get settled in. Then they knew to leave her alone. Fiona soaked in the tub while Luna sat on the floor and kept watch. The house was quiet—it didn't hum and breathe like her house did. Fiona was grateful for David and Elizabeth's hospitality, but she ached for her cozy home.

Sitting in the tub, she quietly sobbed.

How had it come to this? Why couldn't I save Llwyd and why couldn't I defeat that darkness? Why me? Why this horror? Why now? Why did I run away like a coward?

A flood of self pity, grief and soul-deep melancholy for everything she lost washed over her like a tidal wave. This was a wave she couldn't surf; it was too big to ride. All she could do was drown in it—there was no hope for coming up for air.

Letting herself go, she sank into gloomy depths of despair where it was cold and ink-black; where she saw shudder-inducing images and faces that made her shiver despite the scalding bath water steaming like a volcanic hot spring. She let go of all she knew, of all she loved—she released her dreams and her hopes and they drifted away like balloons on the wind. She gave her anger and despair to the night. She let it all go. She slowly slid downward into the water while a song echoed in her ears.

Give up and let it go
Give up and let your life flow...[14]

---

[14] *Give Up and Let It Go*, Francis Dunnery, From *The Gulley Flats Boys*,

She held her breath until her lungs threatened to burst. As she slowly emerged from the water, she opened her eyes. Whatever internal battle had just been waged, Fiona acknowledged it by simply saying to herself, "So be it." As she watched foamy water swirl down the drain, she sent her ugly feelings down with it. Steely, disciplined resolve, that's what she needed now.

She climbed out of the tub, dried off and put on the warm, comfy clothes that Elizabeth had laid out for her. She climbed into bed and Luna jumped up with her.

"Looks like we'll start a new adventure tomorrow, Luna. Let's hope we're up to the challenge."

Luna snuggled next to Fiona, his mistress and protector. He would follow her anywhere and do his best to protect her as well. Luna let out a grief-filled mew. Fiona held him.

"Yes, I know. No more Llwyd to instruct and annoy us. No more Kailen to ride atop your back. No more checking on Sebastian and his family—it's all going to change and it will just be you and me for now. We're probably safe tonight, but we can't stay here. Soon, others will come and we need to be miles away. I'm so sorry if I've let you down, Luna. I'm so sorry for all of this— for bringing all this woe upon us."

Fiona reached for her iPhone, hoping to find solace in music.

She put her music on "shuffle" and said "well, luck of the draw—let's see what comes up, maybe it will give us some insight, eh?"

The magic music genie made a selection which brought levity into Fiona's thoughts.

"How appropriate that Michelle Lewis was chosen..."

She is nowhere and everywhere, nowhere and everywhere
Nowhere and everywhere at the same time
She's as shady as cheap sunglasses, but as perfect as this

October Monday passes

> *To a draggin' your-soul-around-town rhythm*
> *Always in such a hurry, but never too fast*
> *Playing chicken with delivery boys and tag with the subways*
> *Searchin' alleys for proper company, she's jumping in and out*

of cracks

> *And she's got everything that you lack*
> *Well she entered unnoticed, you won't feel it when she*

leaves.[15]

Fiona and Luna drifted into a facsimile of sleep as the music played quietly in her earbuds. It was a long night filled with vivid images; a psychedelic mix of haunting and comforting scenes. But deep, healing sleep eventual came to Fiona—a sleep she desperately needed.

Sleep, the gift of the Greek god Morpheus, settled and healed her troubled mind.

---

[15] *Nowhere and Everywhere*, Michelle Lewis and Wayne Cohen, from Lewis' album *Little Leviathan* © 1998 Wannabite Music/BMG Songs/Wayne's World/ASCAP

Among the Smoking Ruins

MORNING CAME AS it always does. The sun rose and peeped through Fiona's window while birds began chirping their symphony. Fiona stirred, then popped up with a start.

"Oh, Luna, it wasn't just a dream, was it?" she said while looking out through the alien window of her friends' house. "I guess we can't hide in here forever; it's time to get up and face whatever else might come our way."

With Luna in tow, Fiona padded to the bathroom where she washed up and slipped into yesterday's clothes. Elizabeth had washed them during the night, hoping to rid them of the smell of smoke. It was a lovely gesture, but the ghostly remainder of sulfur and charcoal lingered. They made their way downstairs where they found David and Elizabeth puttering around. Elizabeth started heating a pot of water for tea while David stood and stared out through their back door.

What do you say to someone who has lost everything? What language can ease their pain? What vocabulary can play on the drawstrings of hope?

The words he found were insufficient; they hung in the air and swirled about Fiona like wind currents stirring piles of dried winter leaves.

"I'm so sorry, Fiona," David said. "You can stay with us for as long as you'd like, ya know."

"Thank you, David. I'm not sure what I'll do, to be honest. The first thing I'd like to do is go back and take a look around. I know Luna is anxious to get out there as well—of course, after he's dined," giggled Fiona as she glanced at Luna to see him diving nose-first into a food bowl.

Finding a bit of appetite, Fiona sat with David and Elizabeth and grazed on their breakfast fruit and pastries while talking about this, that and the other thing. They skirted the issue of how Fiona's house caught fire. Elizabeth placed her hand on Fiona's.

"You don't have to pretend with us, Fiona," she said. "We know."

A wave of confusion crossed Fiona's face.

"You know what?"

Elizabeth and David exchanged a look.

To David, Elizabeth said, "Shall we see if she'll come out?"

David shrugged.

"Let's try," he said.

He stood and addressed empty space—he appeared to be talking to the wall.

"Ancamna, don't be shy. Show yourself." He stood and waited for a handful of seconds, then shrugged. "Sometimes she appears and sometimes she doesn't."

Giving up, he sat back down and popped a plump red grape into his mouth. A largish faerie walked into the room—she was completely naked except for a loose red ribbon wrapping her body from neck to thigh. She was one-foot-tall with froggy green skin and wore a long sword in a sheath. This faerie was different from the ones Fiona had seen before; she was full-figured with long, pointy ears and eyes like slits—she had long, droopy wings like burial shrouds.

Luna looked up from his food bowl.

Another faerie, no big deal.

He returned his attention to his crunchy breakfast.

The faerie stood with splayed legs and looked up at Fiona. Fiona tore off a shred of dried apricot and handed it down. The faerie accepted the morsel and chewed it thoughtfully.

"Llwyd was my friend," the faerie said.

Instantly, tears flooded Fiona's eyes.

"He didn't deserve to die alone," she said.

A hard expression settled on the faerie's face.

"You didn't kill him, The Thinn Man's trolls did and don't you dare dishonor his memory by dismissing his sacrifice—there is a time to stand and fight and there is a time to run. The Queen is right, you're not ready, but there's no time to train and prepare, that's our dilemma. Llwyd told you to flee and to respect to his wisdom, flee you must."

Fiona's voice was flooded with emotion.

"I'm such a coward."

The faerie studied Fiona's face.

"Yes, that's true, you are, but that's irrelevant. It matters what you *do*, not what you *feel*. But, know this, Fiona, when you call, we will come. We might share dear Llwyd's fate, but we'll die with The Thinn Man's blood on our swords. Your true test comes when it's time to defend Minerva's life, what will you do then?"

Fiona filled with an instant irrational defiance. She wagged her finger.

"I don't know any Minerva and I hope I never do."

The faerie laughed.

"Cling to that thought, Fiona."

With that, she turned and marched from the room.

Fiona turned her gaze to David, then to Elizabeth.

"You are in the circle of magic," she said.

Elizabeth laughed.

"The fringes of the outer circle."

Fiona reached out and they clasped hands in a circle.

"Can I say a few words?" David said.

Fiona shrugged.

"Of course."

David closed his eyes and took a deep breath before speaking quietly.

"Let the spirit move in us like a fish in the water, like a hawk in heavy air and like a woman with her man." With those words, Elizabeth squeezed David's hand. "Let us enjoy the gift of every living minute and dream of the day where the one-spirit soothes all sorrows."

When he was done speaking, they sat and let silence settle on them until Luna, demanding attention, grew bored and rubbed against Fiona's leg.

"You're right, Luna, we should leave these good people. We're safe for now, but it won't last."

"Let me pack you a bag," Elizabeth said, "we can spare food and warm clothes."

Fiona held up her palm.

"No, I don't know why, but it seems I should go as I came—with nothing."

Standing by the Bug, they shared hugs and kisses and soon, Fiona was on her way. She decided to stop by the house where Luna prowled the perimeter hoping to find Kailen, but all he found was a bit of Kailen's charred hat. He then scampered to Sebastian's burrow and beckoned for him to come out. They talked and talked and then talked some more. Luna said that he and Fiona were leaving; that made Sebastian dreadfully sad. He promised Luna that he and his family, as well as the other forest pixies and gnomes would continue to watch over the land. They would sow what magic they could into the tortured Earth to help it heal and to rid it of the evil blood. He told Luna he'd spread the word far and wide that any gnome, pixie, faerie, sprite or elf should help them if possible. Sebastian asked if he could ride atop Luna to say a proper goodbye to Mistress Fiona.

Luna bowed and said, "It would be my greatest honor, sir."

He returned to the house to help Fiona look through the rubble.

Fiona searched through the ashes where she found patches of oily-black goo that seemed almost alive—lingering and hissing before dissolving into the Earth. She came upon the spot where she'd last saw Llwyd. She knelt and said an incantation of peace. Tears ran down her cheeks and into what she thought must have been his ashes. In that moment, a small voice came upon the breeze.

"I'm still with you Fiona—you're not alone. Remember what you learned. I will always love you."

Fiona looked down and saw a bump in the ashes. Rooting through the debris, she found the brass bulb of his staff. It was still warm. She brushed it off, kissed it and put it in her pocket. After more searching, she found crystals—gifts from Sean—and a handful of seashells. All her CDs and books and clothes and furniture and herbs and artwork—gone.

Everything.

Gone.

"So, this is what's left of my life," she said quietly to herself. "A brass knob, a few worthless shells and Sean's crystals. Dark magic breeds dragon fire—the unholy fire that consumes all." Shaking her head to dispel the imagery, she walked away from the steaming ruin. "Luna? Luna, where are you?"

Looking around, she saw Sebastian riding atop Luna like the proud elder he was. Standing in the charred grass, she waited patiently for their arrival.

"Mistress Fiona, I come to you offering my utmost sympathies for your loss."

"Thank you, Sebastian."

"We and all the creatures around here will watch over this sacred Earth and we will work to restore it and rid it of the evil seeping into the ground. I already sent word on the wind that any creature that happens upon you and Luna should treat you with respect and offer their services. You are a friend and protector to us all, and we should take care of you as well. My dear, my family and I will miss you with all our hearts. Be well and travel safely. May you be blessed in your travels. I pray you and Luna find happiness and peace once again. There will be songs sung and tales told of you and your adventures here in this enchanted house. Neither you nor Luna will ever be forgotten."

Tears ran down Fiona's cheeks—she extended her hand and Sebastian climbed in and nestled. She brought him before her face.

"Sebastian. You are a true love of a gnome and I will never forget you. You are a gnome amongst gnomes and it has been my honor to live side by side with you. Please be safe and keep your family safe. I hope you understand that Luna and I must leave. To where, I don't yet know, but the wind will show us the way."

She kissed her fingertip and placed it on Sebastian's cheek, then put him back on Luna's back.

"Luna, take Sebastian back to his home, then we'll be on our way."

While she watched, Luna marched away with Sebastian riding like a baron. When Luna returned, they piled into the Bug, where, in the usual ritual, Fiona rubbed the dash and started the engine. Stalling to stretch these final moments with her home, she let the car warm up. She looked in the backseat to see if Luna was settled in and saw Sean's backpack. It made her laugh.

We're not completely stripped of resources—we have Sean's road gear. I wonder what all is in there?

She slowly backed out of the driveway.

"So, this is how it ends. I don't know where I'll go or what I'll do but you have not seen the last of me."

She said those brave words but deep down she was still awash in sorrow, grief and fear.

Unbidden words formed in her mind.

Eyes I dare not meet in dreams
In death's dream kingdom, these do not appear:
There, the eyes are sunlight on a broken column
There, is a tree swinging and voices are in the wind's singing
More distant and more solemn than a fading star.[16]

One day she might feel better, but today wasn't that day, no, by far, not yet.

---

[16] *The Hollow Men*, T.S. Eliot

The Birthday Party

SEAN AND MINNIE cuddled on the floor next to the rock-protrusion in the living room. They were cozy and snuggled together—and engrossed in a conversation about Flix.

Sean cocked his head.

"Flix fills you with *considerable intrigue*? It always surprises me how many adult words you know for an eleven-year-old."

Minnie's eyes flooded with tears. She turned to lean her forehead against the wall.

Sean thought about what he'd said.

What is the problem?

He reached out to touch her shoulder; he gently turned her around.

"Minnie, what is it? Whatever I said, I'm sorry."

"I-it's nothing."

"No, Minnie, it's not nothing. Please honor me by telling."

She sobbed for a moment before speaking.

"You keep calling me eleven, but I'm not eleven. I turned twelve and no one noticed."

Sean's heart fell like a meteor.

For the love of the Elements, she's right. In all the work and

183

play and learning and planning and building, we forgot. Now what?

"Is that all it is?" he said. "Then I know something you don't."

She was suspicious while coyly peeking up at him though dripping eyes. One of Fiona's words popped in her head. *Blarney.* But, sometimes, even if you know *blarney* when you hear it, it's irresistible. A gleaming lightning bug of hope waxed in her belly.

"What?"

"It's a secret I'm not supposed to talk about, but—come closer."

She looked left, then right, then leaned closer to him with her head tilted back. Sean whispered as if the walls had ears—which they did, of course.

"Around here we celebrate birthdays twenty-two days after."

She worked the numbers through in her head before shouting. "Then that means the party is—tomorrow!"

She threw her arms around his neck.

"Minnie, keep quiet—it's not a secret-surprise if the whole blessed world knows about it."

She covered her mouth and giggled before moving her lips a fraction of an inch from his ear and speaking ever so softly.

"I'm going to wear my green dress," she said.

Tomorrow came as it always did, but only after a restless night. Minnie could scarcely sleep, what with images and ideas of her impending party prancing about in her head.

What has Sean planned for me?

While Minnie tossed and turned, Sean did much the same, for he had no ideas or a plan. In all honesty, he had forgotten about Minnie's birthday and was now at a loss for what to do to recover. He muttered and fretted.

"How careless of me to let such a momentous day slip by. To a wee one, they are the most important days. I'll simply have to come up with *something.*"

At long last, sleep overtook both of them and soon enough,

dawn came. Minnie came running and squealing into Sean's room the next morning, singing her heart out…

"Today's the day, today's the day, today's the daaaaaaaay, today's the day!"

Sean couldn't help himself—laughter erupted.

"My goodness, Minnie, did you sleep at all last night?"

"Nope," she giggled in reply.

"Well then, let's venture downstairs and have breakfast and talk about how you'd like your special day to go, shall we?"

Sean took Minnie's hand; they skipped and twinkle-toed downstairs.

As soon as they entered the kitchen there was a chorus of "Happy Birthday, Princess Minnie," resounding from every corner and hidden niche. Minnie blushed and squeezed Sean's hand.

Sean looked down and said, "My fair young princess, what would you like for your birthday breakfast?"

Minnie patted her finger on her lips and pretended to think—as if she didn't already know full well what she wanted.

"If I might, I would love fresh strawberries and cream, warm bread and cheese and berries and honey—and a fresh glass of spring water."

Sean never grew tired of this child. While other children demanded cake and candy, this young one wanted little more than fresh fruit and cheese. Sean's eyes teared up while looking down at her. Such a love this one was, such a love.

"I think we can arrange that feast."

Minnie went to the table to take her seat. While waiting, Flix wandered into the room and sat down next to her. Making sure Sean was busy in the pantry, he produced a special stone rounded and polished just for this occasion. Flix could be a fickle little creature, but deep down he loved Minnie as much as any soul in the house.

"This marble, Miss Minnie, will only activate in your precious hands. When anyone else picks it up, it will appear plain and simple, but when *you* pick it up, the colors will swirl and change. In time, you will learn what the colors mean, and eventually the colors will learn your moods and adapt to your ways, but most importantly, when the marble goes completely black, then be *en guarde* for trouble coming your way. Keep it close and keep it safe."

Minnie examined the stone with wide-eyed enchantment. Just when she thought she had prankster-rogue Flix figured out he went and did something nice.

"I will keep it with me forever, master Flix."

She impulsively reached out, grabbed him in her little hands and pulled him close so she could hug and kiss him. Flix squirmed and protested, but deep inside, his body was filled with boundless joy. Sean looked at Minnie and winked while Flix wriggled and complained.

"You can unhand me at any time, my princess—I've had quite enough, thank you."

"Oh, sorry."

Minnie promptly put him down, whereby Flix brushed himself off and straightened his jacket. A chorus of giggles could be heard throughout the kitchen.

"Flix," said Sean, "it was wonderful of you to make Minnie such an exquisite gift. Thank you so much."

Flix bowed to Sean and tipped his hat to Minnie. She pretended like she would hug him again—he squealed with alarm and scurried off.

Minnie turned her attention to her marble and watched the colors cascade and flow, much like gymnast's ribbons. It was beautiful to watch, both mesmerizing and soothing.

Sean placed a plate of food in front of Minnie and sat next to her with a cup of tea to watch her gobble the fruit and cheese. They laughed and talked and sketched out the day. What would they do? Minnie's day would be orchestrated and mapped out by no one other than her herself.

After a spell, Minnie decided it was high time to get dressed in her green party dress, so off she raced up the stairs, skipping and humming as she went.

While getting dressed, she heard a little voice.

"Ah-hem, Mistress Minnie?"

Minnie looked down and saw a sock goblin standing sheepishly at her feet. The little female creature was no more than eight-inches tall and was most colorful in feature.

As everyone knows, sock goblins collect socks. They don't take both socks, because they don't enjoy matching socks—symmetry is boring and mundane for colorful creatures such as these. In supplication, this one offered a pink and purple striped sock, one Minnie thought was lost forever. She lowered herself to sit cross-legged on the floor before the goblin. Brimming tears overflowed in her little eyes.

"My sock, one of the last pair my mommy gave to me. Have you had it this whole time?"

The sock goblin simply nodded her head.

"It's okay, it's such a pretty sock—I can understand why you'd want to have it for your very own."

The sock goblin looked down, then back at Minnie.

"Well, since it's your birthday and all, I thought I should return it to you," she said while extending the offering to Minnie.

Minnie reached out for the sock and gingerly took it. She held it up and rubbed it against her cheek; it still had the faintest smell of her mother on it. For a moment she was lost in thought, and began to sway back and forth as her mother had rocked her. As a tear worked its way down her face, the long lost sock caught it and twinkled. As if echoing from a long distance, Minnie heard her mom's voice.

"Happy birthday, my darling Minnie. I love you. Happy."

Minnie looked down at the sock goblin who, still as a pebble, sat and studied Minnie's face.

This had to be the *best* birthday ever.

Minnie leaped up to her dresser and grabbed another sock. This garish one was rainbow-striped and sure to appeal to the little goblin.

"I'd like you to have a gift in return," she said as she handed it over.

The sock goblin jumped up and seemed to levitate, though she was an earthbound being and had no wings.

"Oh, thank you, Princess Minnie. Thank you so very much. Here it is *your* birthday and you give *me* a wonderful gift. Oh thank you, thank you, thank you."

With a running start, she ran up and jumped onto Minnie's lap and wrapped her long arms around Minnie's neck and gave her a kiss on the cheek. The sock goblin then scampered off from whence she came—leaving Minnie sitting on the floor shaking her head with wonder and grinning from ear to ear.

Minnie finished getting dressed and then ran downstairs. She found him sitting on the patio taking in the early afternoon sun. She jumped onto his lap and momentarily took his breath away.

"Sean, Sean, let me tell you about the sock goblin..."

Once Minnie was all done with her breathless tale, she stopped to take a drink of rose water and sat still—waiting for Sean's response.

"Now what, Sean, now what? It's already been the bestest birthday ever."

Some of the flower faeries flew over and put a daisy-chain wreath in Minnie's hair; she giggled and giggled.

"This is better than any silly old paper party hat any day," Minnie said. "Thank you."

The faeries gathered around and performed an elaborate, complex dance for Minnie's entertainment. When they were done, they pulled Minnie into the grass and let her join their faerie ring dance. Sean watched as Minnie sang and giggled.

"Such a carefree life she has," thought Sean.

Deep down he knew it wouldn't last but for today at least, it was here and wonderful to watch. Sean clapped to the tune and even joined in with his battered lute. After a while Minnie plopped on the grass where the faeries fluttered about sniggering and tickling.

In exhaustion, Minnie sat in the grass and looked at Sean. She had never been happier. From his isolated hut across the meadow, up hopped the Fachan wearing his best party scarf—smiling in the endearing way only a Fachan can. He stopped momentarily to allow Sean to tie a red-ribbon bow in his hair while Minnie chuckled with delight.

The Fachan plopped down next to her.

"I hoped a silly bow in my wisp of hair would be an adequate birthday present. What else do I have to offer? Nothing, that's what."

Minnie leaned over and hugged her dear friend around the neck. Sean saw a little tear trickle down his face; he knew the homely Fachan had never felt such feelings before.

What love this child brings to our world. Yes, we have hope now, is what ran through Sean's head.

Minnie and the Fachan sat and chatted and laughed in the grass and had a merry visit.

Throughout the course of the afternoon, various magical creatures came to call. Fairies and sprites, gnomes and pixies. centaurs and minotaurs, butterflies and birds of every sort—each bringing a small gift, trinket, song or story. At one point a giant arrived with his family. They said they were passing through the realm nearby, heard the ruckus and decided to stop in. They were on a journey westward and opted not to stay, but wanted to extend their well wishes to Princess Minnie. Sean knew better. They had walked many miles out of their way and this was a tremendous honor. Minnie was gracious and somehow seemed to understand.

As twilight stole the day, Sean snapped his fingers and the whole yard was suddenly ablaze with a thousand candles. Minnie let out a gasp.

"Oh, Sean, I want to learn how to do that. Please may I know?"

Sean looked over the gaggle of assembled guests and pondered the question.

Was this his decision alone? Why not just ask?

He took a deep breath before holding up his hands to get the attention of the crowd.

"Do you think Mistress Minnie is ready for her first lesson in practical magic?"

Minnie shuffled her feet and looked shy; she'd never had such an audience before. Suddenly, she felt nervous while the group consulted among themselves and discussed the question.

After what felt like a long time, there came a resounding "Yes, Princess Minnie is ready," from every creature present.

The loud enthusiasm helped Minnie recover her confidence.

Sean bent down to whisper in her ear while making elaborate gestures with his hands. Minnie looked puzzled.

"That's all it is?" said Minnie.

"Yup, that's all," said Sean. "Think you can do it?"

"I can try," countered Minnie.

With that, Minnie took a step away from Sean. Sean reversed his spell so all went dark. Minnie said her incantation and waved her arms about as if they were seaweed swaying in the gentle ocean. Something sparked off in the tree, but didn't stay alight.

"Keep trying, Minnie," whispered Sean, "don't give up."

This was a test and all eyes were upon the young Princess.

"I can do this," Minnie muttered. She repeated his whispered words. "Focus my energy to allow the spirit fire to be released— nothing else exists besides me and the thousand candle spirits. Blend my energy with fire energy."

Sean whispered to her.

"Yes, Minnie, close your eyes, visualize the flame and play with it. Make it grow taller. Now shorter. Now make it flicker.

Visualize energy around the flame until you can't stand the heat. Now snap your fingers, wave your hands and see what happens." He whispered and coaxed and cajoled until she not only heard the words, but she *became* the words. Minnie, the spell, the words, the fire energy—all were one.

All the sudden Minnie heard noises. Awed gasps and whispers. She felt an intense heat.

She opened her eyes and saw a thousand diamonds of candles aflame—some that sparkled multicolor like rainbows. The assembled crowd burst into a round of applause and there was an outburst of singing and cheering.

"Well done, Minnie, well done," said Sean as he scooped her up and swung her around. "With rainbow-diamond-sparkles— that's remarkable," he proclaimed as he pointed to several that glowed like fireworks.

This indeed was the best birthday ever.

Minnie's party went on well into the night, with never-ending supplies of food and drink, mirth and merriment. Guests floated in and out like the tide, but Sean and the Fachan stayed by Minnie's side the entire time.

At one point Sean looked down at the Fachan and said, "If Minnie grasped the thousand-candle spell so quickly and even went beyond it, there will be talk, and talk will be carried upon the wind. Keep an eye on her, my dear friend. With so many guests, anyone could be hiding in plain sight. She must never be alone."

As the night wore on, the moon and stars shone brightly upon the affair and Sean saw Minnie finally beginning to tire; it truly had been a most magical day for Minnie and her new family. She ran to Sean and jumped onto his lap. The Fachan hopped after her and jumped into the chair next to them.

Minnie looked up at Sean with utmost love in her eyes. She looked over at the Fachan and held his hand.

"What a family we are," said Minnie.

She put her head down on Sean's shoulder and closed her

eyes. Sean rubbed Minnie's hair as he felt her relax into him. He looked over—the Fachan still had the red ribbon in his hair, if you could call it hair. He snored like a hibernating bearcub.

"Wonder what he's dreaming of..." mused Sean.

Just as Sean was about to join them in sleep, he heard music carried to him on the wind. Faintly, it came from far, far away with a barely recognizable tune and words.

Through the darkened fields entranced, music made her poor heart dance,

Thinking of a lost romance—long ago—somewhere just beyond the mist,

Spirits were seen flying, as the lightning led her way,

Through the dark—in the shadow of the moon, she danced in the starlight,

Whispering a haunting tune, to the night...

Shadow of the Moon...[17]

Sean felt a jolt run through his body. He looked up to the trees as the nocturnal Selene alighted atop a branch. As much as he didn't want to disturb the young princess, it was time.

He gently shook Minnie awake.

"What—what is it Sean?" she said as she rubbed away accumulated sleepy dust in her eyes.

"It's time to say goodbye to the day and sleep, Minnie."

She opened her mouth to protest, but stopped.

It was enough.

"So it is," she said.

She wrapped her arms around his neck. Missing Fiona with every cell, he carried Minnie inside and up the stairs. She didn't stir as he tucked her covers under her chin.

---

[17] *Shadow of the Moon*, © 1997 Ritchie Blackmore and Candice Night, from the recording *Shadow of the Moon*, King Midas Music

Lonely is the Night Filled with Despair

FIONA'S EYES WERE grainy and her head kept sinking toward the steering wheel. Overhead, the cloud cover was solid and the sun was obscured, so she was unsure what time it was. In addition, she wasn't exactly sure *where* she was, though she knew she was vaguely headed south as she wound along endless serpentine back roads in the creaky purple Bug.

How long had she been driving? Twenty hours? Three tanks of gas? Four stops for bad fast food coffee and to let Luna find a sandy place to pee? What is the right measure of time when you're on the road without a destination? Regardless, her day of travel needed to end soon; she was more asleep than awake and her mind flitted randomly from memory to memory and from driving decision to driving decision. Left? Right? Straight?

Dowsing rod. The steering wheel jerked in her hands and made her think of a dowsing rod. Why did this come to mind? She'd held a Y-shaped dowsing rod stick in her hands exactly once—when she was eight. Her father's brother, Uncle Porter, wanted to dig a cistern to supply water for his livestock—he hacked a forked section of willow branch with a Buck knife and handed it to her. Porter was a short man with a huge stomach; he was like a huge, round boulder and when he was in his ale and laughed, his belly vibrated in oceanic waves. He was more like a water balloon than a man.

She remembered the conversation well.

"What do I do with this?" she had said.

"Hold it like so," he replied while holding his hands out in front of him. "Walk across the field and stop when the end gets pulled toward the ground. Not the little tugs—let me know when you feel the big one."

"The big one, Uncle Porter?" she said. "I don't know what you mean."

He handed her a wooden stake with an orange ribbon tied on the end of it and pointed toward the field.

"Go," he said.

This was one of her few vivid memories of her father. A no-nonsense man, he was not a big drinker like Uncle Porter and sipped his ale from a pint-sized jelly jar. The Georgia sun beat down on them like liquid fire. As always, he was a scold.

"Brother, I can't believe you invited us to come all the way down here for this nonsense."

If there was one thing her father hated, it was claptrap. How he ended up with Fiona's mother, a flame-haired, scatterbrained woman who made pocket money by baking endless sweet cherry and almond pies for friends and neighbors, was one of life's mysteries. Her father was an executive for the largest oil company in the world, so they had access to plenty of money, but Fiona's mom still baked pie after pie for the fancy ladies of their upscale golf course community. Her pies made her one of the most popular women in the neighborhood—not necessarily with the ladies, but with their husbands and even at fifty dollars a pie, she could not keep up with the demand.

Time slipped. Another memory took over as the random tangle of history swirled in Fiona's weary mind.

Her mother gathered her long skirt and kneeled before Fiona.

"How do we keep them coming back?"

"By never making the same pie twice, Mommy," Fiona said.

"Right. So, what shall we put in today, Fiona?"

Five-year-old Fiona pressed her palms to her temples and thought about it.

"Apricot," she said.

"You want me to put an apricot in the cherry-almond pie?"

"Yes."

Her mother laughed.

"I was hoping you'd say ginger root because I bought a fresh batch at the farmer's market, but as it happens, apricots are in season and I have a perfect juicy one we can use."

Keep them coming back by never making the same pie twice.

Where did that thought come from? I was thinking about the dowsing rod. I'm losing my grip on reality.

Fiona held the forked-twig in front of her and walked through the field with dried wheat ears rustling against her cotton dress. The twig seemed to be alive and it sometimes twitched. She looked over her shoulder. Uncle Porter waved her on. The twig twisted to the left and she followed it, then it dived toward the ground, pulling out of her hands and gouging scratches into her soft skin.

"Ouch," she said.

She turned back to the house.

"Stab the stake in the ground, Fiona," Uncle Porter called out.

She did, then walked back across the field, running her hands through the wheat grain—scattering grasshoppers and bumblebees. The wheat spoke to her—not in words she could understand, but in images of the ancient windswept prairies of the Levant. Wheat was a key partner in twelve-thousand years of shared human history—the field told her, so she knew.

In the shade of the porch, her father and Uncle Porter still argued.

"There's no scientific evidence that dowsing actually works," her father said.

"I don't care about science," Uncle Porter said. "I just want to know where to start digging with my dag-blasted backhoe—and now I know."

"Unadulterated, undiluted twaddle."

Uncle Porter raised his mug in salute.

"But nothing but the very best, premium quality twaddle." To Fiona, he said, "If I recall correctly, there's cold lemonade in the 'fridge. Oh, and my mug could use a topping off."

Funny that—his beer mug *always* seemed to be in need of topping off.

She fought the steering wheel; it seemed alive and really wanted to make an upcoming left turn.

"Damnation," she muttered before giving up.

As they drove by, she tried to read a road sign so she'd have an idea where they were, but her eyes failed. After the turn, the car purred along the twisty road for a few miles and skirted a large, boggy pond. Just beyond the pond, there was a gravel-paved turnout. The car jerked to the right.

"What?" she said while fighting the wheel. "We're in the dead center of nowhere. Let's not stop here."

It was another battle she lost—the car slewed onto the gravel and promptly died.

"What's this?"

She turned the key and the car stubbornly refused to start. Stroking the dashboard did nothing this time.

"Hellfire," she muttered before getting out of the car.

With her hands on the roof, she stretched her back and looked around.

Woods. Marsh. Meadow. Gray sky.

She was not even sure what state she was in. New Hampshire? West Massachusetts? Wherever it was, it was a place with no shortage of dreary woods, marsh and meadow. She kicked the car.

"With friends like you..."

On a high branch, there was a smudgy blob. Not Selene, but one of Selene's brothers or sisters. With her mind, Fiona reached out. Female spirit. Sister.

"Hooo," the owl said before taking flight and disappearing into the woods.

"*Boo*-hooo," Fiona replied. She kicked the car again, but the only damage was an abused nail on her big toe. "With the day I had—losing my house and my best friend."

It hit her. Sean was a lover. Elizabeth and David were friends. She had lots of other friends too, but Llwyd was her very best friend. She didn't even like him that much, but he gave his life to give her time to escape. He deserved a better friend than her.

Oh, Llwyd. I'm sorry.

She kicked the car again, but with her other foot—now both were sore.

"Crud-poop," she muttered. "I'm a loser."

She turned a complete circle and tried to decipher why she was dumped at this godforsaken place. With everything in her, she reached out and got nothing back. She wanted to scream and tear out her hair.

"I traded a cozy fire and a hot cup of tea for emptiness—for nothing, nowhere."

In a dark territory beyond exhaustion, she gave in to despair with a few tattered lines of dark poetry haunting her thoughts.

The angel folded you up like laundry,
Your body thin as an empty dress.
Your clothes were curtains hanging on the window
Of what had been your flesh and now was glass.[18]

---

[18] *My Mother's Body*, Marge Piercy

Sunlight waned as the landscape folded into night. It was already cold, but got colder as the day died. Mist formed over the swamp and drifted over the road while the evening wind gathered strength. Was she supposed to wait for a ride? The road was deserted. Maybe no one ever comes this way and the next truck will pass her moldering skeleton.

"What am I supposed to do?" she whispered.

There was no answer, so she said it louder and louder until she was screaming and hoarse.

"Is it too much to ask? A sign. A hint. A clue. Anything."

She opened the car door and Luna jumped out. Purring, he wove around and through her legs. He stopped and sank his claws into her leg.

Must he be so annoying?

"Ouch, dammit, not now, Luna," Fiona said.

He sniffed the air and then bounded across the road. He stopped at the road's shoulder and stared at her for a few seconds before disappearing into the gloom.

Go ahead, cat, leave me too. I'm not worthy of your friendship, either.

Semi-catatonic, she was in an emotional fugue of distressed confusion. In circles, she thought of Sean, Llwyd, the smoking ruins of her home and everyone she hated, like the Queen, the Black Faerie King and the mysterious Minerva who was not now her friend and never would be. An image of Minerva formed in her mind—a hag older than the Queen—with a hooked nose, warts and fingernails like talons; an ugly old beast with a scattered mouthful of black teeth.

Maybe I'm supposed to wander in the woods where I can suffer and die without anyone else getting hurt. Is that the grand plan—the best outcome of this sad tale of woe and misery?

She fell to her knees and the cruel gravel stabbed through her jeans and pierced her knees. The pain felt like truth.

At a time like this, that's what I deserve. Not comfort. Agony.

Why did I run away and let Llwyd die alone? No good person would do that.

"Okay. No ride? I should wander in the woods like a lost soul until hypothermia claims me? I can do that. I will."

Her ears echoed with a half-remembered song from her father's old vacuum-tube stereo.

Oh, oh, oh, step right up and take a look at a fool
He's got a heart as stubborn as a mule
C'mon everybody, he's good for a laugh
And no one could tell his heart is broken in half[19]

Hooo, cried the owl lost deep in the woods.

Hooo-cares, she thought while gathering her stuff from the car.

Car keys, wooden staff, Sean's backpack. With a windup and overhand toss, she threw the keys as far as she could and listened for them to land in the bog. The bullfrogs stopped their mocking croaks for a moment and she heard nothing but dead silence.

Not even the satisfaction of a splash. Perfect.

Standing by the side of the road, she imagined what she looked like: a hopeless road bum. With her first step off the road, cold swamp water rose over her ankle and soaked through her sneaker and sock.

Yes, that's it, she thought. This is what a coward deserves: a thorough drowning in fetid water and quicksand. With another step, the other foot also became muddy and soaked with cold water. The absurdity of her situation struck her and she laughed.

Not only am I a coward, but I'm stupid.

She did not bother with trying to find a path, she just walked forward and dared the swamp to swallow her whole and leave no

---

[19] *Goodbye Cruel World*, words and music by Gloria Shayne, as sung by James Darren.

trace behind. A cloud of mosquitoes hovered around her head. Apparently they liked coward's blood just fine.

Have at it. Enjoy.

After the first mile, she suspended all thought and just walked. Straight ahead? In circles? She didn't know and didn't care. She walked through fatigue into mindless exhaustion until she couldn't lift a foot for another step—there she collapsed in the mud.

No one would ever find her rotting body in this lonesome nowhere, so she composed her own epitaph.

Here lies Fiona Pascälle, coward and loser. Good riddance.

Closing her eyes for what she assumed was the last time; she gave herself up to the night.

It doesn't matter, it's just a physical body made of rotting meat. Goodbye. Farewell, cruel world.

Call it what you will: spirit, soul or otherworldly essence, but *it* was halfway out of her body when she reopened her eyes.

Voices? Did she hear faint voices?

She strained her senses and saw a hint of a flicker of light.

Unless she was mistaken, it was a campfire, but there was no strength left in her body, so there was no way she could find out—she had no energy left to even call out for help.

That's funny, she thought. As the cliché goes, so close and yet so far away.

She looked down and saw she was standing. She was more surprised to see her feet begin moving—now she was walking. Not quickly, but walking nonetheless, stumbling along with one tired foot set in front of the other.

Luna Makes His Way

HE STOOD WITH his paws on the inside of the Bug's window—staring out into the night. Selene's sister was perched on a high branch and just outside the bramble there was a small, thin figure sitting on a deadfall branch. The night was alive with possibility.

"Why must mistress Fiona behave like this—I understand her despair, but truly, there is a time to curl in a ball and lick one's wounds, but this is a time for action," mused Luna. "Is she going to *ever* let me out? There is plenty to explore. It is most annoying and I'm honestly not sure how much more I can take. If I were to carry on in such a manner each time I failed to catch my prey or earn some treat, nothing would ever get done. How long have we been driving anyway—feels like forever and a day. I generally don't mind traveling with her but in this state it is MOST dreadful."

He sat in the car waiting for Fiona to open the door, but she was busy having *another* tantrum—this time, because the car knew something she didn't—that she was exactly where she needed to be. And there, by the woods pixie, it was as clear as anything—that was where the trail began.

Finally, Fiona cracked open the door. In a fraction of a flash,

Luna slipped through the gap. He rubbed against her legs.

Branch. Trailhead. Dry pathway.

She ignored him, so he used his claws. Not to draw a lot of blood, but to get her attention.

Dry pathway!

"Ouch, dammit, not now, Luna," Fiona said.

Really, mistress Fiona?

He walked across the road to examine the woods pixie—cautiously he sniffed and approached slowly.

Friend or foe?

The pixie was a small figure of a man with brown skin—rather ragged in appearance. Luna was used to seeing merry elves and gnomes, pixies and sprites—he was unsure of the nature of this one. Back at the car, Fiona was still breaking down. Luna turned to watch her car keys arc through the air. He had an impulse to go back again and try to get her attention.

"Let her be, Luna. Fiona needs to sink before she can swim again."

"I don't understand humans."

The little man shrugged.

"You're right—their ways can sometimes be wrong-way mysterious."

"What kind of forest creature are you?" Luna said. "I'll bite you in half if you mean us harm."

The little man laughed.

"Friend or enemy? If only things were always that simple. Yes, Luna, I *am* a different sort than you're used to—my name is Elcor and I am a creature from the deep-wild. I will not harm you, so be not afraid. Your trials and tribulations were carried on the winds to us and we have been on the lookout for you and your mistress Fiona."

Luna stared into the woods. The route was lighted like a garden path; it started with a hop from rock to rock, then along a deadfall cedar, then on a dry patch skirting a pool of fetid bog before disappearing in a patch of holly.

"Will you help her find her way?"

Elcor filled his lungs with cool air and released it slowly.

"She not in a state where we *can* help her. She's closed, not open. In this state, she'll have to find her own way."

"But she'll make it?"

Elcor shrugged.

"We think so," he said. "Probably. Maybe."

"What should I do?"

"Go ahead. When you find the fire, make yourself known and introduce yourself to Nellie. They are a motley crew, but they are good people. Wait for her; if she makes it, you and Fiona will find a safe place to hide among them."

Luna sat and looked at little creature.

"Well, my good man, I quite like your suggestion. Resting sounds like a splendid suggestion. However, I do not wish to be skinned and roasted. Are you quite sure they will welcome me?"

"Bring Nellie this mushroom as a gift." From his shoulder bag, Elcor produced a special brown mushroom with green spots. "Carry it by the stem though, because, if you get even a smidgeon of the cap on your tongue, you will be in for one wild ride. Take the time you need to rest and recharge, Luna. Rediscover your cat-like ways. Find the hunter in you. Find the strategist. Find that inner warrior cat that has been sleeping. You will need all these skills in the days to come because the battle is brewing and enemy forces amass. Danger closes in on us like a vulture circling its thrashing prey. Fiona will make her way to the fire—right now she must struggle through on her own."

For an instant, Elcor rested his hand on Luna's head, then he turned and strode away. Luna sniffed the odd little mushroom before gingerly picking it up—being careful to only take the end of the stem in his mouth. After taking a last look back at Fiona, he walked into the dark woods.

Rocks. Fallen cedar. Dry patch.

Luna walked and walked before stopping for a breath. Something heavy passed while he hid among the roots of an old stump. He took inventory of where he was and what he was going to do next.

The forest was filled with sights and sounds and there were bountiful hazards, but they were easy skirted. A faint scent drifted on the breeze. He put his nose to the air. Meat, fire and earthy-smelling humans is what came back to him. He crouched low and let his nose and senses guide him; he found himself at the edge of a clearing where a band of misfits stoked a fire against encroaching darkness. A hunk of meat roasted over the fire and the smell was intoxicating—it had been hours and hours since he'd last eaten. He sat and surveyed the scene.

A large, oafish human wore some sort of animal pelt while a friendly looking woman tended to the cooking. In addition, a rather cranky looking man perched on a log.

They look harmless enough.

He took a deep breath, raised his head up high and walked right up to the woman and dropped the mushroom at her feet.

She looked down at him. Her eyes twinkled as she looked at Luna and he knew he was both welcome and safe.

"What do we have here?" She reached down and picked up the mushroom. "A furry friend bearing a gift. Welcome my fine fellow."

She stroked his ebony fur.

The grumpy man spoke.

"Eh, what's that Nellie? Found yourself another mangy critter, did ya? Looks like another mouth to feed to me. Shoo it away."

"Shut your gob, not on your life. There will be another joining us shortly. Mind your manners. Be quiet and don't make any trouble."

"Ehhhhh," garbled the man as he threw up his hands returned his attention to his stein of ale.

"Never mind him, my noble cat. You'll be fine. Stay close to

204

me and all will be well. Rest and recharge. Your mistress will be here soon."

Humans touched by magic never ceased to amaze Luna. How they knew what they knew he would never understand and right now, he didn't care. Nellie gave him a few scraps as a snack before returning her attention to tending her roasting meat.

Luna took a deep sigh, yawned and drifted off to sleep. Soon enough, Fiona would join him. Until then, yes, he would sleep.

A Campfire in the Woods

THE FIRE WAS bigger than she first imagined—and farther away. In between, hazards were still plentiful; for one, she was barely able to extract herself from a hungry patch of hard-working muck pulling her toward the center of the Earth, but, by dragging her body out inch-by-inch with the tangled roots of a swamp willow, she was able to find a safe, semi-solid patch of ground. There she lay for an hour or ten gasping for air and listening to her overstressed heart pound in her chest.

She heard faint voices from the people around the fire and tried her own, but it was more of a croak blending seamlessly with the other noisy bog creatures—the good folk around the fire did not hear her.

She wiped a gloppy mess from her face and looked up. The fire was near—so near she could feel—or imagine feeling—the skin-drying, life-giving thermal radiation. Only another thirty feet to go, maybe fifty, tops. She'd already walked seven hundred miles in this swamp; it would be a cosmic irony if she couldn't make it another fifty feet. Sixty, tops.

She rolled onto her back and studied the patchy sky—looking for stars. Of course, the cloud cover was blanket-solid and there were none to be seen. Even the traitorous moon hid its shameful face and she was completely alone—except for a whirring bat chasing mosquitoes. Once on her back, she rolled over and found her knees. Once on her knees, she found a crouch and from the crouch—with the help of her staff, found her feet and soon walked again. A shambling shuffle of a walk, but the fire grew closer and soon enough, she stood outside the circle of people around the blazing fire.

On a spit over the fire, a woman turned the blackened carcass of a small animal. The odor coming from the poor dead creature was irresistible—Fiona's mouth flooded with saliva. The woman turning the spit wore a green-velvet wenches' dress—her copious breasts were on display like fat, freckled loaves in a baker's shop window.

"We have our visitor," she said.

One of the men—with his back to her—leaned over the fire to carve off a slice of roasting flesh with a huge knife.

He spoke.

"That's news? I could smell her an hour ago."

The woman scolded him.

"Shut your yap, Nick. I'm Nellie," she said. She stood, waved her arm in an expansive gesture and spoke in a formal olde-English form of invitation. "Make your tired bones at home by our fire."

Without turning, the chewing man spoke with a harsh tone.

"Tell her to go away and find her own fire—there's no room here."

Fiona took a step forward. The blistering fire was hot and already mud dried and flaked off her skin. One of the men across the fire was a huge black man who seemed to be wearing a bearskin as a coat. He stood and towered over the fire.

It was impossible, but to Fiona, he seemed eight-feet-tall.

He lifted a staff as big as Fiona's leg and poked the rude man in the chest. The rude man tipped over backwards and left a vacant seat on the fallen log they used as a bench.

"There's room now," the giant said with a rumble of a voice.

The woman tending the fire laughed.

With an eye on the tumbled man's knife, Fiona quickly stepped over him and settled on the log in his place.

The fallen man stood and brushed leaves from his tunic. He brusquely shoved at the shoulder of a man who looked remarkably like Benjamin Franklin.

"Scoot your scurvy ass."

"Take your odiferous pottle elsewhere, swag-bellied lout."

Fiona held her hands out to the fire.

"Fiona," she said in a quiet, mousy voice. "Fiona Pascälle. That's my name."

The woman carved off a generous hunk of steaming meat, skewered it with a giant silver serving fork and handed it to Fiona. Her greedy mouth craved its taste, but she hesitated and looked at it skeptically.

"What are we eating?"

"Dog," Nick said. "Border collie, I think."

"Shut your gob, Nick," Nellie said. "It's an old goat. Don't worry about it, the goat had a good, full, goaty life, and it's okay. *We* feed the worms when it's our turn. Now, the goat feeds us. The tragedy would be not enjoying its earthly flesh—letting it die in vain."

Fiona tasted the hot meat—it was delicious. She tried not to seem greedy and gobble the offering too quickly, but it was impossible. With the first morsel quickly consumed, she looked at the roasting carcass and craved more.

Nick waved his knife. With an antler hilt, the blade had a nasty blue glint in the firelight.

"I don't think the goat was thinking cheery thoughts when it faced death by my blade."

Nellie pointed her carving knife at Nick.

"Shut the hell up," she said. "You already know me." She pointed at Ben Franklin. "When he's not playing the First

American, he does insults for two dollars a pop."

Ben stood, doffed his hat and bowed.

"I also do compliments, but they are a dollar more. I'm not akin to these lisping hawthorn-budded, swill-buckets. I love thee, none but true-penny thee, and thou sweet, nose-herb smilet—for there's nothing ill that can live in the temple of your glorious soul."

The rude man snorted.

"For a fecking buck you get robbed," he muttered.

The huge man reached over the fire with a hand like a mutant catcher's mitt. Shaking his hand, Fiona felt like a paper doll.

"Little John," he said.

Nellie laughed.

"His real name is Andre, but he'll answer to either name. He's my common-law. If you can knock him off the log in the center of the Faire, you win a thousand dollars."

"Not bloody likely," Andre said. "Ain't happened yet."

The woman continued, "The sweet-tempered man who warmed your spot on the log is Nick. The dog is Leonard and we don't know the cat—he just turned up a couple of hours ago."

Cat?

Fiona peered through the fire and scanned the circle. Barely visible, there *was* a napping cat. Black. Luna lifted his head and blinked his yellow eyes at her.

"That's my cat. Luna."

Nick snorted.

"Nobody owns a cat. The cat owns you."

Andre gestured with his gallon-sized mug and spoke.

"Ale or hot tea? Either will chase the dreary chill from your bones."

Fiona's eyes were still glued to Luna's.

"I'd sell Luna's soul for a cup of hot tea," she said.

Andre pulled the cork bung from a cask and refilled his mug.

"Suit yourself," he said.

Nellie tilted a cast iron pot and filled a pewter cup with

steaming black liquid—thick as crude oil. She passed the cup to Ben, who waved it at Nick. Nick refused to take it, so Ben reached around him to hand the cup to Fiona.

She breathed the steam deep into her lungs before blowing across the surface to cool it. When it seemed safe, she took a tentative sip. Scalding-hot, it was a simple brew, just loose-leaf black tea doctored with apple cider and cinnamon sticks, but it was perfect and heavenly—and fed a tiny spark of hope deep inside her. Hope was not something she felt she deserved, so she pushed it down deep.

Thank you.

She realized she only thought the words and that was insufficient.

"Thank you," she said.

Nellie nodded.

"No problem," she said.

"Parasite," Nick mumbled.

Fiona had enough of Nick's surliness. She elbowed him in the side as hard as she could.

"Shut your poxey mouth," she said.

Andre laughed.

"You tell him, girl."

Nick scooted over an inch and rubbed his ribs.

"Ingrate," he said.

Over the next couple of hours, Andre carved pieces off the goat and passed them around the circle while alternately feeding bits to Leonard and Luna. Luna pretended to not be much interested, but thoroughly consumed every piece before grooming his whiskers and waiting for more.

Soon, Fiona was still filthy, but dry and feeling very nearly human, though every time she felt a smile brewing, she thought of poor Llwyd and her nascent cheerfulness dissipated. She looked around the circle.

"I really appreciate your hospitality, but you guys are not

serious, right? These outfits? What's the deal? Costume party? You're kidding around?"

"Damned right we're serious, swamp creature," Nick said.

"Don't pay any attention to him," Nellie said. "RenFaire." Fiona looked puzzled, so Nellie continued. "You never heard of a Renaissance Faire? A reenactment of an Olde English harvest festival? We make enough money in a couple of months to keep us going all winter."

"It helps that we live on old goats and almost no money," Nick muttered.

"In the winter when the Faire is closed, we camp out. When the weather improves, we work on fixing the winter damage and preparing for opening day. It's a great gig for people who hate desks and crave freedom."

"This might sound strange coming from a complete stranger, but I don't have anywhere else to go. Can I stay at your camp? I'll keep to myself—I won't cause any trouble."

"Here's my vote," Nick said. "I vote she moves along and takes her drama down the road."

Fed up, Ben Franklin finally spoke to Nick.

"You, sir, are an antediluvian miscreant fripoon and the idol of idiot worshippers—a man with no enemies, but who is intensely disliked by his friends." [20]

Nellie laughed.

"Stuff it, Nick, this is not a voting thing." She turned her attention to Fiona. "If you want to hang out, no one will stop you. As Al Gore famously said, 'there's no controlling legal authority.' But, I have to warn you about the new owner and his manager."

Andre belched—it was a long, deep impressive performance. When he was finished, he spoke with his deep-rumble voice.

"Owner and manager," Andre scoffed. "There's something very wrong with those people. But, we won't see them until June

[20] Adapted quote used with apologies and a hat-tip to Oscar Wilde.

211

or so—which might be a good time for you to clear out."

"That's utter tommy-rot," Nick said, "I get along with the new management fine and I'm sure they share my opinion of tussie-mussie squatters." He turned his head to spit.

"And you," Ben Franklin said, "are a beef-witted, toby-jug applejohn made to sing small."

Nellie continued, "The doss—accommodations—are, uh, rustic. Outhouse, no hot water, that sort of thing. The owner doesn't turn on the power until we start the prep work for the season. But, if you're looking for a place to hang loose for a while..."

"It sounds, perfect," Fiona said. She held out her cup. "How's the tea holding up?"

Minnie Learns a Secret Spell or Three

MINNIE AWOKE AS she always did, with a smile on her face and thankful she was now in this enchanted house with Sean and his magical friends—in her young body with its unfolding awareness. No moment passed when she wasn't grateful for what she'd been given. Always, her thoughts were balanced by memories of her mother and all she'd done for Minnie in her short time in the earthly plane.

Today she felt a tingle run through her little body as soon as her toes touched the floor. Something special was in the air—though she didn't know what. As she stretched and yawned and became fully awake to the potential of the day, Flix scampered in.

"Good morning, Mistress Minnie, I trust you slept well?"

Minnie plopped on the floor—face-to-face with master Flix. She was always very careful not to offend the little pixie. While she and Flix did not start off as the best of friends, they were now very close and Minnie didn't want to risk doing anything that might send them back to square one.

"Why, yes, I *did* sleep well, but I feel something strange in the air today—some sort of curious energy. Do you know of any special adventures or lessons planned for the day?"

With that, Flix got a twinkle in his little eyes and said, "Why, yes, I do, Minnie. I will teach you out-of-the-ordinary magic today, if that's alright?"

Minnie let out an uncontrollable, impertinent, high-pitched squeal that made Flix cringe—then she scooped him up.

"I get to learn new pixie magic today? From youuuuu? Oh my, yes, that would be wonderful, Flix."

She pulled him closer so she could hug him. Flix had learned not to protest too much at these open displays of affection, though he'd much rather prefer it if they didn't happen at all. Soon he'd had enough—he squirmed and demanded to be put down.

He couldn't avoid a hint of sarcasm. "Great. If I survive being squeezed to death, I'll meet you downstairs where we will have breakfast. Then you and I will retreat outside to have our lesson."

With that, Flix bowed and took his leave.

In record time, Minnie washed, dressed and virtually flew down the stairs. As if having wings on her heels, she raced into the kitchen where she nearly knocked Sean into his buckwheat pancake batter.

"Slowwww down, twinkle toes, the world isn't ending today."

With that, Minnie plopped down in her chair and let Sean know Flix was teaching her pixie magic today. Sean raised an eyebrow and looked over at Flix.

"Nothing dangerous, right, Flix?"

"Oh, no, no, no, Sean, nothing of perilous sort—just simple spells that might come in handy somewhere down the path."

Flix and Sean exchanged glances and Sean understood at once. This was to be magic meant only for Minnie and her upcoming battles with whatever forces were coming her way.

"Very well, Flix. I trust you take care of the Princess and see that no harm comes to her."

"But of course, my lord, of course."

With that settled, they sat down to a breakfast of hot buckwheat pancakes, fresh huckleberries and maple syrup brought to them by the forest gnomes. Minnie raced through her food at record speed—Sean wondered if the child even tasted his labor of love. He sat back and laughed as Minnie sat in the chair swinging her legs back and forth, quite unable to control her energy.

"Okay, okay, you two run along," he said to them.

Minnie jumped up and gave Sean a sweet, sticky, syrupy kiss on the cheek. "I promise to be safe; Flix will look after me."

Flix piped in, "Not to worry, Master, we'll be nearby in the rock garden, not far. We'll be safe."

Sean trusted Flix, but sometimes pixie magic could be unpredictable. However, if this was to be part of Minnie's education, then so it must be. Standing in the doorway, he watched Minnie skip away with Flix on her shoulder. A princess and a pixie—what a magical pair, thought Sean with a smile.

Minnie and Flix soon reached the rock garden. It was a lovely place infused with peaceful beauty. Among the rocks and flowers, a stone path wound around in a spiral meditation labyrinth. In the middle sat a boulder with a pool carved in the top—a pool of clear water decorated with floating lilies where butterflies and hummingbirds frequented to rest or get a drink. This garden of peace and magic was a place where one could rest, recharge and reconnect to the earth—which is why Flix, on this warm, quiet morning, chose it for his classroom.

"Now, Minnie, you know a spell is thought brought to life and words give meanings to our thoughts and feelings, thus, they have to be chosen very carefully. Words can cut deeply and leave eternal wounds—they can be a weapon used to protect, defend or attack. In fact, did you ever realize that *words* and *sword* contain the same letters?"

Minnie had to confess she did not know that and took a moment to write the letters in the sand—she liked seeing things for herself. Once she saw the letters she giggled.

"You can also make drows and rowds."

Flix leaned over and studied the letters with intensity.

"What? Rowds? You're right, but wait, those aren't real words and you're a bad little girl for trying to fool a pixie."

Giggling, she lilted her head backwards and spread her arms.

"No, I'm not bad. I'm the last truly sweet and innocent person in the universe."

Flix looked down and used his foot to scatter the sand and obscure the letters. If her bold statement had come from anyone else he would proclaim it as self-deception and madness, but he knew Minnie to be pure of heart and spirit. For an endless few seconds, he sat and absorbed the moment. Like all beautiful experiences, he wanted to capture it and make it last forever. But, as always, there was work to do.

"Ah-hem, where were we?" muttered Flix to himself. "Ah, yes, a magic spell is thought captured in words—the meaning is special and reserved for you and you alone. Your words float outward into the universe with energy and intent and the mysterious universe takes those words and intentions and creates a physical force. Everything has an inner certainty, a way of being, an essential natural state and a need to align with its central truth. But, things can transform into what they desire or what you can convince them they want to be. Do you understand? This is why words are so important—when you give voice to your thoughts, they can create and modify the world around you."

Minnie nodded at Flix wide-eyed.

"You must connect with the elements; they are all around us—and within us as well. We are made from them. They *are* us and *we* are them.

"The North is connected to the Earth. The Earth is mystery and manifestation of thought, the keeper of time and memories. Magnetic flux lines emerge from the North and these lines flow through us. When you need to be reminded who you are and what you must do, when you feel lost and need grounding, go to the Earth. Put your hands into it. Smell it. Let it guide you.

"The East is connected to the Air—the Air is the beginning of all things, the breath of all life. Air provides you with your voice and your ability to think. Balance, truth and justice are the gifts offered and provide illumination to light your way. When you are lost in the dark, when you need to clear your head and find your voice, inhale the Air and reach for its spirit.

"The South is connected with Fire. Fire honors our individual and unique spirit and will spur you onward when you feel weak and lost. The Fire can't be tamed—it is fierce and creative, complex and combustible. It is found within each of us; it is that spark within that never goes out. When you are too scared to go forward, too scared to go back and too scared to stand still, seek out the inferno in your soul and unleash the Fire.

"The West is connected with Water. Water is the tide of our lives; our lives past, present and future. The Tide is the sister to our beloved Moon. Water washes us clean and loves us no matter what we have done or what we have yet to do. Water remembers but does not dwell—all things come from and return to the Water. When you need of healing, reflection or intuition, find Water and drink in its cleansing wisdom."

Flix took a moment to pause and catch his breath. Was this too much for the young Princess to take in? He looked at her and saw the glimmer of understanding in her eyes. No, this was fine—she drank it in like a person who finds an oasis after being lost in the desert.

Flix went on to speak of working magic with the moon and the sun, the planets and the stars. He reminded her of the different trees and their leaves and what they could do. He briefly went over different herbs and their properties. All the while Minnie sat there, never once did she fidget or get bored.

Flix realized it was time for a break.

"Shall we break for tea and a snack?"

The mention of food broke the spell.

"Oh, yes, please," said Minnie.

With that Flix disappeared and then returned with a basket

and stoneware jug. That was just what they needed to revive their life blood.

"What now, Flix?" asked Minnie.

He thought it over.

"Okay, I have one for you." He pawed through his kitbag and produced an orange and held it a foot away from her eyes. "Watch this carefully," he said.

He rotated it so she could see it from all sides and while she stared with solemn intensity, the orange shimmered and transformed. Then it was not an orange, it was an apple—a shiny, mottled green-red Fuji apple.

She laughed and clapped her hands with delight.

"How did you do that? Can you change it back?"

"Change it back?" he said. "Probably not, but I'll show you what I did." He pulled another orange from the bag and handed it to her; she held it before her shiny little eyes. "What do you see?"

She shrugged.

"An orange."

"Do you see an orange that would like to be an apple?"

"No," she said, thinking. "I see an orange that is happy to be an orange."

"Tell it. Look deep into it and give it permission to be the glorious, beautiful apple it always wanted to be. It's made of waves and space and can be an apple if it wants to."

"No, it still wants to be an orange."

"Sell it, Minnie. Be persuasive. Believe it yourself, then *transfer* that conviction."

With eyebrows furrowed, she concentrated. In a flash, she no longer held an orange in her hands—she held a shriveled little red apple. She turned it in her hands while they laughed.

"It was a grumpy orange and wanted to be a sour crabapple."

"See if it wants to change back," Flix suggested.

She held it directly in front of her face and focused for a full minute before giving up.

"No, it's happy being a crabapple." She took a bite and screwed up her face. "A nasty-tasting, bitter-sour apple." She cocked her arm and tossed the apple across the tall branches of the labyrinth. She rubbed her tummy. "I feel it inside me. It's alive."

"Its spirit will abide in you forever," Flix said.

He could not decipher the look on her face as she thought about his words.

"Is that it?" she said. "Is there anything else?"

"That's a very good question, Minnie," answered Flix. "I'm trying to figure out that very answer as we sit and chat—trying to sort out exactly what you may need to have in your bag of tricks as we go further and further down this path. I'll figure this out soon enough."

Minnie took that as a cue to not bother him for the moment, so, with Flix's teachings swirling in her head, she got up and began exploring the labyrinth. While letting sunrays warm and soothe her—radiating deep in her being—she worked her hands and fingers in this motion and that. Today was another great day—Minnie bowed her head to give thanks.

Flix watched the young princess walk the labyrinth. Only a tender twelve years of age but so wise beyond her years; so strong and powerful, yet still so naïve and gentle. Princess Minnie truly was a wonder. What magic should he teach her? Something known only to his folk—something that could be filed away and only pulled to the forefront should that time ever come?

The air was warm and still—slumber's call was irresistible.

Just for a minute.

He put his head on his kitbag and was deeply asleep, instantly.

Skipping around the labyrinth, Minnie explored neglected pathways while the green walls grew taller and taller like overhanging hedgerows.

Overhead, the bright sky was a washed-out strip of blue; she walked in deep, black shadows. The outside world faded away to nothing until she was left only with spider webs and thorny brambles for company.

Tiptoeing, she passed a papery wasp's nest. Careful to keep her distance, she moved slowly to avoid disturbing the buzzing horde in any way. The oversized bees had bodies banded by black and vivid yellow and had evil glints in their beady-cold eyes. No warm-blooded sympathy lived in them.

She stopped to study a huge black beetle crawling in brown leaves and gravel.

She poked it with a twig.

"Where are you going in such a hurry?" she said.

"You shouldn't be here," it replied before disappearing into the bramble.

Curious.

When she stood and brushed off her knees, she was startled by a figure sitting on the deadfall tree that terminated the pathway.

"Ah," she said. "You startled me."

She'd seen trolls in one of Sean's books—not the happy volumes he read to her at bedtime, but in a slim, leather-bound book hidden away high on a shelf. He hadn't told her *not* to explore his bookshelf, but he did not make it easy—she had to stack thick books on a chair to reach the top shelf, then lean over precariously to reach the dusty ones on the end.

In the sketches, most trolls were stocky, but this one was rail-thin and missing an ear. An angry red scar trailed down his neck like a thunderbolt. He stood up and took a bold, arrogant stance with his hand on the hilt of his scaled-down rapier.

Laughing, he said, "You are what everyone is afraid of? *You?* I've killed more fearsome creatures with a belch and the flick of a finger."

Standing in front of the curiously thin troll, a kernel of fear blossomed in Minnie's belly. Head to toe, she took inventory. No staff. No marbles. The red jewel was tucked away safely back at home.

What *did* she have?

Patent leather shoes, a leather belt, cotton underclothes and a pair of blue ribbons in her pigtails.

She knew as certain as night follows day; this little troll would kill her. She could *see* her crumpled body bleeding in the mossy gravel. She could see the tears of her friends. She could see her mossy gravestone under an oak tree.

Goodbye, my friends, farewell.

Minnie's Hard Lessons Continue

"GOOD SIR, I bid you greeting. Isn't it a fine day for a stroll?"

The troll stopped approaching and looked at her with wonder.

"For what might be your last words—idle, mundane comments about the weather are what you choose? Remarkable."

A black spider, who, with legs spread, was bigger than her hand, walked up beside him from behind. Without a thought, he drew his sword and speared it.

"It can be as easy as that to dispense with a minor annoyance."

Deep inside, she knew she was going to die. Oddly, the realization did not bother her. Everyone dies and it wasn't fair that she carried on after her mother took her last breath.

It's all okay.

Here spirit left her body and drifted up beyond the maze hedgerow and into the breezy sky.

Oneness.

That's what death is. The dissolution of the individual and a merging with the grand everything. When the day comes, that's what happens.

I'm lighter than air.

It didn't hurt. She felt fine. Better than fine. All of her cares and worries dissolved.

A voice filled her ears.

No, not yet.

It was the old Queen.

You're not dead until you are dead.

What a silly thing to say, Minnie thought.

The word popped into her mind. Tautology. A banal, self-referencing, meaningless, circular argument.

Where had she seen that word before? She had no idea.

The world is not done with you yet. Ask for help and it will come.

In an instant, she was back in her body. Taking a deep breath, she looked around for a weapon.

There was nothing.

She reached out with her mind.

Okay. Fine. I can use a little help here.

Beyond the gentle breeze in the hedgerow, there was nothing.

The troll took a deep breath and looked around.

"This is sad. Really. After all that was said about you, I expected a more worthy challenger. Well, so be it, it doesn't matter. The Thinn Man's gold will spend just as easily, regardless of how easily I earned it."

The Thinn Man.

She thought back to selecting produce at the food co-op with her mother—it seemed like a trillion years had passed. The troll made a mistake by mentioning The Thinn Man because it made her angry. She could scarcely control an impulse to scream.

"You are the kind of man who, when given a choice between making a friend or making an enemy, choose the bad road."

"That's no better," he said. "False Princess Minerva took a bad road. I'll make sure it's carved in your gravestone. Too bad they'll have to bury you without your head because it's going back with me in a sack."

She gritted her teeth.

"I'll give you one last chance," she said. "Disappear now and I'll spare your life."

Snickering, he leaned over and put his hands on his knees.

"It's a wonder how hard it can be to tell the difference between courage and stupidity."

She spread her legs, took a solid stance and slowly lifted her hands, palms up.

He raised his blade.

"There's not much magic more powerful than a sword. And against a blade forged by my grandfather in Iona? Who did he forge it for, you might ask? We will not speak of that." He took a step forward until the rusty tip was six inches from her naked neck. "Say goodbye, Minerva."

She flicked her eyes to his leg. He cocked his head and looked. A giant black spider crawled slowly up his trousers. He lowered his blade and flicked it away.

Glacially, she raised an index finger to point behind him.

The path was alive—it flowed like an ebony river; a tsunami of spiders.

"No," he said. "This is not happening."

"Yes, it is," she whispered. "Sorry."

Desperation filled his voice.

"I'm sorry. You win. Peace. I'll go back and tell the Thinn Man I could not find you."

"Too late," Minnie said.

In a handful of seconds, the screaming troll was overrun. After collapsing to his knees, he fell over and was a writhing lump in a carpet of writhing arachnids. In minutes, they tore him apart and carried away the pieces leaving only dry bones, his sword, sheath, leather trousers and jerkin. Then, all the creepy beasts were gone except for one.

Minnie took a deep breath, then kneeled and held out her hand. The hideous spider climbed on and she raised it to her face to look into its black, gleaming eyes. There were six, two big ones and four small. It was a hunter. Venom glistened on its fangs and moistened its cheliceral teeth. With a minuscule movement from the spider, she'd be bitten and doomed.

"I am in your debt," she said.

Spiders don't have vocal chords and cannot speak.

"Yes, you are," the Queen spider said. "When you see a spider in your house..."

"Yes?" Minnie said.

"Stop stepping on them."

Minnie shivered.

"But, what if I save one and later, it creeps up from behind and bites me?"

The Queen spider's fangs twitched.

In her vivid imagination, she could feel the bite, the pain and the mortification of her flesh and her ultimate death in writhing pain. But, there was no bite. Minnie lowered her hand and the spider walked off. In a few seconds she was gone. Minnie felt empty and sad.

I want flowers and sunshine, but, for every sunny day, there is a cold, lonely and rainy one.

She couldn't tell if the little voice came from within her or was carried on the breeze. With her miniature shoe, Minnie toed the sword. She thought about leaving it, but decided not to. Picking it up, she studied it.

Unimpressive.

The grip was wrapped with filthy leather stained black with ground-in soil and old sweat. On the pommel and quillon block, there were oval lumps covered with dirt. The pitted blade, except for the last sixteenth inch, was crusty and corroded. The very edge, though nicked, was shiny and sharp. Deadly sharp. It had tasted death, she knew it. It filled her belly with revulsion.

She slipped the ugly blade into its sheath and slipped the sheath through her belt. While walking back on feet that felt like they weighed a million pounds, she passed the bee's nest—this time she didn't care, she walked by without her earlier respect and fear. A squadron swarmed out and approached. She looked them intensely and spoke with firm conviction.

"No you won't."

The bees turned in midair and returned to the nest while she continued walking. After a few wrong turns and a break, she found her way back to Flix. For a few minutes, she stood over him and watched him snore. He woke with a start.

"Ah-ha!" he proclaimed with his index finger waving in the air. "My dear Minnie, there you are." Sensing her sad, troubled mood, he sat up and rubbed his eyes. "Minnie? Are you okay?"

She shrugged.

"I'm all right," she said.

He pointed at the sword.

"What did you find? Can I see it?"

"I'd rather you didn't."

"Okay," he said.

He desperately tried to think of a way to lighten the atmosphere.

"I know, let's make you an angel bag."

Minnie wrinkled her nose. She couldn't help herself, she was intrigued.

"An angel bag? What's that?"

"Ah, yes, that's the thing, we'll concoct a dangerous angel bag for you to carry around. You can only use the bag once. Should you choose to activate it near fire, the bag will burst into flames and the dangerous angels will fly forth and go after your attacker—and they will not relinquish until your attacker is no more. How's that sound?"

Minnie shuffled her feet.

"It doesn't sound very nice, Flix."

Flix looked down, then looked back up to meet Minnie's gaze. He didn't like putting it forth like this but there was no other way—time was drawing near and the Princess needed to be aware.

His eyes were dark and grave.

"No, it's not very nice Minnie, but at some point, you will encounter those who are not nice and wish to do you harm—or, they will go after those you love and cherish. In those instances, you will have to choose between saving yourself or your loved ones, or relinquishing."

The words hung in the air for a long time.

They already have.

A fragment of melody drifted through her mind.

Where is my innocence?
Where has my blindness gone?

In the far distance, an owl hooted.

Must I still pretend to be young and carefree?

Finally, Minnie spoke quietly.

"All right, Flix, let's make this bag. I pray I never have to use it, but at least I'll be prepared."

Flix and Minnie roamed the magic garden to find angelica root, angel garlic, angel wings, angel's turnip and dried angel's trumpet seedpod. Once their supplies were gathered, he and Minnie spoke the words that were infused into the herbs. They came alive to hiss and moan. Minnie shivered as the herbs took on a life of their own. Flix instructed them to only activate further when in the presence of the Minnie's staff, as the fire from her staff would release them in all of their fury. They then wrapped the herbs up in a red cloth bag and tied it tightly. With her spirits restored, Minnie assured Flix she would keep it with her, nearby and safe.

"Ah, and I have one more for you, Mistress Minnie. One you can practice and may not seem as dark to you. How's about learning the Explosion Breath spell?"

Minnie giggled.

"Wouldn't that simply be if I didn't brush my teeth for a long time?"

Flix couldn't help but laugh too.

"No, Minnie, I think that would be called the *Rotting Breath* spell."

That was the tension breaker they both needed.

"Well then, my young princess, it's quite simple really—or I should say, quite simple for someone of your caliber. Explosion Breath is a secret Dragon- or Half-Dragon, Fire-based spell, but this spell can be used by human people too, but only if they are granted the power of the spell. We pixies mastered it over time and I think you too can master it, after a bit. What you need to do is control the heat in your body and *aim* it—much like you did when you focused your intent in the thousand-candle spell. Use your breath, collect the air and convert it into heat in your body. When you're ready, let it burst out and it will come out in an explosive fire blast-breath. Down the road, after a lot of practice, you will eventually be able to make the fire blast come around you like a protective ring. I've not done it in a while—would you like to see me try?"

Minnie vigorously nodded.

Flix climbed to the top of the boulder, thus increasing his energy. He stood in the direct sunlight. Minnie watched him breathe in and out, in and out, looking remarkably like the bellows for a fireplace. After a time, neither a long or short, Minnie saw Flix begin to turn pinkish, then reddish. He then opened up his mouth and out shot fire just like that of a dragon. It was not a gentle flame but an explosive one full of red, yellow, orange and black tints. Minnie jumped back in surprise. The flame circled Flix to ward off potential attackers and protect him. After a bit, Flix opened his eyes to not only look at Minnie, but also to admire his work. Eventually he let his mouth close and the flames slowly disappeared. He dropped down to the boulder and Minnie rushed up.

"That was amazing, Flix, truly amazing."

"The only thing Minnie, is when the spell is cast in its most complete, pure form, it can leave you a bit tired, so keep that in mind." With that, Flix reached into the pool of water and took a nice deep drink. "Ahhhh, that cooled me down some."

Minnie scampered off a ways and began practicing her Explosion Breath. Flix burst out laughing because it looked as if Minnie would hyperventilate. After much trying and failing, coaching and listening, Minnie finally emitted a small spark.

"Yes, Minnie, it will take time, but, I've no doubt you will master this and much sooner than you think. My only request is that you practice this spell outside, as the fire you produce is very volatile. I don't think Master Sean would like his house to be burnt down just yet. Do we have a deal?"

Minnie nodded.

"Well, my dear one, we've been out here the better part of the day. I think we're done for now. What do you say we head in for dinner?"

Minnie walked over and gingerly scooped up Flix and put him on her shoulder. Together they strode into the house and washed up for dinner. It had been a long day for them both, but an eventful day none the less.

Once they were cleaned up, they went back downstairs and told Sean about their time together. She even dragged Sean outside so she could practice her Explosion Breath again. The tiniest of sparks flew from her wide open mouth and that was enough to make her giggle and elicit a round of applause from both Sean and Flix. As she scampered back inside, Sean picked up Flix and put him on his shoulder.

"Run up and get ready for bed, Minnie," Sean said.

Like lightning, she ran off—leaving Sean and Flix to talk privately.

"Thank you Flix for teaching her today. Do you think she'll be ready?"

"Yes, my master," responded Flix, "she'll be ready. But then again, she'll have to be, won't she?"

"Yes, I suppose she will—for the sake of us all, she will have to be ready," said Sean. "What's with the sword?"

Flix steered his eyes to the side.

"I don't know, Sean," he said. "I wish I did, but I don't. I'm sorry I didn't come back with the sweet and innocent girl I left with."

Sean sighed and looked around the room. Unconsciously, he sang a wisp of song.

Flames to dust, lovers to friends
Why do all good things come to an end? [21]

"Will we ever be forgiven for all of our sins?" Sean said.

Flix spread his hands in supplication.

"If there was ever a time for a drink? Perhaps a wee spot of Mackinlay's Scotch?"

"Yes," Sean said, "agreed. A wee spot. Or two."

---

[21] *All Good Things (Come to an End)*, ©2006 Nelly Furtado, Tim Mosley, Chris Martin, Nate Hills from the *Loose* recording.

The Book

MINNIE AWOKE FROM her afternoon nap to the sounds of Sean and the Fachan in the garden chasing butterflies with wispy nets. They were supposed to be weeding, but Sean always mixed work with fun—it was as if he didn't know the difference.

Silly man.

Today they sowed seeds in one of the side gardens and she could hear Sean singing as he dropped seeds into their holes, then the Fachan would come along and stomp with his one massive foot—he laughed and laughed as he hopped along behind Sean.

Every once in a while you'd hear something like, "A little more gently with these ones, they're more delicate—yes, yes, just with your big toe, just like that."

Minnie sat up in bed giggling to herself she slowly pushed off her covers, stretched, yawned and rubbed the sleep from her eyes. She still loved afternoon naps; it was a time of integration and relaxation—she was in no hurry to abandon these solitary hours.

"Hmmm, I guess I'll go out and help Sean," she whispered to herself.

Just then a faint twinkling faerie flew by. This faerie was not the usual gossamer fleck of fluff on the breeze; this one was more like a glowing ember cast from a campfire.

"No, no, follow meeee...come play in the librareeey..."

The library? Huh?

Nothing in the house was off limits, but Minnie had rarely ventured by herself into that secluded room—it wasn't locked, but she didn't feel the pull to investigate very often. When she walked by that room, she always felt like she was being watched. Not in an evil manner, but with naked, thirsty curiosity.

"Hmmm, maybe today would be a good day for a little peek into that mysterious place," said Minnie. "One should never ignore an invitation from a faerie," she said while giggling and padding off on bare feet towards the library.

This time, the library was alive. As she opened the door she heard many whispers...

"She's here—she's here."

"Ooh, how pretty she is."

"She's more clever than pretty."

"Pluck me from my prison shelf."

"No, *me.*"

"No wonder I always felt like I was being watched from here—you *are* all watching me, aren't you? You're alive."

She stood in the center of the room and inhaled the dusty life of the ancient and wise books full of stories, memoirs, recorded history, mad dreams, silliness and frivolity. After spinning in slow circles for a minute, she sat cross-legged in the middle of the open floor, closed her eyes and listened to the whispering voices. A dead-serious voice caught her attention in the mild cacophony.

"Up here—look at me and see what I can show you..."

Minnie opened her eyes. She let her senses guide her to a shelf in the corner.

"Closer—you're getting closer my young princess."

Minnie squinted and looked up, up, up into the dim corner. The ceiling seemed too far away for the size of the house. With an edge showing, she spied an exceptionally ancient-looking book that seemed to glow. Minnie wheeled the library ladder to the spot and excitedly climbed. As soon as she placed her little hands on the book's spine it sent a jolt of electricity through her. She recoiled and nearly fell from the ladder before regaining her balance and wrapping her arms around the rungs like a lifeline.

"Ouch, you nasty beast, you shocked me," she said to the book.

"If you want to read me enough, you'll chance to touch me again."

"Why? You'll just shock me again. Why should I do the same thing twice and expect a different outcome?"

"Some locks spring open when you repeat the combination."

"True that," Minnie said, considering.

With piqued curiosity, she reached out her little hand, tentatively at first, for the book. The shock was more powerful this time, but she did not recoil but pressed harder on the cover until it relaxed and felt cool. With tingling fingers, she pulled it from the shelf and examined it in faint light coming from a dusty skylight. Well worn, the faded red cover was blank—the title had long before been rubbed off. It smelled older than time itself with a nasty underlying odor of rat scat, dead toads and vomit.

Carefully cradling the book, she worked her way slowly down the ladder and plopped on the floor.

"Let's see what you want to tell me," she mused while opening the cover.

As she turned the old and worn parchment pages, her little eyes grew wide with wonder. Holding the pages close to her face, she studied the illustrations and captions. There were things she did not want to know. There was a whole section on how men and women make babies.

"You put what where?" she muttered with distaste. She squirmed on the floor. "Looks painful. There must be a better way."

She set her mind to being a virgin forever and with flying

fingers, whiffled through the offending pages. She did not care about the proper ways to kill an evil baby under a full moon, how to convert a leek into sweetgrass or turn your enemy's entrails into snakes.

Worthless, all of it worthless.

"Yessssssssss, Minnie, yesssss—this is a book of dark spells and not for the faint of heart," hissed the book.

Minnie tried to throw the book off her lap but she couldn't release it.

"I don't want to know this dark stuff," she said in a panicked voice. "I don't want to hurt people."

The book assumed a calmer and more measured tone.

"Settle down, child. Virtue does not come from weakness. Virtue comes from being dangerous, but controlling your power. When push comes to shove, will those trying to do you harm show you mercy and excuse your ignorance? Have you so quickly forgotten the troll in the labyrinth?"

How did the book know about the one-eared troll?

With that, Minnie settled herself down and started taking in all the spells that rolled before her eyes:

Pain Rituals

Kill Yourself in the Afterlife
Soul Trap
Projecting Nightmare Spells
Blood Stop Magick
Ancestors Curse
Death by Fire
Death by Ice
Death by Kindness

It went on and on, page after page. Minnie was horrified and excited at the same time at the lessons of human-animal anatomy, botany, incantation of love, hate spells, despair, spirit worship, transcendence, infrastructure, logic, dark arts offense, last resort offense, alchemy, charms and metaphysics.

She was fascinated by a short chapter explained the proper mechanics and incantations of digging an outhouse—who knew handling human waste could be so complicated? Absorbed, she spent an inexplicable half hour studying this chapter.

"Yes, child, take it in. Take it all in. The words will pass through into your minds' eye and flow through your skin."

Dark Arts Offense

...look upon your target and imagine a demonic hand squeezing the air from him or her. Allow energy to flow through your body and out through your hands—Kali! Hera! Kronos! Tonic! Air as nectar thick as black onyx.

Cassiel, by your second star, hold my victim as in tar...I OWE YOU PAIN! [22]

A chill ran up the length of Minnie's spine. Squinting, she read the footnote:

The Dark Arts offense imbues the caster with the power to harm your enemy with the black arts—and as always, there will be backfires and ebony-fires that drain energy, blank out memory and there is always a chance of self-binding. [23] *Every sharp blade cuts two ways. You can't defeat evil without taking some of the evil inside yourself. If you stare into the void, the void stares back into you—with power comes responsibility.*

After she read those words, the book slammed shut and flew back

---

[22] Adapted from:
http://www.spellsofmagic.com/spells/spiritual_spells/binding_spells/3818/page.html
[23] ibid.

onto its shelf.

"I'll be here when you're ready for more. Tell no one of your lessons today. Some things are best held as secrets."

A fragment of song from one of Sean's old records echoed in her mind.

Wish I didn't know now what I didn't know then...[24]

Secrets. It seemed as though she was becoming a sad and unwilling expert in creating and keeping them. Her hand itched for the thin troll's sword and she knew if she had it with her now, she would cut herself with it and leave long bloody trails in her secret skin to feel the pain she deserved for being a bad little furtive girl.

She fought an impulse to rip off her pretty dress and tear at her hair and scream forever and never stop. Instead, she sat and willed every muscle in her body to relax from head to toe. She needed to stop broadcasting and let things flow.

One lingering, high-pitched voice worked its way through her defenses.

"You are not responsible for all the evils of the world, just a few of the worst of them. All you can do is try to generally leave things better than you found them and no worse, unless you feel like it. It's never easier to create than destroy, so take it easy, little girl. Give more than you take or take more than you give, it only matters when you take sides. You are an imperfect tool in the hands of a mystery or a perfect tool in the hands of a mad creator."

She stood and cocked her head to try to locate the source of this squeaky little voice. To her left. Up. Up. On tippy-toes she was able to reach a thick book—a huge book almost six inches wide. She tilted it to read the title.

---

[24] *Against the Wind,* © 1980 Bob Seger, from the recording *Against the Wind* by Bob Seger and the Silver Bullet Band.

Pathways to Inner Peas

She puzzled over the title before reading the authors' names.

Oliver von Wienerschnitzel and Laurel Hardcrabble.

She pulled it down and barely held onto it as the five-pound tome fell into her hands. Grunting, she dropped it on the room's center desk and leafed through it. There were no words, only pictures of empty playground equipment and abandoned toys—a thousand thick pages of color photographs of swaying swings, teeter-totters, absurd yellow ducks on springs, hobby horses, red wagons and dolls. The book was ludicrous. Silly. Absurd. Insane. Pointless. The last picture she looked at before giving up and slamming the book shut was of a rusty tricycle with forlorn, tattered rainbow streamers drooping from the handlebars.

"You're stupid and heavy," she said to the empty room. "Move yourself back to the shelf."

Ponderous like a blimp, the book slowly rose in the air and slipped into its place on the high shelf—she followed it and once it was settled and still, placed her hand on its warm spine. She grokked the bottom-line message of the massive book.

You'll go insane if you try to make sense of everything.

Not speaking out loud, she projected the thought with as much power as she could.

Thank you.

"Sometimes to fill your belly, you need to bite off more than you can chew," the book said in response.

"What the seven damned hells does that mean?" she muttered.

From a million miles away, she could hear Sean calling.

"Minnie, let's start working on dinner," he said.

"Good idea," Minnie replied. After leaving the library, she closed the door firmly and did not look back.

Settling in at the Off-Season RenFaire

THE HOUSE THEY let her live in wasn't a *real* fake house because there was no insulation—during the few hours of blue-sky daylight that evaded the clouds, blinding streams of light poured through holes and seams in the rustic cedar slats and tarpaper the place was built from. It wasn't completely hopeless because the roof was solid—the eaves, cedar shakes and tarpaper had been competently selected and installed, so the interior was dry and dusty.

In idle hours, she pondered what the isolated building was used for. Off the beaten track of roaming RenFaire tourist herds, the shack was not used for retail sales. Access was via a muddy truck-track in the back, so perhaps it was used for storing silage or nosh for the service animals; it had a feed store smell about it.

When she first spotted it—before claiming it by throwing down Sean's backpack—it was completely empty. She picked it for its secluded isolation. No one would bother her there and more importantly, she would not bother anyone else. She was a coward and deserved to be alone. She deserved to freeze in this unheated hovel and warranted the uncomfortable sleep on a barren, prison-like wooden bench. She earned the misery of spending the rest of her hopeless life in this forgotten, friendless hut.

These were the nature of her scattered thoughts as she sat on the bench with her hands running through the tangled mess of her filthy hair—flicking mud-scabs and dried leaves from her clothing. She heard someone swishing through wet grass and weeds, followed by a knock at the door.

To herself, she laughed bitterly.

Perfect. Probably the sheriff with an eviction order or the owner's factotum with a shotgun bearing the friendly suggestion she move her act down the road.

"It's open," she said.

Of course it's open—there's no knob or lock.

The creaky door opened inward slowly—it was not the Sheriff. Instead, it was a pre-teen girl dressed in torn jeans and Mumford and Sons t-shirt—wearing an absurdly huge leather parka with wolf fur around the hood. She looked like an Iditarod musher.

Something was thrown across her shoulder and at first glance in the dim light, Fiona thought it was a limp corpse, but, on closer inspection, it turned out to be a dusty cushion from a lawn chair. Once her eyes adjusted to the scene, it was one of the most beautiful things she'd ever seen. She couldn't help herself—her knees weakened and she flicked her eyes to the wood-slat bench. The girl smiled—showing a mouthful of silver braces—and arranged the cushion on the bench, patting it into place and fluffing it up.

"Ain't much," the girl said in a buttery southern accent.

Arkansas?

Fiona's eyes flicked around the room at the useless nothing she owned—walking stick, the plastic sack with her crystals and seashells and Sean's backpack.

Seashell?

Fiona held out a hand to stop the girl from leaving and rooted around in the plastic bag. Inside, she found a blackened coil of conch shell. Rubbing her thumb on it, a bit of iridescent pink shone.

"I don't have anything," she said.

"Thanks," the girl said, shrugging. "We're always looking for things to use for necklaces and earrings—this is perfect."

The girl turned to leave and stepped off the stoop.

"Wait," Fiona said. "What's your name?"

The girl waved over her shoulder.

"We'll get to know each other later," she said.

Fiona watched the girl trudge away until she disappeared on an invisible path through a tangled bramble of blackberry vines. She turned to admire the cushion. Cushions like it could be bought at garage sales all day long for two dollars each, but it would make a world of difference at night compared to sleeping on bare wood.

She didn't deserve it, but there lived a molten dollop of warmth deep in the pit of her stomach. She tried to focus on it to kill it, but, slippery, it moved around and lived on.

Her eyes flicked to Sean's backpack and for the umpteenth time wondered what-all it held, but before she could start an inventory, there came another knock. When that visitor was gone, there came another. Throughout the afternoon, there were a steady stream of visitors—all bearing invaluable gifts.

Soon Fiona had a kerosene-filled hurricane lamp, a stack of dog-eared paperback thrillers, two plastic gallon-jugs of water and a foot-long Saran-wrapped sandwich made from a home-baked French roll, thick ham slices, green chilies and butter.

In addition, she had an olive-green surplus wool blanket, three quilts, a jelly jar of amber honey, cups and spoons, a rocking chair (which came with a warning that the rockers had been re-glued that morning and it should not be used for a day), a wool Sherpa hat, a Bic lighter, a watercolor sketchpad half-filled with pictures from a dabbling artist who apparently only had only two colors to work with (salmon and indigo), a hibachi charcoal grill (the man who brought this looked around and wryly commented,

"Looks like I don't need to warn you about ventilation.") and string-wrapped bundles of kindling and firewood.

As darkness fell, she looked at all the loot and craved a teapot—and scolded herself for being greedy. Had the gifts stopped with the lawn chair cushion, it was already more than she deserved.

Cold. It was bitter-cold. With the wool Army blanket around her shoulders, she lit a match and stoked the hurricane lantern and the hibachi. There were running footsteps on the porch and something heavy was dropped. By the time she got the door open, there was no one to be seen, but at her feet sat a dream come true: a battered and blackened copper pot.

"Thank you," she called out into the night.

Faintly, a voice called out in return. Man, woman, child or something else? She couldn't tell.

"You're welcome," it said.

She had no tea, but was undaunted—she could take the lantern outside and find blackberry leaves to make a perfectly acceptable tea. The old leaves would be bitter, but there was plenty of honey. And there was peppermint in her swampy surroundings, she could smell it. In addition, the woods were filled with wild-gather herbs, mushroots and medicinal mushrooms when you knew what to look for.

Who needs factory teabags when Mother Nature is so generous?

She felt a momentary surge of bold self-confidence and optimism.

Put me on the moon and I'll make tea from rocks and dust— and it'll be healthy and enjoyable too.

This was too much joy—she thought of Llwyd and pinched the skin of her arm—twisting until tears sprouted from her eyes. She deserved pain, not satisfaction, then felt embarrassed when she realized what she was doing.

This is stupid. Feeling sorry for myself won't bring Llwyd or

Sean back. Stop it, Fiona, just stop it. Use your head. Obviously, something out there loves you even if you don't; otherwise, your cold body would be rotting in the quicksand.

To distract herself, she looked at the cover of one of the thrillers, but it didn't grab her—she was not in the mood for murder and mayhem. She scanned her pile of loot and thought about what was missing.

It would be nice to have a pillow.

She even got up to look on the porch to see if that dream had come true too, but there were no more treasures to be seen.

Except?

She bent down to examine a clump of orange leaves and recognized pumpkin-colored Laetiporus sulphureus mushrooms. Chicken of the Woods. Delicious with the ham sandwich, but useless as a pillow. She laughed at her covetous self—then her eyes fell on Sean's muddy backpack.

I lugged that bloody thing halfway across New England to be my pillow?

So be it, brush it off and it will be fine.

After carefully placing the mushrooms by her dinner sandwich, she hefted the backpack. Was this finally when she'd find out what she'd been carrying around? Standing on the edge of the porch, she beat on it with her hands to dislodge the worst of the mud. Something tugged at the corner of her eye, but she knew she should not react. She stood quietly while absorbing and assimilating slow information.

The best information is slow information.

She continued brushing the backpack and gradually turned her head.

"I see you, little man," she said.

His skin was golden-brown—he looked as if he'd been bronzed. Rail-thin, big ears, big eyes, green pointy hat. Longsword hanging from his belt. No wings. He had a ragged scar that stretched across his face like a fissure.

"Did *you* bring the mushrooms?"

The little man shook his head.

No.

"You are welcome to enter my home."

"Elcor comes and goes as he pleases. In. Out. Doesn't matter. Beyond that, you are our guest, not the reverse."

"Of course," Fiona said. "What brings you to *my* stoop?"

The little man shrugged.

"I heard something whispered on the wind and I wanted to see for myself."

"Me," Fiona said.

"You," came the reply.

"And now you know."

"Yes. For now, all is well, but over the span of time, this is not a safe place. Not for you. Not for the other humans. Not for us."

"I'll leave tomorrow if you tell me where to go."

Elcor sighed.

"Truly, I don't know. I wish I did. Some say—perhaps this is as good a place to die as any. Llwyd was no friend to me and my kind."

"I'm sorry to hear that."

"But he wasn't our enemy either." As if deep in thought, he turned to look out into the dark woods. He appeared to make a decision. "Don't eat the lilac brown boletes—people eat them elsewhere, but they are not safe in these woods. The hedgehog chanterelles are fine, actually, better than fine, delicious, superb."

Holding his sword at his side to keep it from flopping, he hopped from the porch.

"Farewell, Fiona."

I didn't tell him—but he knows my name.

He continued, "You have things you need to work through, we understand. But when the time comes, here, there, or elsewhere, call us and we will come out and die by your side."

"I'm not who you think I am—I'm homeless and broken. There's nothing left inside."

"From my point of view, you don't look homeless."

Fiona glanced inside at the flickering lantern.

Home?

When she looked back, Elcor was gone and there was no sign he'd ever been there.

Fiona sighed.

Funny—I have no idea where I am, but others can still find me.

Arranging the scratchy blanket around her shoulders, she went inside and piled more wood on the hibachi. Her desire to explore Sean's backpack had waned, but she pulled it onto her lap anyway and reached out with her mind.

Where are you, Sean? I need you.

When she realized what she was doing, she clamped down. This was not a safe thought or wish to entertain.

To distract herself, she unzipped the backpack and the first thing she saw was a paper-wrapped packet bound with a lavender ribbon. She raised it to her nose and recognized it instantly.

Hand-rolled pearls of Chinese white tea—Dragon Phoenix Jasmine. All day long she could drink seeped blackberry leaves and be perfectly happy as long as the wild-blueberry honey held up, but the Dragon Phoenix Jasmine tea was considered by many to be the best commercial tea in the world. If she was allowed only ten more cups of tea in her life and she could have anything she desired, DPJ would fill one of the cups.

She closed her eyes and breathed in deeply.

Oh.

Oh.

Thank you, Sean.

Fiona, Not Listening...

MINNIE WAS UNHAPPY in repeating their invitation chant, but meekly, she did. After silence reigned a few minutes, she complained.

"I don't think she'll come."

"What?" Sean said. "Of course she'll come. We built this place for her and she must. It's not safe for her out there—we can build our strength and when you get older, your power will grow. In a year or two, we'll be ready, really ready. Open the door so Selene can fly in and let's call out to Fiona again. She'll come. She must."

In a prime example of wishful thinking, the house was decorated for Fiona's welcome. In fact, the pixies had made a banner of dried dandelions, golden-heart violets and Brown-eyed Susans that spelled out the word: Welcome. Sean arranged pillows around the house-rock for the callers. He clapped his hands.

"Everyone, please take your places."

Sean was on Minnie's right and the one-legged Fachan squatted to Minnie's left. Minnie clutched her red stone in her right hand and a blue in her left. The rest of the circle was formed with the sock goblin, woods faeries, forest pixies and sprites. They all settled in place and waited for a moment, then with a beating of her powerful wings, Selene hovered over the rock and slowly settled. There she groomed her frost-white wings and stared around the circle.

Like Minnie, she was skeptical.

"Hoooo," she said with a morose tone.

Sean flicked his fingers and the candles in the room sprouted flame. Though the door was open, the air outside was still and the candles did not flicker. Through clear skies, moonlight flooded a north-facing window. He looked around the circle and nodded.

"We're ready," he said, then he kneeled, took Minnie and the sock goblin's hands and the circle was complete. They closed their eyes and he began singing the song he'd agonized over all afternoon.

> *The front door is open and the tea is abrew*
> *The bedding is clean and the bath towels too*
> *Three pies in the oven, and four plates of blue*
> *The only thing missing, my dear love, is you.*

Minnie could not restrain the thought.

Dear Sean, fortunately, you're a far better carpenter than poet.

Impatient, Selene rustled her feathers. Mentally, Sean reached out to Fiona, but found her mind locked down and frozen.

Fiona, come home. I built a house for you. It's safe and warm and we can love and live and train and learn and get ready for the trials ahead. There's wine and tea and music and love and you will adore dear Minerva as I do—as we all do.

For an endless stream of minutes, nothing came back. Far away, Fiona was awake—sitting on a porch and reading a paperback thriller.

Why won't she respond?

Giving up, Selene took wing and skirted Sean's head. A bit of white fluff drifted in the room's air and landed on Minnie's nose.

Keeping her hands entwined, she giggled and puffed at the downy feather until it drifted to land on The Fachan's cap.

"Fiona," Sean cried. "Please."

A thought came back from Fiona as cold and solid as a steel rail.

I don't care to hear Minerva's name mentioned ever again.

Aggravated, Sean got up and snuffed the candles one-by-one with his naked fingers.

"Damn you, Fiona, you're stubborn as an old mule—you always have been and you always will be."

Minnie slipped her marbles into the pocket of her gingham kitchen apron and patted him on the back. With tears in his eyes, he turned and collapsed to his knees before her and wrapped her in his arms.

"I don't know what to do," he said.

"It's obvious. When the time comes, *we* have to go to *her*."

Sean held her at arm's length and looked into her eyes.

"Goddamn it, Minnie, Goddamn it all to the backdoor of Hades, that's too dangerous for us. We're safe here—here we must stay."

With a stern look on her face, Minnie pointed at the forest pixies and sprites.

"Watch your language around the children," she said.

Apples

WITH A MIND fuzzy from napping, Minnie emerged from a fitful sleep filled with images of a barren field with mysterious apples flying from a clear blue sky. Of late, her dreams were filled with nonsense—places that didn't exist, impossible situations and people who acted irrationally and against their nature.

She reached out to search for Sean. In place of the warm comfort she usually got back from him, she sensed only an echoing emptiness.

"Sean? Where are you?" she called out.

After rubbing sleep from her eyes and running her fingers through her tangled curls, she ran down the hallway, skidded to a stop on stocking feet and then backed up. Peeking through the library doorway, she found Sean pacing back and forth.

"What's up, buttercup?" Minnie said.

Sean looked up from the book splayed in his hand.

"Oh, sorry, didn't see you. Good nap? All rested and ready to take on the world?"

His cheery words sounded *off* to Minnie. His tone was world-weary—his was wrung out. She cocked her head like a dog confused by its human. He took off his reading glasses and rubbed the bridge of his nose.

"I'm sorry, little one. Truly, I hope you rested well. I'm just a bit preoccupied..."

248

His voice trailed off into a whisper.

Minnie scampered in and plopped into an adjoining chair.

"What can I do to help?"

Her earnest eagerness brought a hint of smile to his lips.

"Do you have a magical transporter up your sleeve?"

"A what?"

"Oh, never mind—I was being silly. It's abundantly clear we need to go to Fiona and drag her sorry butt home, but things have been good here and I've been stalling. I'm working on a teleportation spell, but the pages flip at random and the stupid words in the stupid book keep changing. Nothing works." He gestured to a half-empty wicker basket of green apples. "I've been sending out apples, but who knows where they go—when they decide to go anywhere at all."

"You got us here without any fuss."

Sean stared at her with an exasperated expression, then reached out and tweaked her nose.

"Right, and I needed you to remind me of that."

Minnie reached out for an apple and studied it before taking an exploratory bite.

"A bit tart for my taste," she said.

"You certainly are."

"Ha, whatever. May I take a look, Sean? You know, sometimes I'm extraordinarily good with troublesome spells..."

Like an unruly toddler, his first impulse was to push her away and say *I can do it*. But, it was true, he struggled—the magic world was often a foreign territory to him. He took a deep breath. An essence of maturity is accepting a helping hand when it's needed. He sighed.

Maturity can be such a drag.

If only I could banish adult responsibility, reasonable compromise and unselfish accommodation to the deepest depths of hell...

In an odd gesture, he closed his eyes and slowly raised his

hands—palms-down—like they were floating in the air of their own accord. After a few seconds, he dropped them to the desktop.

"I'll take any help I can get, Minnie," he said.

She closed her eyes and held out her hands, palms up, and waited. It took a solid minute, but a book eventually drifted from a tall shelf and settled, open-faced, on her hands.

"I could have done that," Sean said.

"Shush," Minnie replied. "I'm concentrating."

Sean angled his head and studied the spell.

"I already tried that one. Didn't work."

Minnie set the book on the desk and fished around in her blue drawstring bag for a clear stone. With a flick of a finger, she rolled it to Sean.

"Take a look," she said.

He leaned over and looked into the marble. Inside, Fiona sat on a rustic porch talking to someone unseen. Sean's heart flopped. Her hair was tangled and wild—he yearned to reach out and push back an unruly strand.

"I see her."

"I think you'd better gather your travel gear, Sean. When you're ready, we'll go."

Sean stared at the little girl for a long moment. Nonchalantly, she reached out for the apple and took another bite.

"You didn't need to make it look so easy."

Minnie shrugged. She held out the apple on her palm and in the blink of an eye, it changed into a peach; a beautiful, plump and juicy peach with two bites taken from it.

"No one likes a show-off," he said.

With a broad grin she took a bite and immediately spit the glop onto his desk.

"Yuck. Bad apples make worse peaches."

"I'll make a note of that," said Sean.

Skunk in the Coop

AFTER A WEEK of keeping to herself, blocking entreaties from the outside world and wallowing in depression and despair, Fiona settled into her new life with a growing, cabin-fever malaise. Other than gift packages left on the stoop, no one came around to bother her, but she heard work being done—trucks coming and going and sometimes, when the wind was right, children playing—chanting and singing silly songs. Sometimes she could see Luna at the edge of the copse that surrounded her little house, but the little traitor would not come when she called.

She stayed clean by washing with hot water heated by her hibachi, but her grooming was imperfect and as the days passed, she looked more like a wild wolf-woman and less like the cultured, civilized hippy-woman of fading memory. She did not forget who she was or her past life, but the painful images were tucked away and buried while seeds of bitterness, anger and regret took strong root—no more was she the whimsical woman of yesterday in love with what was and dreaming of what would be. Inside, a steely resolve grew. Her heart was no longer in control; her head now ruled. She deserved this sad life of isolation and solitude.

Over and over on a dilapidated, battery-operated cassette

player, she played a haunting melody by Eddie Vedder which spoke to her new self about how she felt about everything around her.

> *Have no fear, for when I'm alone*
> *I'll be better off than I was before*
> *I've got this light, I'll be around to grow*
> *Who I was before, I cannot recall*
> *Long nights allow me to feel...*
> *I'm falling—I am falling, the lights go out*
> *Let me feel, I'm falling*
> *I am falling safely to the ground, ah...*[25]

In the mornings, she would find a tin bucket on the porch and it would be filled with enough food to last through the day. It was never anything fancy, just simple fare of porridge and sliced peaches for breakfast, a French-roll sandwich for lunch and stew or chili with hard rolls and butter for dinner. But, with the tea, it was plenty. More than plenty—it was bountiful and beautiful. All by itself, the butter was a joy, lumps of salty, home-churned clotty gold spread across black-flecked, home-baked rolls—a Queen could not ask for a better treat.

All the while, eyes in the woods watched, relentlessly watched, but it was clear: as long as she wanted isolation, her wish would be granted.

She had plenty of time to do a compete inventory of Sean's backpack. In a pail of cold water, she scrubbed his dirty underwear and filthy socks and taught herself a couple of simple songs on his wooden flute. He had a ratty Tam O'Shanter cap she enjoyed wearing; she packed his Borkum Riff into the bowl of his clay pipe and sat smoking on the front porch while rocking in her chair.

On the fifth day, she gave thought to forgiving herself.

Was there a pathway back to life?

---

[25] *Long Nights,* ©2007, Eddie Vedder—from *Into the Wild*

To be human is to inevitably be flawed and weak. She was a coward, but she lived and as long as she lived, she could remember Llwyd and honor his memory.

What else can I do?

Life was for living, not for wasting.

While sitting on the porch with Sean's backpack on her lap, she noticed a hidden slot covered with a crude Velcro closure. There was paper inside which she fished out and flattened. It was poetry. Bad poetry—was that why he hid it so well, or was he embarrassed by the maudlin sentiment?

Fiona, when the birds sing, they croon your name

The next lines were crossed out, but she held the paper against the light and worked out the words.

Fiona, when the stars dissolve, the sun takes the blame
Fiona, my heartbeat, my breath, my life, my soul
Fiona, my precious, your love fills me like a bowl.

Searching for inspiration, he'd made a list of words that rhymed—or sort-of rhymed—with bowl. Owl, bowel (this word was crossed out with heavy strokes of his pencil), gall, coal, dowel, foal, howl, hole, jewel, stole, toll. At this point, he gave up and worked on a bad limerick instead.

There was a maggot named Scott
I hated that dimwit a lot
Like a snake in the grass
I kicked his lame ass
And pissed on his boreal plot.

She wondered if he was confused and meant *burial* instead of *boreal*—or if he attempted some esoteric point about the cold winters and warm summers of the boreal north woods.

After he gave up on the limerick, he attempted a haiku which was also inept.

Your skin, like silk, your—
Breasts, like loaves baked in heav-en
Taste of salt and honey

For some reason, the absurdity of his secret scrawls broke the back of her depression. She tried not to, but could not stop laughing. In laughing, she forgave herself and slowly gave up her self-assigned isolation; she felt as if it would be okay to begin to face the world.

A nut-brown chickadee flitted to the edge of the porch and cocked its head. Fiona flicked a crumb of bread across the porch. In an instant the crumb and the bird were gone. She got up and brushed off her skirt and faced the woods.

"I will wander and not wallow," she said to the trees.

While wandering, the first person she found was a boy. From the shadows, she studied him. With black, nappy hair and milk-chocolate skin tone, he was a mixed race child about twelve years old. He muttered curses under his breath while half-heartedly working at converting a pile of dry splits into kindling with a rusty old hatchet. Hidden by the trees, she watched him curse and complain—then she stepped into the light.

"Who are you angry with?" she said.

The boy jumped as if an icicle had slid down his back.

"You shouldn't be sneaking around like a jackal."

"I'm sorry I startled you."

"You shouldn't be creeping around like a—creep."

The failure of his vocabulary reminded her of poet laureate Sean and brought a smile to her face.

"Who are you so angry with?"

"My stinkin' father. He says I can't come in for dinner until I fill this wheelbarrow all the way to the top. We have kindling, lots of it up the butt, but here I am working like a dead Roman servant. It's not fair."

"Maybe I can help you?"

He looked at her with the calculation in his eyes.

"Maybe you can," he said. He handed her the hatchet and brushed the moss off a stone—then down settled to watch. "The pieces should be no bigger than an inch across or Dad will kick my ass."

"Okay," she said.

After the sedentary week in the hut, the sweat and ache in her muscles felt good—she needed physical activity. While she hacked the firewood, the boy maintained a steady patter and she learned his name (Philip), about how much he hated home schooling, how evil was his twisted devil little sister Amy and why he had been assigned the kindling splitting chore.

"All I did was throw a skunk in the neighbor's chicken coop. You want to see scars, I'll show you plenty. That rooster needed to die." He lifted his pant leg and it was true, his shins were pockmarked and raw. "Why do stupid chickens need spurs anyway? God hates me."

She buried the hatchet in the chopping block with a satisfying thunk, then turned and stretched her back while mopping perspiration from her brow.

"You put a skunk in with the chickens?"

"It's not like it squirted—not much anyway—and I would have gotten away with it too, but Amy told. I'd like to throw her in the coop and let the chickens peck out her spying eyes."

"This is not your regular chore. You're being punished."

His eyes shifted down and to the left.

"Never said it was regular."

"I suppose I'd better let you finish up."

He studied the heap in the wheelbarrow.

"I think we got enough." He turned his eyes to her—studying her appraisingly. "You could push the mother-baker a lot easier than me."

She leaned over, put her hands on her knees and laughed, then spit on her palms and rubbed them together.

"Lead the way, Prince Charming," she said.

She pushed the heavy barrow while he led the way down a cart path, then across a weedy, overgrown parking lot. A paved road from the main entrance led along the grand entrance to a large square in the center of the Faire.

She looked up at the lurid signs.

Magic Wand Antiques and Curios and The Henna House— Body Art, Permanent and Temporary Tattoos, Face Painting and Glitter. He studied the angle of the sun and pointed between the two buildings.

"There's time," he said. "Leave the barrow."

In a fraction of an instant he scurried between two buildings through a gap barely big enough for her. When she came out into the sunlight again, he stood impatiently at the edge of the forest.

"Walk where I walk," he said.

He ducked under the branch of beech tree and was gone. She stooped and nearly had to crawl, but beyond the tree was a deer trail and she caught a glimpse of him racing ahead. With her hands trailing through sword fern fronds, staghorn sumac bushes and young black gum tupelo, she took her time and followed along. Ten minutes in, she heard him hiss. She turned and spotted him at the edge of a bog. When she stepped off the path, he gestured for her to watch her step.

"You'll go up to your knees in muck if you don't watch out."

After stepping over a boggy patch, she kneeled beside him and watched him put a hunk of beef jerky in the mouth of a snare. The snare was large—large enough to catch a man.

"What are you trying to catch?" she said.

He studied her face before answering.

"Gator," he said.

"Gator?"

"Don't tell me there ain't none because I seen one."

"Okay," she said.

Once the snare was arranged to his liking, he got up, brushed off his knees and worked his way back to the path—carefully walking around the patch he'd warned her about. Once she found her way back to the path, he was gone again.

This struck her as amusing and she laughed. Philip is fleet of foot, she mused. She slowly walked along the trail. It had been ten minutes since she'd seen him, but she enjoyed the declining angle of the sun, the diffuse and filtered light and the increasing gloom of the woods. The path forked and she could not see the scuff of his footprints—it was as if he'd taken a step into the unknown. With her arms outstretched and her eyes closed, she twirled and tilted her head back. The glory of verdant life burned in her core like a bonfire.

"You're like a blind fool," he said.

She stopped spinning and looked up—he'd climbed twenty feet up into a white oak where he rested in a cleft. It was a nearly perfect climbing tree with sturdy branches starting just above her head.

"Too bad you don't climb," he said. "This tree likes it."

"Who said I don't climb?" she said.

She looked around. Rock. Deadfall pine. Low branch. Easy.

In thirty seconds, she worked her way around him and mapped a path to the last sturdy branch that would support their weight. It had been years since she climbed—since she was a tomboy teenager—but the freedom and nugget of fear of heights deep in her gut was at home and made her feel fully alive. On her belly, she inched up and settled in and waited until he joined her.

"Where you been, slowpoke?" she said.

"Shut up," he said. "I don't even know you and I feel like I've been waiting half my life for you to catch up."

From the branch, they were high enough to see over the canopy of forest. A mile away, smoke drifted skyward from the

RenFaire.

"In these north-woods, a gator?" she said.

"Or a wild pig or bobcat or something. It was almost dark."

She smiled.

"Right," she said.

"You're in my tree, so you gotta answer my questions."

"Whatever you say, treemaster."

He poked her with a knuckle.

"Don't make fun of me. What's a Tax Lion?"

She pondered.

"Do you mean a Tax Lien?"

"Maybe. What's it mean?"

She shrugged.

"If the government says you owe them money, then they reach out—", she pinched an inch of his belly visible between his trousers and shirt and tugged on it, "—and take it."

"Oh."

"Where'd you hear it said?"

"Dad was talking to a guy. Never mind. In a field, I seen a bull mount a cow. It was gross—I wanted to puke. Is that the way human babies are made?"

"Did you ask your Dad?"

"Yeah, but he didn't tell me nuthin'."

Fiona thought for nearly a minute.

"There are several ways for a man and a woman to make a baby—that's one of them."

She almost laughed at the look of concentration on his face, but stifled it. She rested her head on her forearm and looked out over the forest. The sun had nearly dropped to the top fringe of the canopy.

"What about..."

"You only get three questions," she interrupted, "so make it a good one."

He stuffed a knuckle in his mouth and spoke around it.

"Never heard that rule."

Holding up an index finger, she did not speak out loud, but mouthed the words.

"One more, that's it."

From the look on his face, she could tell he had a million questions. With an intense expression, he sorted through them all to find the *one*.

"I been having dreams," he said. "Bad dreams, mostly. Do you know anyone named Minerva?"

She turned and studied his face—under smudged dirt and a scattered constellation of freckles, it was wind-chaffed and sunburned.

"No, I don't," she lied. "It's getting dark—we should be getting back."

Absolution with a Hug

IT WAS FULLY dark when, under Philip's direction, she dumped the barrow-load of kindling into the galvanized livestock water tank they used for firewood storage on the front porch of their little cottage. She stood on the first step and turned to give him a handshake—slapping palms, the back of their hands, a fist-bump and pointing her index finger at him.

"See ya," she said.

He finished the phrase.

"Wouldn't want to be ya."

She stepped off the wooden stair onto the gravel of their entry path.

"Where you going?" Philip said. "You're staying for dinner."

He pushed open the front door and shouted at the top of his lungs.

"Mom, I brought a pet, can I keep it? I'll feed and water her every day."

Fiona recognized the two voices merged into harmony—Andre-Little John's bass and Nellie's shrill mezzo-soprano.

"No!"

"Some thanks—I worked my hands to pulp filling that dad-blamed barrow to the tip-top with pigeon-poop kindling."

Andre filled the front door like a cork in a bottle. He looked over the top of his reading glasses at the heap of kindling, then at Philip and Fiona. His deep voice was like an earthquake rumble.

"Let me see your hands, Fiona."

She laughed and looked at them herself before holding them out for Andre's inspection. They were patchy with pitch. A broken blister seeped on the palm of her right hand.

With a hairy knuckle, he tapped Philip's head.

"Go wash up for dinner, Tom Sawyer," he said. As Philip slipped past, Andre spoke to Fiona. "One of his core competencies is to get others to do his chores for him. How? I don't know—it's a mystery. Come in, Fiona, we'll find salve for your abused paws." Over his shoulder he said, "Nell, we'll need another plate on the table."

"Not enough—no can do," Nell said. Squinting in the fading light, she leaned backwards from her dish washing station to peer into the front room. "Oh, Fiona, it's you. Sure, no problem, there's plenty."

After careful doctoring with his curiously gentle hands, Andre pointed at the dinner table.

"Give me a minute to finish the newspaper, then dinner should be ready. Here's my suggestion, use a glass of Nell's blackberry wine to lubricate your patience."

Philip's voice drifted down from the loft he'd climbed.

"Pour me a snifter too."

Andre's voice was thunderous.

"Silence your gaping maw, bad-boy."

The table was made from a huge wire spool and the wine was stored in a two-gallon stoneware jug plugged with a rubber stopper. While Andre settled in his massive chair with his *Wall Street Journal*, she poured an ounce into a battered tin cup and took a tentative sip. The sweetwine caressed her tongue like a fiery liquid explosion.

"Damn, that's good," she muttered while topping off her cup—filling it to the brim.

"I use dandelions and Rudesheimer yeast," Nell called out from the kitchen.

"Nell will fill your head with flowery nonsense, but to really understand how wine gets made, as opposed to preserved, you need only understand fermentation. Everything else is flourish."

"You never seem to mind the *flourish* when it's in your glass," Nell said.

Andre raised his giant mug and winked at Fiona.

"I'm an ale man," he said.

Nell brought in a steaming cauldron and put it on the spool-table.

"I hope you like chili beans," she said, "and it's the last of that old goat. Do you like it spicy? I went a little heavy on the Ancho chili—this pepper seems to bite more than I'm used to."

"If Nell warns you—that means you're about to meet the man."

"You can use her chili sauce for paint remover," Philip called down from the loft.

"They complain," Nell said, "but there's never much in the way of leftovers. Besides, it's not that hot—there's no Habanero, Ghost Chili or heaven forbid, Carolina Reaper in this sauce, but for anyone who likes hot, I can make hot. This lame-ass crew is a bunch of light-weights."

On her next return, she brought a platter of corn muffins with a clay crock of butter and a block of homemade, lemon-yellow cheddar cheese.

Fiona thought back to her last meal—breakfast was a thousand years ago, or so it seemed.

"I'd eat a goat hoof—raw—if that's all you had."

"Good. There's nothing a cook likes more than a hungry mouth to feed."

A voice from the darkened corner of the front room startled

Fiona.

"Hunger is the best pickle."

Fiona peered. A little girl peeked over the top of a picture book. She too mixed the races of her mother and father, but had generally Caucasian features with wavy, dark-brown hair. The book had a vivid, tomato-red cover. *Alexander and the Terrible, Horrible, Very Bad Day.* Fiona racked her brain. Philip had mentioned her—what was her name?

Ah, Amy.

"Amy," Fiona said, "I didn't see you there."

"She's a reader," Andre said. "She disappears into her books."

Fiona smiled. She knew it instantly—this was no figure of speech, this little girl could literally disappear into a book.

"Everyone has bad days," Amy said. "Sometimes bad weeks. You're not alone."

With that comment from a six-year-old waif, a weight lifted and Fiona felt free—as if all her sins had been absolved.

"Can I give you a hug?" Fiona said.

"Don't get any on ya," Philip called down from the loft.

After a shrug, Amy slipped a pheasant feather in to mark her place and put aside her book.

"Pay no attention to the creepozoid mutant," she said.

Fiona leaned over and picked up the little girl and wrapped her arms around her.

"I love you," she said.

"I know," Amy whispered. "I love you too."

"Let's eat," Andre said.

Philip poked his head over the edge of the loft. His curly hair caught the light like a halo.

"It's about beetle-blasted time," he said. "I'm on the south side of starvation."

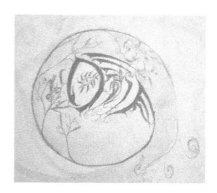

Travelers

MINNIE WOKE TO see Sean sitting in a rocking chair by her little bed. Napping with his head tilted at an uncomfortable angle, it looked like he'd been there a while—he wore clothes from the day before. An old book was splayed on his lap.

"What?" she said.

He started and the book fell to the floor. After rubbing his eyes, he leaned over and picked it up.

"I've been reading and reaching out—calling to Fiona, but she's not responding. I don't know why, but simply put, she's not coming. It's time—time to go to her—fetch her and bring her home."

Sitting up, Minnie's eyes sparkled. Reaching out with her mind, she tuned into the music on the wind. Selene hooted and Minnie looked up and smiled. In less than a heartbeat Minnie was fully awake and ready.

"Wait—can I get my sword and staff? And, do I have time to pee first?"

Sean laughed.

"Yes, yes, go do what you must, but don't dawdle. And, I don't think we'll need any swords—it can stay here."

Minnie ran inside and came back out dressed in striped thick cotton tights, cowboy boots, a little skirt and a hoodie. She had her new stone safely zipped into her pocket along with the angel bag safely tucked away. In her hand was her walking staff—she looked every bit an explorer and enchantress and properly ready to find Fiona. She walked toward Sean who looked upon her like a proud poppa.

"You ready?" he said.

"You betcha."

There was a fluttering at the window.

Sean looked at Selene.

"Show us the way, my dear Selene, show us the way."

The owl swooped away toward the woods.

Sean was already packed; he shouldered his knapsack and held out his hand. They walked down the stairs and out the front door.

They walked toward Selene and the woods, but as they entered the shade of the tall trees, there was a shift. A slip and a slide. Then they were in trees, but not the same trees.

Instead of morning light, ferns and holly, there were deep, dark shadows, bramble and swamp.

The moon moved. The wind changed scent and direction.

The travelers had traveled.

Luna Meets Friends in the Woods

LUNA PADDED THROUGH the woods muttering to himself.

"Does my Mistress think of me as nothing more than a traitor? How can she remove herself so far away from herself and her obligations? Does she think the whole world is against her?"

"Yes, Luna, that's exactly the situation," said Elcor.

By now, Luna had become accustomed to Elcor's abrupt comings and goings.

"Fiona lost herself, Luna. She's detached from her spirit-self—many of us question her worthiness. We thought she'd awaken with Sean's coming, but all she did was rediscover her heart. Then came the Queen and all that woke in her was useless rage. Last came Llwyd—with Llwyd we held out hope, but his time passed more quickly than we imagined possible. This will sound like a cliché, but Fiona must make the inner journey to find herself. The flame still flickers, but she has a very far distance to go. The time of test quickly approaches when she will need all her skills and wits, but for now, all we can do is watch and hope. But enough of that, Master Luna. Follow me—there are visitors in the forest."

Luna turned to look at Elcor with renewed interest.

266

"Come along," said Elcor as he began walking along a path that was invisible to human eyes.

Deep in the forest Luna stopped in his tracks—he smelled a familiar scent upon the breeze. Looking at Elcor, he twitched his tail. Without words, Elcor knew Luna's thoughts.

"Yes Luna, he has returned—and he is not alone. Go, meet him and help him to set up camp."

Slipping through the forest's shadows like an ebony ghost, Luna ran ahead, then crouched among the fiddleheads of a young patch of ostrich ferns and waited for the visitors. As soon as the footsteps passed, Luna leapt unto the back of the one who passed, then climbed the man's shoulders.

"Well, I'll be, if it isn't Master Luna," said the man. "I was hoping you weren't lost somewhere along the way," he said as he nuzzled Luna's head. "Your fur has grown thick and you appear more like a jaguar than a house cat."

Pleased, Luna purred loudly, something he'd not done for ages.

Sean stopped walking and Luna jumped down to the path.

"May I introduce you? Minerva, please meet Master Luna."

Minnie squealed.

"He looks just like my stuffed, Luna-pet back at the house."

She bent down to pet the cat which studied her with a quizzical expression. He'd heard Mistress Fiona, Llwyd and the dreadful old Queen mention "Minerva" before, but somehow he pictured a much different person. This was a sweet little girl. Luna looked up at Sean, who seemed to understand.

"Yes, Luna, this is the Princess Minnie. I'll introduce you properly once we set up camp. Will you show us a good spot to rest for the night?"

Luna mewed approval and led the way with his tail straight up in the air—appearing every bit the confident jaguar he had truly become inside. As he walked he heard the murmurings in the forest.

"They've come, they've finally come."

"The armies are amassing, time is short."

"I thought Princess Minnie would be bigger."

Luna led Sean and Minnie to a clearing in the woods and stopped. Elcor appeared and bowed.

"Welcome to the forest, Sean and Princess Minnie. This is a good, safe spot to camp. We've been keeping an eye on Fiona. She arrived in rough shape but seems to be slowly regaining her sense of self. Get settled in and I will gather our friendly compatriots."

With that, Elcor was gone.

Sean and Minnie set to pitching their tent, gathering wood for a fire and setting up a meeting place for their allies who would be soon engaged in this war.

Luna explored the tent and then sat next to Sean.

"Luna, I need your help watching over Princess Minnie. The Darkness draws ever closer—keeping Minnie safe from harm is our paramount duty. Will you help?"

Luna looked up at Sean—part of him wanted to run from responsibility and enjoy the delicious freedom of the wild. He could take care of himself; Sean had been nothing but trouble since Fiona first brought him home like a stray dog. But, in truth, Sean was simply the messenger of things to come, things that were set in place long, long ago. It was Luna's duty and honor to do as Sean asked. With that thought, he mewed his answer and walked over to sit on the log next to Minnie. Minnie looked at Sean and grinned from ear to ear.

"He's an amazing cat, Sean. Majestic and fuzzy and lovable at the same time. I'm sure he's been through a lot. I can't wait to bring him home with us; I'm sure he'll love the house.

With slow, gentle strokes, Minnie petted Luna. In those moments, Minnie passed some of her energy into Luna, who purred with utter contentment. They could now understand each other's thoughts; a strong bond was now formed. Luna would protect Minnie as he did Fiona, and Minnie would fight for Luna's life if need be.

Sean looked on and shook his head.

"Such an amazing one you are, Minnie."

While Sean drifted in thought, Elcor reappeared.

"Might I interrupt? I would like to bring forth those of the forest who answered our call for help. Luna spent his time with us forging alliances and making us all united and ready for battle. If you are rested enough, we would like to sit and tell you of all we've observed since Fiona arrived."

At the mention of Fiona's name Sean took a deep breath. He wanted to rush and see her and fall into her arms. Yet, at the same time, he was fearful of what he would find. So much had happened—so many changes; so much intensity and death; so much anger and sorrow. Just so much of everything—perhaps more than Fiona could bear. Deep down he knew Fiona would return with him and Minnie, but at what cost? He shook his head just as one who shakes cobwebs off the end of a broom—there was no time for such thoughts now.

"Yes, please bring forth whomever you feel we should meet. I will start a fire and cook some food and we'll sit here until the telling has been completed."

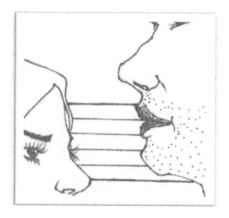

Fiona Finds her Soul Mate

FIONA PUSHED HER bowl away.

"I couldn't eat another bite," she said.

"That's good," Philip said, "because you didn't even leave any scraps for the field mice."

Andre patted his massive stomach.

"We'll see how full you are when dinner settles and you get a look at Nellie's apple cake with hand-crank ice cream. If I ever get fat, that will be why. Philip, you might well get started with the ice cream churn."

"I have to do everything around here. It's not fair."

Andre winked at Fiona.

"What do we always say when you say something's not fair?"

Philip hunched his shoulders and spoke in his deepest voice.

"Thank you for pointing that out."

Fiona laughed at the caricature of his father.

"Get busy, boy, or I'll flay your hindquarters with a switch."

Philip insolently stuck out his tongue, but immediately busied himself with filling the pine-slab ice cream bucket with rock salt and rough shards of dirty-looking ice. Bigger chunks were put in a cotton sack which Philip lustily beat into smaller chunks with a fireplace poker.

"You guys don't have electric power, but you have ice?" Fiona said.

Andre shrugged.

"We're about at the end of it, but in the dead of winter, we haul it in from the quarry pond and store it in an icehouse. The old ways can be good-enough. Makes good ice cream."

"It's also good for cold storage of the old goats we use for soup," Philip said.

Nell poured a heavy cream mixture into his ice cream canister.

To Fiona, Nell said, "I hope you like huckleberries."

Fiona's eyes filled with tears. She could already feel their magical texture on her tongue.

"To me, they taste like an endless summer."

Nell laughed and held out the double handful of dried berries scooped from a sealed bin.

"Then I'd better find more."

"I'll crank first," Amy said while pushing Philip to the side.

"Mom," Philip complained, "she wants to go first while the cranking is easy."

"You can go last if that would work better for you," Andre said.

Philip took a deep breath and aimed his eyes upward. The poor lad wondered if the spirits above were fully aware of his burdens.

"He's going to bring us boundless joy when he's a teenager," Andre grumbled.

The image of a sailboat tossed on a stormy sea filled Fiona's head. She laughed.

"Yeah, that should be fun."

While Amy, with two hands, worked the hand crank, Fiona followed Nell into the kitchen area.

"Help you clean up?"

"I can always use a hand," Nell said. "But, let's start the tea first."

"Oh, I have a treat for you," Fiona said. She reached in her pocket and carefully pulled out her silk-wrapped packet of Dragon Phoenix Jasmine pellets.

Nell studied the offering and put a hand on Fiona's cheek.

"Ah, the very best tea in the world." She pushed Fiona's hand back. "But we can do better," she said with a big grin.

Nell poured five cups of steaming tea. Checking to make sure Fiona was not watching, she tippy-toe reached to a top shelf and retrieved a dusty vial. She removed the stopper and took a whiff.

"Oh, boy," she muttered. She carefully put in a single drop, then considered. She then dropped in another. "Hold onto your toque, Fiona," she whispered.

The ice cream was nearly finished—Andre's colossal muscles strained as he cranked the final series with beads of sweat gathered on his brow. A few minutes after finishing her tea, Fiona stared into the crackling fire. She took her bowl of ice cream and ate every bite, even cleaning the melted residue with an index finger, but didn't say a word.

After clearing away the dishes, Andre and Nell kissed the kids and herded them up the ladder to the loft for bed. He put his beefy hands on her shoulders and inclined his head toward Fiona.

"Did you go a little overboard?"

"I hope not," Nell replied. "Let's see if we can draw her back."

Andre pulled his chair around and took Fiona and Nell's hands to make a prayer circle. They sat in silence for a few minutes before Nell began to chant. Andre's voice joined in and after a few minutes, Fiona added to the harmony. Over and over they sang with the pitches and resonance changing with each iteration of the words.

One with the spirit, one with the Earth,

One with the cycle and one with the Mother.

Was it hours or minutes? They did not know, but slowly Fiona came back to the Earth and her body.

Her slow words stretched like taffy.

"Yes, Nell, your tea *is* the very best," Fiona said.

Nell opened her mouth to reply, but was interrupted by a knock on the door.

"Shitte," Andre whispered.

"Can we pretend no one is home?" Fiona said with a dreamy, disconnected voice.

"No, he knows," Nell said. "He's the owner's man—that makes him God of the RenFaire. He comes and goes as he pleases."

"Fiona," Andre said, "don't trust this man. His soul is—he doesn't really have a soul, does he?"

"I rather don't think he does," said Nell.

"No matter what he says, don't let him in, here," Andre said while stabbing her in the middle of her chest with an enormous finger.

The Thinn Man was tall, just as tall as Andre or a smidge taller, but where Andre was built like a mountain, The Thinn Man was twig-wispy and slight. To Fiona, it seemed as if his face writhed with squirming ornamental scars, but when she focused her eyes and concentrated, his skin turned smooth like polished ebony. His voice was smooth and modulated like a radio disc jockey.

"I finally get to meet the legendary Fiona Pascälle," he said. "I am honored."

He lifted Fiona's hand to his mouth and kissed it. She thought she felt the trace of his dry tongue across the back of her hand, but quickly decided that was impossible—she must have imagined it.

"It was a pleasure to meet you, sir, but it's late and I should get back to—to the place I'm camping."

"Oh, I don't think so," he said. "That wouldn't be right, not at all—not after I've heard so very much about you and waited so very long to meet you."

His black eyes bored into her and she felt as if every strand of her DNA was being weighed and measured. His eyes drifted downward to where turncoat nipples pressed against the rough cotton of her shirt.

I should have remembered to wear my bra.

After an eternity of uncomfortable moments, his eyes drifted downward to the center of her fertility. There was nothing subtle or disguised about his naked desire and while part of her squirmed with creepy aversion and distaste, another part—a big part— flushed with steamy heat. Sean was a good and attentive lover, but she knew it—this tall man was a masterful, skilled expert and would give her orgasm after orgasm. His seed would fill her and it would be like the last piece of a cosmic jigsaw puzzle finally sliding into place so she could admire the smiling face of the Goddess. This was something she craved very much.

"Every woman comes to me as a virgin," The Thinn Man said cryptically. "You and I will make Antony and Cleopatra seem like schoolchildren playing doctor under a tree."

He recited a few phrases.

Age cannot wither her, nor custom stale
Her infinite variety: other women cloy
The appetites they feed, but she makes hungry
Where most she satisfies.[26]

"My cabin..."

"You're through with that nasty cabin," he said. "After the concert, we'll go wherever you like. London? Rio? Mecca?" He laughed and the texture of his laugh was smooth like perfect

---

[26] From *Antony and Cleopatra*, William Shakespeare, the First Folio of 1623.

sateen sheets. "Even Beans Corner, Maine, if that's your desire."

"Wait, what concert?"

The Thinn Man cocked his head and looked with feigned irritation at Nell and Andre.

"She doesn't know about that? Tsk-tsk. You are in for many treats, my dear, and tonight's concert is but only one. I will be there at midnight, of course I will, but I have many miles to travel between now and then to prepare. Let's not agonize over the decision—after an afternoon of carnal indulgence at Hôtel d'Aubusson, let's have espresso and let Alain Ducasse serve us twice-baked almond croissants at my favorite sidewalk table—*Benoît* on the rue St-Martin. There is only one perfect place this time of year for lovers, and that's Paris, of course it is, and always will be."

He took her hands and slowly drew her close and leaned down to kiss her. The kiss was not much, just a brief press of the lips, but the tingle passed through her body all the way to her toes.

"You are mine, Fiona, and I don't intend to share you with anyone," he whispered. "*Au revoir*, my sweet."

Letting his fingers linger on Fiona's hand, he turned to the door. Just before exiting, he pointed a bony finger at Nell and Andre.

"Don't do anything stupid," he said.

Without looking, Fiona dropped back onto the couch and returned her stare at the fire. Nell put her hand on Fiona's shoulder.

"Fiona," Nell said, "The Thinn Man—he's not what he appears."

"Isn't he wonderful?" Fiona said with dreamy peace in her voice. "Paris."

Nell and Andre exchanged glances.

"Double-shitte," Andre said.

Talks in the Night with Friends

THE TALKS CONTINUED late into the night. As darkness came, Sean instructed Luna to take Minnie to bed.

"It's been a long day, my precious one and you need your sleep. Luna will stay in the tent with you. Go get washed up and snuggle down for the night, okay?"

Minnie could barely get herself ready for bed, but she did manage. She gave Sean a hug and kiss goodnight and she and Luna went into the tent to sleep.

Once he was sure Minnie was sound asleep he turned toward Elcor.

"Now we can speak more freely. Tell me what you know."

Gathered around were gnomes and pixies, sprites and dwarves, woodland creatures on four feet and two diminutive dragons. All reported in on the coming of the Dark One. Rumors that they'd heard concerning The Thinn Man and Trevir, the Black Faerie Prince—tales brought to them upon the wind of their fast approach.

They were looking for Minnie and Fiona and would not stop until they were vanquished. They told Sean of the last battle at Fiona's house, and how neither the house nor Llwyd survived. They shared all they knew, both fact and gossip. Sean listened intently to every morsel and let it all seep in. He neither judged nor commented; he simply acted like a sponge and trusted that his instinct would shake out the truth.

In the wee hours of the morning the talking was done. Sean sat back and looked up at the night sky.

"So, the Darkness comes to this place. It approaches as silently and stealthily as a wolf pack hunting its prey and it will watch from the shadows and look for the weakest link and enter in that way. We must all be on high alert from here on out. In the morning, Elcor, I would like for you and Luna to lead Minnie and I to Fiona. I'd like to watch her unseen for now. I need to see how she is and assess her. Are we in agreement?"

Elcor nodded his head.

"It won't be easy for you to see, Sean. She is much more of a wild woman now. It may or may not be for the best, but it is how it is. And the Thinn Man, he has powers of—persuasion—and we should not underestimate him. As we hear, he intends to claim Fiona as his own."

"Understood," said Sean, as he cast his eyes downward. "For now, my friend, let everyone go and sleep for the rest of the night. You are all free to remain here or venture home. There are no secrets here, what's ours is yours. What is paramount is keeping Princess Minnie safe. They will come looking for her and they must not be allowed to take her."

"We pledge ourselves to you and this cause, Sean," said Elcor. "Nothing will happen to you, Fiona or Minnie. You have our word."

With that, some left to sleep in a quieter place and some remained around the dying fire. Sean beckoned to Luna and they found a place in the shadows to talk privately.

"Where are the rest of the forest creatures?" he said. "There should be many more."

"They would not come when I called," Luna replied while licking a paw and grooming his whiskers.

"Is there no hope for more?"

"There's always hope, but I will have to seek them out and ask them for their service. Some will join us, some won't. Some we'll see on the battlefield—fighting against us."

Sean sighed and leaned back against a tree.

"Go, my friend," he said. "Do the best you can."

On stealthy feet, Luna disappeared into the gloom.

"I wish you good fortune and safe travels," Sean whispered into the night.

He crawled into the tent with Minnie and looked on her innocent face.

Oh, Minnie, what's to come of us?

It had been a very long, eventful day and he welcomed the sleep that quickly came to him—his mind drifted as consciousness faded away.

"Soon, Fiona, we will be together again—soon, my love, soon..."

The Futile Emissary

MOONLIGHT STREAMED THROUGH thick branches and dappled the forest floor in creamy patches.

"Ho, ho, ho."

The mocking voice seemed to come from all directions—left, right, up and down. Luna was dizzy from turning in circles.

"Púca, please."

The King Púca laughed.

"Ho, ho, ho."

Luna squatted on his haunches and caught his breath. There came a rustle of brush, which startled him.

"Elcor? I know you're near—show yourself and stop lurking."

"Me—lurk? Never! Your mutterings can be heard in the forest from river to meadow—they led me right to you. King Púca drives you mad? That's what he does."

"The Fomorian refused to commit, now the King Púca won't stand still and let me speak to him."

"Sengann was merely waiting for you to pay tribute—all it took was a squirrel tail and a handful of acorns. When the time comes, you can count on the The Fomorian. They are brave fighters."

"You're following me around?"

"Don't ask questions—just say thank you."

Luna raised a paw and scratched his neck vigorously. Then he shrugged.

"Thank you."

Elcor stroked the ebony fur on Luna's head.

"You were masterful with the Gwyllion; they would never listen to me. Strengths and weaknesses."

"I hope you have a trick up your sleeve for the Púca. If he'd just stand still for a minute..."

Elcor smiled.

"The pranksters will never help us, but I can make him appear." He raised one hand and rested the other on Luna's head. "It would work better if we say the words together."

Frozen like the sap in a winter maple
Captured like a butterfly in a net
A mouse in a trap, a fly in pitch
Púca stand still, King Púca trapped

"That's not poetry and it doesn't make sense," Luna said.

"Take this as another lesson," Elcor said with a grin. "It doesn't have to make sense as long as it works."

Luna sighed and repeated the words. Over and over they recited the chant.

"I'm here, you can stop already."

"One more time," Elcor whispered, "or he'll be right back at it."

King Púca groaned with pain and spoke with a resigned tone of voice.

"Stop. Please, stop."

"You get a few minutes," Elcor whispered, "no more, so make it quick."

Luna walked to the King Púca who rested on a patch of moss—the Púca had a body like a furry frog and had pointy, mouse-like ears on his head. His deep-set eyes were buried under folds of loose flesh and a billygoat beard.

"Trolls," Luna said. "Death. Despair. When Queen Fiona calls, we will win if we stand together."

"Fiona is not the Queen. She's a coward and she'll never be the Queen."

Luna raised a paw—claws extended—to bat at the King, but Elcor restrained him.

"Let me try," he whispered. He took a step forward and spoke in a bold voice. "You'll be frozen for a hundred years if the Black King wins."

A small bat fluttered by. The King Púca reached out and grabbed it. He studied it as it wriggled in his hand before stuffing it in his mouth.

"The Black King will have to catch me first." With that, the King Púca disappeared. "Ho, ho, ho," he said with a disembodied voice. "Though, you can have this much: when the time comes, we'll see what we see."

Elcor shrugged.

"I tried to tell you," he said.

Luna turned and with the bitter taste of defeat in his mouth, muttered to himself while striding through the forest. Elcor hurried to catch up.

"We'll see? Why must all selfish creatures be so stubborn and difficult?" said Luna. "And, the more supposedly superior, the worse they are—all I'm trying to do is reason with them and all they want to do is push back and fight among themselves. We'll see—we'll see—what in tarnation is that supposed to mean? What's there to *see* about the approaching darkness? What's there to analyze about joining forces for the common good? For a species supposed to be so superior, I'd say they're anything but genius."

"Well, my fine friend, there is a fine line between genius and insanity, and truth be told, it really depends upon which big toe the rock happens to fall on that day."

"It would help if you spoke sensible sentences."

Elcor laughed.

"Sorry," he said.

Luna sat down on his haunches. He was tired and worn out, but he knew he couldn't stop.

Elcor continued, "Some grievances transcend time and space—bad blood and grudges get passed along through lore and legend to the point where the current grudge-holder may have no real concept of the absurdity of the logic."

"In the face of this very real threat," Luna said, "it boggles my mind why unification requires any thought."

"My dear friend, not everyone is as forgiving or as advanced as you. Some wounds run deep, older than time—and to be fair, some grudges are based on horrible crimes which should not be forgiven. Neither you nor I should sit in judgment, all we can do is try to facilitate the change and hope reason prevails. Enough of this, who has joined thus far?"

"The Redcaps are holding out but I suspect they will sway with the wind, malevolent little trickster goblins that they are. Surprisingly, the Gytrach and Gwyllion pledged their support— they would like the world to be rid of humans but as they are a steady supply of food for them, they see value in keeping a few around. All the pixie and gnome clans are assuredly on our sides. The Wood elves are with us, and they will try to convince their cousins the Ellyllon to join as well—though they're a gentle sort who do not want trouble but trouble will find them if they don't step in, so I felt it best to leave that field of conversation to the elves themselves."

Elcor nodded his approval.

"Any water folk willing to join us?"

"The selkies for sure, as their range isn't completely limited to the shoreline. The kelpies are willing to join in."

Elcor patted Luna's head.

"You've done well, Master Luna. You are weary and in need of rest—we can only do so much. When the circle is needed, we won't be alone."

"Will it be enough?"

"Uh..."

Luna stopped and rested his head on his paws.

"Go ahead and say it. 'We'll see.'"

"Sorry," Elcor said, "but that's just the way it is sometimes."

The Concert and Fiona Meets the Black Faerie Prince

LIKE A CHILD, Nell stripped Fiona down to her skivvies. She stood back to study Fiona's figure and shook her head with wry humor.

"I remember when *my* breasts laughed at gravity."

She then dressed Fiona in a peasant skirt and blouse and added layers to protect her from the bitter cold. Though conscious and gradually regaining her wits, Fiona was passive and let Nellie do what she wanted. Taking her hand, Nell led her to the main room where Andre waited.

"Concert?" Fiona said. "Tell me."

Andre nodded with approval at Fiona's finery.

"Every year," he said, "on this special, off-season night, we have a concert. This is the real thing, not street buskers in rented costumes."

"Some of the RenFaire performers are very talented," Nellie complained.

"Yes, they are, but this is a special show for insiders, friends and families—it's not the kind of experience you can buy from Ticket-Bastard."

"Who is performing?"

"You'll see. We have our main performers, but there are always mystery guests. Don't worry, you'll like it. Ready? Let's go."

As soon as they stepped off the porch, the lights from the central square could be seen. There were torches hanging from trees and in cast-iron tiki lamps stabbed in the ground. Most of the light and heat came from a thirty-foot pile of logs blazing lustily and driving away the chill. There were three hundred people in the audience and they were closer or farther from the fire depending on how cold-blooded or warm-blooded they were. Almost immediately, Fiona began shedding layers. Under the stars, the air was crisp and bracing, but she was not cold.

In a key central location, there sat two giant wicker chairs. Nellie led Fiona by the hand until they stood before the angled pair. There were flowers arranged in bundles around them—interleaved with glowing candles. Between the chairs was an odd statuette of a pregnant woman with green skin, wild hair with twigs and butterflies woven into the tangled mess. The woman's bulging stomach was painted like the Earth while her left breast was a glowing sun and her right breast was the cold, gray moon. More mysterious was Sean's bodhrán leaning against the nearest chair.

Who brought that out?

"*Someone* will have great seats," she said.

"We'll move them if you wish," Andre said. "Forward? Backward? Left? Right?"

"What?" Fiona said.

There was a tug at her dress. She looked. A pre-teen girl offered a giant clay mug filled with what looked like steaming broth. Fiona recognized her from the morning deliveries at the cabin.

"Perhaps I've had enough magic tea for one night," Fiona said.

Nell looked at the ground and scuffed the Earth with her boot.

"Go ahead," she said. "It's okay. He didn't have a role in

making it."

Fiona lifted the mug from the girl's grasp and took a sip.

"Hot chocolate. Perfect. Thank you."

The girl curtseyed and scampered off.

"I could get used to being treated like a Queen," Fiona said.

"You *are*—"

Andre stopped speaking when Nellie elbowed him in the ribs.

"Who is the other chair for?" Fiona said. "The Thinn Man?"

"No," Nellie said. "His boss. Sit. Sit."

Raucous sounds came from the stage—the atonal jingle-jangle of lutes and guitars being tuned. The tuner was a talented player—after each tuning, he played a flurry of cascading arpeggios on the varied instruments before gently placing them on their stands.

"When it's cold like this, they have a hell-bitch of a time keeping the guitars in tune."

Fiona turned to see who spoke—it was a young man about fourteen years of age. He was strikingly handsome with wavy auburn hair and emerald green eyes—dressed in perfectly creased slacks and an open-collar shirt. Every extremity gleamed in the flickering firelight—there was a diamond stud in his left ear, a giant Rolex watch on his right wrist and gleaming gold chains on his left wrist and around his neck. In the sleeves of his shirt: heavy silver cufflinks and on his head was a sort-of crown made from intertwined brown roots and green tendrils of English ivy. With his head bowed, he kneeled before her and a troll quickly slipped a satin cushion under his knee to keep his trousers from being soiled.

Her heart twitched in her chest.

Troll.

She didn't like trolls.

This troll had an obsequious glitter in his eye. He spoke with a froggy voice.

"Madam, may I present The Black Faerie Prince."

"Please, call me Trevir," the young man said.

The seconds stretched like rubber with the fire crackling and assorted twanging coming from the stage. Eventually, Fiona realized they were waiting for her to say something.

A battle raged inside her—should she show gracious, diplomatic politeness and see where the situation led, or should she tear out the troll's throat with her teeth?

What was in Nell's tea? She felt disconnected, not herself, like an observer of a staged drama. It was not right: the tea defused her anger and made her feel as if it was okay to betray Llwyd's memory.

He's been gone a long time. Life is for the living. It would be good to be Queen if only for a night or a lifetime.

"Uh, you may rise, I guess," she said. The boy stood and the troll brushed invisible lint from his slacks. "Can we rid ourselves of the horrid beast? I don't like trolls."

Trevir laughed.

"Of course."

He gestured with a dismissive flick of his hand. The troll nodded and, after shooting Fiona a glare filled with angry malice, turned and walked away. As Fiona watched, the troll marched through the crowd which paid no attention at all.

Was he invisible to the others or, here, were trolls an everyday, normal experience?

"I hope you don't blame me for the attack on your house—I had nothing to do with that. I want peace, not war. I want unification of the magic worlds and the ordinary world too, while we're at it—this senseless mayhem has gone on far too long and for what? None of us really even knows what we're fighting about. It's time to bury the sins and crimes of the past and clasp our hands for a glorious future."

"Uh," said Fiona.

The young man laughed.

"I meant to bring all that up later and here I've poured it all out at once without ceremony—or foreplay, as The Thinn Man would say. I've gone this far, so I might as well say the rest. I am asking for Minerva's hand in marriage—not now, of course, she's far too young, but we should seal the promise now and spend the next decade planning the most incredible wedding celebration ever."

"I don't know any god-damned Minerva and I wish the name would stop popping up like a bloated corpse in a river."

"Oh, Miss Fiona, you have an evocative way with words, there's no questioning that. Look, the band is ready and waiting for your permission. Sit, sit, there will be plenty of time to talk about our business later."

Fiona sat and stared at the stage. Dressed in olde-English finery, the musicians stood like statues with their guitars and pipes and drums and tambourines. Fiona slowly raised her hands, palms up, and then spread them in a gesture of welcome.

"Please," she said.

The lead guitar player was dressed in black from boots to tall, pointy hat. Beside him, the lovely blonde singer was dressed in a white lace dress. They bowed and with a slippery-slinky introductory guitar line, the heavenly music began.

Watcher

FROM THE WOODS, which seemed to be alive with trolls, Sean watched the concert scene.

What was Fiona doing with the Black Faerie Prince?

He wanted to rush the field and kill everything in his path, but it was hopeless, he'd be killed along with Minnie, Elcor and Luna. Trolls were everywhere—there were thousands.

It was true, Fiona was a coward and his faith in her was futile. There was no war—it was already over and Fiona was at peace with their enemy and laying down her sword. King Custennyn had won. The Black Faerie Prince had won. The Thinn Man had won.

Sean ground his teeth and growled at the thought of The Thinn Man and what he would do to Fiona. According to legend, he was descended from an illegitimate son of Pan and Euphrosyne and knew the ancient secrets of passion and release—a touch of his finger could deliver a woman to the pinnacle of ecstasy. What mortal man could compete?

And there, across the wide field, Fiona sat like a complaint bride waiting for her groom.

Sean clenched and unclenched his fists in futile fury.

289

Music to Fiona's Ears

WITH HER EYES closed, she sat and let the music wash over and through her.

> *There's too many stars for one sky to hold, some will fall, others are sold*
> *As the fields turn to gold, down at the Renaissance Faire...*[27]

After this third glorious song, the band took a break. She leaned over to talk to Trevir.

"This band is amazing. They're just friends gathered to jam? I can't believe that."

Trevir shrugged.

"It's a little more than that. The man in black is considered by many to be the best rock guitarist in the world—he's a living legend. It's not really my thing because I'm more into post-punk dubstep, you know, like Clive Chin or Scratch Perry? You know them?"

---

[27] Renaissance Faire, © 1997 Ritchie Blackmore and Candace Night, Minstrel Hall Music / Daunted Song Music, traditional composition by Tielman Susato.

Fiona made a face and raised her hands in ignorance.

"No clue," she said.

"You should check them out. Anyway, the singer and guitar player are married. They could play the biggest arenas in the world, but he's been there and done that and is simply not interested. You could offer him a million tax-free dollars to play Madison Square Garden and he'd tell you to bugger off. I know because I asked and that's what he said. So, here he is playing music he loves for 271 people."

"271?"

"In this business, you learn to count the crowd. There's more if you count the pixies and the forest sprites." He pointed toward the woods where Fiona saw flashing lights like fireflies. "They never pay admission to anything and don't seem to grasp the concept, so I don't count them."

A thin man with a gray beard—wearing a beret adorned with a silver star—plugged in a seafoam-green electric guitar.

"Who's that?"

Trevir looked up from his mug of chocolate.

"A friend. These guys kick each other's asses. The old guy is damned good at the finger-picking—he drives his black-clad friend crazy, but the man in black is better at flat-picking. They challenge each other to greater and greater heights. Though, like I said, it's not as good as dubstep."

He sang a few lines.

Pum pum come, pum pum go, it's all right
Pum pum come, pum pum go, it's Saturday night...[28]

"What's Pum Pum?" she said.

Trevir shifted his eyes back to the stage.

---

[28] *Pum Pum*, © 2008 Lee 'Scratch' Perry, from the record *Repentence*, Narnack Records.

"I think it refers to a bass drum."

"I doubt that very much," Fiona said.

"Never mind, the band is ready."

Fiona's hand drifted to the side of her chair and encountered the bodhrán. She idly tapped her fingers on it while the band played a quiet, acoustic version of *I Still Remember.*

> *I had a dream of you and I, a thousand stars lit up the sky*
> *I touched your hand and you were gone, but memories of you*
> *live on...*[29]

Sean.

She picked up his drum and quietly tapped on it. With her eyes closed, she let the music carry her away and she found herself beating a counterpoint rhythm vigorously with her fingertips. Two very large men appeared and stationed themselves on each side of her chair.

Uh-oh, she thought.

Too much cowbell?

They've come to break my legs.

Instead, they helped her up and escorted her to the stage. One took the drum, the other lifted her; once up, the other man handed her the drum and, by pantomime, urged her to beat on it.

She turned.

The band—even the man in black—grinned and gestured for her to play. Embarrassed, she stood off to the side and tapped lightly, but the music was contagious and she soon found herself on the center of the stage next to the singer—playing with wild abandon. With skirts flying, she whirled and pranced. Soon, the

---

[29] *I Still Remember*, © 2006 Ritchie Blackmore and Candace Night, from the record *Beyond the Sunset*, Minstrel Hall Music / Daunted Song Music, additional music: traditional.

extended song drifted to an end with the guitarist noodling on his nylon-string guitar. The crowd stood and clapped. Stunned, Fiona stood in the spotlight, perspiring and ashamed. The blonde singer grabbed her hand and dragged her to the front of the stage and, together, they bowed and curtseyed.

Then, somehow, Fiona found herself back in the wicker chair where Trevir smiled and took her hand.

As the evening progressed, a dignified lady came to the stage to sing a song called *Bound for Infinity*. The two women's voices mixed with like sugar mixes with lemon. For the last encore, a scrawny man strapped on a Fender bass and sang a song called *Stormbringer* and that is what echoed in her ears as the show ended and the crowd dispersed.

> *Coming out of nowhere, drivin' like a-rain*
> *Stormbringer dance on the thunder again*
> *Dark cloud gathering, breaking the day*
> *No point running, 'cause it's coming your way…*[30]

Stunned, Fiona sat in the wicker chair as if paralyzed.

"Who was that? He has a great voice."

"The voice of rock. He doesn't do that kind of song very often and neither does the man in black, so we're double-lucky."

She got up and walked to the glowing embers of the massive bonfire. There were no licking flames, but heat still radiated intensely.

"What time is it?" she said. "It has to be three already."

"Four-thirty. The sun will rise soon."

"This has been an evening. I have to get some sleep."

"Oh, no you don't. At this point, you might as well ride the adrenaline until your evening in Paris. Don't worry, The Thinn

---

[30] *Stormbringer*, from the album by Deep Purple, ©1974 Ritchie Blackmore and David Coverdale.

Man knows how to keep a lady—stimulated. He'll be here in an hour or so. The bar, *My Ale Hither* is open for us. Let's get an Irish coffee or Baileys-and-coffee and chat a while longer."

"Aren't you far too young to drink?"

"I'll have chocolate milk."

"I'll nap until The Thinn Man comes—I'm no good to him exhausted."

He put his hand on her arm.

"I told you, he knows what to do. Everything happens in the next couple of hours. I'm sorry, but sleep is not in the cards for you. Cards? Do you like tarot? I'll run a set and tell your fortune."

She pulled her arm from his grasp.

"Look, I don't know why, but I am attracted to The Thinn Man and I'll go to Paris with him and do everything he wants—I'm not arguing that point. Just let me get an hour's sleep and I'll be good to go."

The final song of the evening echoed in her ears.

Dark cloud gathering, breaking the day
No point running, 'cause it's coming your way...[31]

"I'm sorry, Fiona, but I must insist," Trevir said.

She raised her voice and nearly shouted.

"I already said The Thinn Man can use me upside-down and sideways—"

A voice came from behind her.

"Fiona?"

She turned.

Sean.

His face had drained of color.

"Fiona? The Thinn Man? Have...", he glanced down at the little girl holding his hand, "...*things* happened already?"

---

[31] ibid.

Sean.

She couldn't bear the look in his eyes, so she kneeled to be eye-to-eye with the little girl.

"I know you," she said.

"That's Minnie," Sean said.

The realization flooded her mind.

Minnie. Minerva.

Trevir stood up straight and adjusted his cufflinks.

"You're a little earlier than I expected," he said. "We might as well get on with it."

The first ray of the morning sun appeared to set his hair to flame and made his vivid green eyes gleam. At this instant, he was, by far, the most handsome man in the world. He kneeled beside Fiona and took Minnie's little hands and held them to his lips.

"I know you and you know me, Minerva. We're going to be husband and wife if you simply say—yes. I will protect and love you and give you a castle and carriage and promise that all your secret dreams will come true."

Minnie was dazzled by the young man's beauty. Something inside her twitched and her heart fluttered.

Her lips formed to say the word.

"Y—"

Something hard and green flashed through the air and hit Trevir on the shoulder.

"What?" He reached down to pick it up. A crabapple. "Who threw this?" Trevir shouted. He spun in circles, searching. "I'll kill you."

From under an elm tree fifty yards away, the figure of a boy was barely visible in the gloom. He waved his slingshot. In a sliver of an instant he drew back and released another missile. Trevir ducked instantly or he would have been hit again. He grabbed Minnie's shoulders and shook her.

"Will you marry me?" he said.

The mad spell was broken. She wriggled from his grasp.

"No," she said, "I will not."

Kicking up her heels, she ran toward slingshot-boy as if the devil was on her heels. While watching her run, Trevir was hit directly in the center of his forehead with an apple that dropped into his hand. He threw it to the ground with disgust and rubbed the rising welt.

"Damn it," he said.

Philip, Meet Minnie; Minnie, Meet Philip

TEN FEET AWAY from the boy, Minnie's consciousness rose above the Earth's surface and she *saw* herself running across the field; she wondered what she was doing. Her legs slowed to a walk, then she stopped. The boy aimed his slingshot and released another missile over her head.

"I don't really like girls," he said. He studied her face. "What I mean is I *really* don't like girls. Go away."

A few-years-younger girl handed the boy an apple from a heaping pile.

"It's true," she said. "He doesn't; he hates me too. His name's Philip. I'm Amy."

Minnie took another step. Suddenly shy, she fumbled with her words.

"I'm Minnie. Minerva, but people call me Minnie."

"Well, Min-NERD-va, yer about to get beaned if you don't get out of the way."

He released another green missile over her head.

She took another step closer.

"Got another slingshot?" she said.

"No. Boys get slingshots; girls get dolls and tea sets." While holding up an apple, Amy shrugged and grinned. Philip continued his rant. "Beat feet. You belong with your people. Hurry—Dad says things around here are coming undone very quickly."

Minnie looked over her shoulder. Sean and Fiona stood with their heads six inches apart, talking. Trevir was screaming—walking in circles and kicking up clods of dirt.

Philip was right—she needed to go back. Another apple hissed over her head. She took another step forward.

"You don't listen too good," Philip said.

"I'm going to kiss you," Minnie replied.

"No you're not."

She pushed the slingshot aside, raised up on her toes and leaned in—aiming for his cheek, but he turned his head. His mouth tasted of stolen cherries and there was a telltale red stain of evidence on his lips. She stumbled and their teeth rattled together. It was clear: it wouldn't always be easy, but they belonged together.

He pulled back and rubbed the back of his filthy hand across his mouth.

"Gross," he said. He looked over her shoulder. "Blast it. Trolls. They won't hurt you, but we have to go."

He reached down and grabbed a handful of Amy's sweater, lifting her to her feet. He stuffed the slingshot into the back pocket of his jeans.

"I'm going to kiss you again later," Minnie said.

"Not happening, Nerd-va," he said, and with that he was gone.

Standing, she watched the trail and listened to the sound of their running feet fade away to nothing. She turned and on heavy feet that complained about going the wrong way, walked back. In the eastern sky, the sun was a golden orb casting long shadows.

Fiona Calms the Stormy Waters

FIONA RAISED HER hands and screamed at the top of her lungs.

"Everyone, please, settle down."

She put her hand on Trevir's shoulder to stop him, but he shook it off.

"Get off me, bitch," he said. "I will have no more disrespect."

"Fiona?" Sean said.

"Not now, Sean. Let me gather my thoughts."

"That damned kid ruined everything," Trevir said with a voice that dripped with ugly malice. "My trolls will flay him slow."

Fiona looked into the forest; it appeared to be alive with movement.

"Trevir, stop for a minute, let's talk about this."

He stopped and turned. His contorted face was red with anger.

"No more talk—it's time for blood to spill in gallons."

"You're like a hysterical yammering schoolgirl, get a grip. I don't understand anything, but if Minnie agrees to marry you and bind the clans, there will be peace in the kingdom?"

"Fiona," Sean said. "No. We can't..."

"Hold your tongue a minute, Sean, I'm not negotiating anything, I just want to understand the landscape."

"Fiona—"

"Can it, Sean, let me think this through. How long has this war been going? Decades?"

Trevir took a step forward—his face was inches from Fiona's and she counted the beads of sweat on his upper lip (seven). There were flecks of foam at the corners of his mouth.

"Centuries," he said.

She closed her eyes. Where was her staff? Why did she leave it at the cabin? She reached out with her mind and felt for it, then raised her hands. Like a wooden missile, the staff flew through the air and rammed solidly into her hands. She lifted it and tapped the end of Trevir's nose.

"And one word from the mouth of a little girl—a little girl who's been chapping my ass—could end it?"

"Fiona," Sean said.

She turned and raised her stick as if preparing to hit him.

"Damn it, Sean, we should at least consider the option if it saves souls."

"It's too late for options," Trevir said, "I'm going to see you— all of you—die screaming."

"I don't suppose you'd tone down the melodrama for five minutes? Maybe not all is lost—look, Minnie is coming back."

Unified, they turned to look over the weedy field.

It was true: Minnie slowly walked back—dragging her feet in the dirt and taking ponderous strides as if the weight of the world bore down on her shoulders. Fiona kneeled and held out her hands. After a slow minute Minnie stood before her. Fiona held the little girl at arms' length and looked into her dirty face.

"I've been dreaming about you," Fiona said.

"I know," Minnie said.

"Sometimes, for the greater good, we have to do things we don't want to." Minnie nodded. "I don't know exactly what's happening, but I think it's likely we all die here, this morning, unless a peace is forged. Can you feel it?"

Minnie nodded.

"No one can make you," Fiona whispered. "You have to give yourself willingly. Will you?"

"Yes," Minnie said. "For you and Sean and Flix and the Fachan and Selene and Luna and the trees and my mother in heaven and our home, I'll do it."

Fiona stood and, ignoring the shock on Sean's face, turned to speak.

"Trevir, may I present your bride-to-be? Minerva, take his hands. Who can bless this holy union? I can't do it."

Trevir mopped his forehead with an embroidered silk handkerchief.

"You are genuinely ignorant—only the Queen can perform the ceremony, everyone knows that. Everyone but you, apparently." He pointed his index finger at Minnie. "Our sons are going to rule the world." Fiona's staff twitched and vibrated in her hands. Trevir's face twisted into a broad smile exposing his perfect white teeth. "Speaking of the Crone, here she is."

He pointed.

An impossibly tall man dressed from head to toe in black approached, dragging a filthy bunch of old rags. He flung the bundle at Trevir's feet. From under a cowl appeared a wrinkled, tear-stained face.

The Queen—broken and barely alive, but unmistakable.

Minnie stood like a statue with her eyes locked on The Thinn Man.

"Okay," Fiona said, "I'm beyond exhaustion, let's get this done."

Minnie raised her little hand and pointed a dainty finger at The Thinn Man.

"You—," she said.

Unification

ELCOR KINDLED A small fire—a feeble spark in the gloom of the deep forest. With a soul that ached for losing the argument for unification, Luna padded around the circle and looked at each creature in turn.

Veraudunus, the toad king, Selene's spirit-mother: Nemetona, Moccus, the God of the wild boars, Icovellauna, the spring water Goddess, Buxenus, the master of the Elm spirits, Roboris, the Oak master and Black Vaughan, the raven King.

None of them came willingly or seemed open to compromise, but when Luna begged and pleaded and threatened, they agreed to come if only to sit for a few minutes. The atmosphere was charged like a battery—the air was filled with ozone and the scent of sulfur-brimstone and decay.

Overhead, the constellations wheeled and vibrated like they did not know what to be. For an instant the North Star Polaris scooted across the sky to join with the Great Bear-Ursa Major, then the Little Bear, then Draco the dragon, then the Big Dipper-Plough and then became the gleam in the sky devil's eye before returning to join again with the Great Bear.

Luna squatted on his haunches and stared into the flame.

"We don't have to be friends," he said. "We don't have to kneel and worship one Queen. We don't have to embrace the one spirit and we don't have to live. We can choose death."

Veraudunus had a deep voice—a subterranean rumble.

"Too much talk," he said.

Elcor stood and began unsheathing his sword, but Luna raised a paw to stop him.

"Anyone who chooses death over life, just get up and go now. Go in peace and be who you are, we won't stop you." He dropped onto a pile of dried leaves by the fire and closed his eyes. "Go," he said.

The assembled forest spirits groaned and grumbled and glared with unveiled malice at their brothers and sisters around the weak flame, but none left. After fifteen minutes of meditation or sleep, Luna opened his green eyes and appeared surprised anyone was still with him.

"In an hour, far too soon, far too soon, the Queen—"

"She's not my Queen—" Roboris interjected, but Luna ignored him and carried on.

"—the Queen will need our strength, the strength from Sky, Earth, Water and Flame. She'll need us to be *with* her, not as servant and master, not as owner and slave, not as higher or lower, but as a fellow bearer of the life-spirit reaching out a hand for help."

Elcor stood. "I offer my sword," he said.

"I offer my tusk," Moccus said.

"I offer my talons," Nemetona said.

"I offer my beak," Black Vaughn said.

"I offer my—tongue," said Veraudunus, "for what it's worth."

This broke the tension in the circle and they laughed. For long minutes, they couldn't stop laughing. The leaves of the surrounding trees and the stars of the cold sky vibrated in blessed harmony while the reaching rays of the morning sun chased away the night.

Luna nodded to Elcor who drew a shriveled stinkhorn

mushroom from his leather pouch. Holding it above his head, he walked around the circle. When the circle was complete he threw the leathery fragment of toadstool into the fire. For an instant, nothing happened, and then the flame's inner eye opened and the *Alptraum*, elf-dream, began.

Miles away, the Queen cried out in pain and the eye blinked, blinked again, then turned in her direction.

Minnie and The Thinn Man

ON IMPOSSIBLY LONG legs, The Thinn Man strode across the field until he stood before Minnie. From his perspective, she was a long, long way down. He drew his long sword from his belt and kneeled.

"Something to say, imp?" he said. "I killed your mother and I'd kill you in a flicker of an instant if Trevir would let me. What he sees in you, I do not know. To me, you're a pest, a bug—a speck of filth on my sleeve begging to be flicked away."

Minnie held his gaze.

What were her mother's last words?

I love you like a cloud loves a rainbow.

This did not make literal sense. Rainbows love the sun, not clouds. How is it possible for a rainbow to love its enemy, clouds?

It was a line from a poem—a poem from an old book. The only book her mother owned—passed down for generations, mother to daughter.

A lost book.

No, Minnie thought.

Books are never lost.

Not as long as someone, somewhere is reading.

I love you like a pebble loves a shoe
I love you like the red loves the blue
I love you like the dark night loves the glow
You didn't kill my mother, but you stole some precious days.
You brought her end sooner than was necessary. I could have had a
dozen more hugs and a thousand more kisses. I could of have had...
I'm little. I have no power.
That's why I'm gone.
That's why I will pledge myself to the Black Faerie Prince.

Stillness started with a black dot in the very center of her gut. It grew while Minnie slept and something else took over. Something mean and ugly.

She was weak and powerless. She had nothing.

The Thinn Man had power—all the power in the world. He was strong. But, his strength was based on one promise. One vow. It had to do with blood.

She looked into his eyes, deep into him. He was formidable, dangerous, cold and mean. Her backbone felt rigid, like it had been replaced with old iron. It was incongruous and inconceivable, but she was dangerous too. The iconic, ritualistic scars on his face writhed like baby snakes.

She reached out with her dainty index finger and touched the point of his black sword. It was sharp, somewhere beyond sharp, and a pinpoint of blood appeared on her fingertip. In the morning light, it glowed like a ruby. With a dreamy smile on her lips, she spoke with a voice that was weak—it echoed as if from a deep canyon.

"Look here, Walden Longfellow, you've drawn the blood of a virgin princess."

Fiona watched with her heart in her mouth knowing everything hinged on these few monumental moments, but she couldn't avoid the wry thought as she exchanged a glance with Sean.

Walden Longfellow? No wonder everyone called him The

Thinn Man.

From books, Minnie had an anatomical idea of what a virgin was, but the image in her mind was of tulips blooming in the springtime sun; a bulb shooting into flower—the virginal bloom living in the time before the flower opened and exposed its petals to the sun, wind and rain.

She knew nothing tangible about virginity, but knew she was unviolated. Moving very slowly, she touched her finger to the flat of The Thinn Man's blade and ran a streak of rusty blood down its length. In seconds, the blade dissolved and turned to dust. The air stirred and the dust floated away while her finger slipped closer and closer to The Thinn Man's face. She raised her hand from the hilt and touched the end of his nose. He jerked back to his haunches as if receiving an electrical shock.

"This is not happening," he said. "You can't..."

"I did," Minnie said softly. "Now you can die screaming."

While Trevir looked on in wonder, The Thinn Man took a stumbling step backward.

"There was one solemn promise," Minnie said. "In exchange for eternity, you promised your blade would never shed the blood of an innocent princess."

"No," he said. "I didn't. You did."

Minnie shrugged. She put her bloody finger in her mouth.

"You pricked me after promising the old King you wouldn't. All he cared about was protecting his little daughter. He gave you everything."

"I didn't. I wouldn't. You did it." He looked up into the sky and laughed. "I'm safe, little witch, little queynte. You have no power over me."

For an instant, Minnie did not exist. Something old and hateful filled her.

"I curse you," she said.

"What?" he said.

His mouth opened wide, cavernously wide and, as his body

was ripped to shreds cell-by-cell and atom-by-atom, he wailed like a banshee. After a few long seconds, he was gone, leaving only his black suit behind. It collapsed into a heap on the ground.

Sean's face turned as white as bleached bones. He kneeled and gently took Minnie's arm and turned her toward him.

"Minnie?"

She seemed to be only half awake.

"Yes, Sean," she said.

His voice was saturated with despair.

"I think you killed us, killed us all."

"Maybe, maybe not," she replied.

"No, Minnie, you don't understand. The Thinn Man? He was not Trevir's man, he was on loan from his real master."

"I know, Sean. The Black Faerie King."

"We have nothing. There is no power on Earth that can stand against him when he's angry and this, I assure you, will make him extraordinarily angry. Unmercifully angry. If we need compassion, we won't find any in the King, not even a smidgen. Minnie, we're all going to die."

"Sean, no one lives forever, not in one body."

"Hopeless," he said.

He stood and wrapped Fiona in his arms and squeezed her tight. The forest was alive with trolls, but they did not enter the field.

The breeze stilled and the air grew heavy as if all the oxygen had disappeared. There was a weak rumble from the west that built in intensity.

"The King," Sean said. "He's coming."

King, Queen, Checkmate

AT FIRST GLANCE, the King looked like a hobo—the King of vagabonds, bums and thieves—but as he marched closer and closer, his silk rags came into focus along with the trappings of power, including a diamond-adorned watch, a scepter with an ivory pearl as big as a billiard ball, a sable hat, a long, thin dagger on his belt with a massive green emerald on the hilt and eyes that accepted no nonsense and sliced and dissected the commonfolk who dared to waste his time.

Before saying a word, he stood before Trevir and slapped his face, then stood for a few moments waiting to see how Trevir would respond to the insult.

When he finally spoke, his quiet voice was harsh with undertones like the meshing of broken gears.

"You've been a big disappointment to me, boy," he said.

After giving up on any response from Trevir, he squatted on his haunches in front of Minnie and studied her face.

"For all the trouble you cause, you don't look like much. I should bite your face off. I don't suppose you have any intent to bend the knee and swear an oath of fealty to your one and only rightful King?"

Minnie was frozen like ice—she didn't even blink in response.

"So be it," the King said.

One-by-one, he looked around the circle of shocked faces.

"Before I unleash the trolls to tear you limb from limb, are there any final words you care to say? Any of you?"

Collapsed on the ground, The Queen whispered something inaudible.

The King whirled and in an instant stood over her. With his boot, he brutally kicked her ribs.

"What—this mound of greasy rags dares to speak? In my presence, you have the audacity to assault my ears with pathetic whimpering? You could have had the world on a gold platter. We could have been the finest royal couple in history and I loved you, or at least, I loved the idea of you if not your flabby ass and hook-beaked nose. You were on the brink of greatness—in seconds it would have been done and what did you do? From the altar, you ran like a coward, like a filthy cockroach. You scurried away in the night. Go ahead: speak, bitch, say your last words on Earth and make them good ones. I've been waiting for this for a long time."

He pulled the knife from its sheath and rotated the blade to catch the rays of the morning sun.

"Do you remember this blade, hag? You should, you gave it to me as a betrothal gift. Stormbringer—long has it thirsted for the flavor of your blood."

He kneeled and placed the blade at the soft skin under her jaw. She whispered two words. He leaned closer.

"Louder, I can't hear you."

Where she got the strength is unknown, but the words were crystal clear in the air for the world to hear as he pressed the blade up, up, up into her skull.

"I do," she whispered before dying.

"Oh, now you'll say the words instead of running away? Too late, Queenie."

He stood and turned to look at the shocked assembly.

"Now it's your turn," he said.

Minnie slowly raised her hand and pointed behind him. The King turned. The bloody knife had slipped out of the Queen's body and quivered in the air.

"What?" the King said.

"I think you just killed your wife," Minnie said.

"What?" the King repeated uselessly. "No, that's not the way it works."

Thirty years ago, they had stood on a hilltop. She was beautiful in her white gown and veil. All around, thousands. Hundreds of thousands, ready for the wedding feast. It was quiet—like no one even dared to breathe. Everything was done. All she needed to do was say the words.

But, she didn't.

Instead, she ran and like Moses parting the Red Sea, the speechless crowd parted and let her pass. His first impulse was to kill and he realized, she was not his queen, so if he could find her, she was fair game.

My dagger will taste your blood, he vowed.

But, he couldn't find her and as the years passed, gave her no further thought. He found another suitable princess and she bore their one and only son.

Trevir.

Weak Trevir.

Mean Trevir.

Evil Trevir.

He knew what the common folk called his son.

Catsbane.

Horrified at what her loins brought into the world and the blood on her son's hands, Trevir's mother died of a broken heart.

In an instant, these memories filled the King's mind and he felt something he had not felt for a very long time.

A nugget of fear filled his belly.

He stood and looked at each of the faces in turn. The air crackled with electricity and smelled of acrid ozone.

"You don't have the moral authority."

There was a soul-wrenching thrum from the woods while the forest creatures and spirits appeared at the fringe and watched. The Earth shook like jelly and the tall trees crowded around the field. They conferred. They decided. There was a raw power increasing in strength. The Earth rumbled. Thousands of eyes watched while the energy in the air built and built until it seemed the world would crack open and fly into pieces. The trolls lowered their swords, shuffled their feet and stared at the traitorous ground before melting away into the woods.

"It's written," Minnie said, "that the King and Queen share a common fate."

The King's face drained of color and assumed an ashen pallor. The knife drifted in the air and hovered before his chin. He grasped the hilt and, with quivering muscles, held the blade at bay. Though it was powered by the strength of the world, slowly it moved backwards and away.

The King grinned.

"I win," he said. "I always win."

At that instant, a green projectile flew from the sky and hit the King's shoulder—just a glancing blow, but it was enough to disrupt his concentration.

"Oh, no," he said, "no, no, no…"

Those were his last words as the blade slipped under his chin and stabbed upward into his brain. Like a boneless glob of custard, he collapsed in a heap on the stony ground.

Minnie turned and waved at Philip before running like the wind across the field. In an instant she stood before him.

"You're my hero," she said. "Someday I'm going to marry you."

"No you're not," Philip replied. "I don't like girls. Go away."

"Lovebirds, kissing in a lovebird tree," Amy sang.

Before he could escape, Minnie wrapped her arms around his neck and kissed him on the cheek with all of her strength.

"Get off me," he said. "I have to attend to my chores or Dad will whip me silly. Goodbye, little girl."

Minnie laughed and turned her attention to Amy. They hugged.

"We'll be sisters," Minnie said.

"I can't wait," Amy replied.

Back in the middle of the field, Trevir's shock slowly melted away.

"I guess that's it, now I'm the boss."

He turned to Fiona.

"And, until Minnie comes of age, that makes you The Queen."

"No," Fiona said. "I am not your Queen. I am nobody's Queen."

"It's not up to you, Fiona. Look around. The trees give you their power. The decision is made. You have the ring."

She looked at her hand.

Where did that come from?

A red ruby gleamed like blood.

"No," she said.

Trevir pointed at her.

"I believe I'll save the pleasure of killing you for later," he said.

He turned to walk away.

To Fiona, Sean whispered urgently.

"Stop him now while you can."

"I can't," Fiona said.

Trevir climbed into the passenger side of a huge Ford pickup truck. The troll-driver spun the tires in the soft soil and tore up the grass.

Sean's reply was filled with helpless resignation.

"Okay." He turned and shouted across the field. "Minnie. Let's go home."

"Home," Fiona whispered with wonder. "How I love the sound of that."

Cupcakes

FOR THE LAST quarter mile of the trek through the woods, Sean kept Fiona blindfolded while Minnie talked a mile a minute with Luna marching by her side. It was an exhausted troupe, but at the same time, they were at peace and glad to be alive and well.

If one were to look upon the foursome, they would think of them as a normal, happy family hiking with their cat; but so very much had happened since the beginning of their journey. Adventures and travels; new beginnings and tragic endings; magic and worldly lessons, friends found and friends lost; enemies made and those yet to be discovered. Now, however, was a time for rest and integration, peace and prosperity, love and contentment.

"Sean, I can't see with this infernal blindfold on. C'mon and lemme take it off."

"There was once a time you didn't mind a blindfold at all, Fiona," Sean said with naked hunger in his voice. "Come now and trust me as you once did."

A rush of color came to her cheeks as memories flooded her mind—washing over her like the rain on a dry riverbed.

"That's it, Fiona. Ride the wave," he said while holding her hand. "Flow—flow as only you know how."

After a ways, she felt them stepping out of the forest. The air smelled fresh again, and dry. She heard Minnie squeal and scamper ahead.

"Okay, please Sean, I can't stand it anymore."

Sean laughed; Fiona had long forgotten the laugh she loved so much—the laugh that made her forget everything. The laugh that lifted her spirits and gave reassurance that everything was okay. The laugh that made the stars twinkle and sunbeams dance.

Sean removed the blindfold and stepped back to watch her reaction.

Fiona stood stock still, stunned at what lay before her eyes.

"Sean, but how—when—how did you—it's my house, but this is not where it was."

He put his finger up to her lips.

"Shhhhh, my love. The hows and whys don't matter. Welcome home."

Fiona's knees gave way as she started to faint. Sean caught her and laid her gently in the grass. He bent down to kiss and revive her.

"Oooh, that was like Snow White, Sean," giggled Minnie.

"Wanna see me do it again?" laughed Sean.

"One kiss will do just fine—for now," said Fiona as she sat up.

Luna ran up and climbed into her lap, mewing and purring away.

"Yes, Luna, we're home again. We're finally home."

Fiona looked up and saw Minnie sitting in a red-painted Adirondack chair kicking her little legs up and down and talking to a creature seated next to her in a purple version of the same chair. The Fachan wore a wide-brimmed, straw gardener's hat with a red bandana tied around it. He sipped a glass of lemonade through a polka dot straw.

Fiona looked at Sean with a quizzical look upon her face accompanied by a smirk and a raised eyebrow.

"He saved Minnie's life in the forest, so she brought him

315

home. He's not quite a pet; he's her friend. He lives in the little out-building across the way. He's really a love, though first appearances may not lead you to believe that—but first appearances can be deceiving. Do you recall your first impression of me on that rainy night by the side of the road?"

"Yes, I do, my silver-tongued rogue. Had I listened to the logical voice then..."

Sean didn't let her finish her sentence—he silenced her by kissing her again, the kiss of ages gone by and of times to come. It was a kiss of ancient and future memories. It was all that and more, and it was the best one ever.

"Welcome home, Fiona," whispered Sean as he looked deep into her eyes, the eyes of his beloved newborn Queen.

"Okay—enough of the kisssssssing, you two," Minnie said. "Can we please go inside and wash up? I want to make cupcakes with Fiona."

Fiona winked at Sean.

"So, this is what it's like to have a demanding spoiled child, eh?"

"Oooh, I want to help too," yowled the Fachan.

He hopped on foot and chased after Minnie.

"Eating all the cupcakes is not helping," Minnie said.

Watching them run, Fiona and Sean laughed as they followed into the house. The stories went long into the night. All the while, there was eating and drinking, baking and tasting, singing and dancing. German chocolate cupcakes, chocolate with chocolate frosting, red velvet, vanilla with vanilla frosting, and the list went on and on. At long last, as the sun began to rise, Fiona carried Minnie up to her room and laid her down into her bed.

"Sleep well, my beautiful princess. I'm sorry I ever doubted you. You saved me, you saved Sean. You saved us all. You are truly a wonder, my little one. Sleep well."

She bent down and kissed Minnie on her forehead. Minnie was already fast asleep, but Fiona knew Minnie heard her words.

She stood in the doorway watching the princess sleep. Sean came up behind her and wrapped his arms around her waist. Hand-in-hand, they left the room and walked to the kitchen.

"She's amazing, Sean. So young yet so wise. She's been through so much—she's lost so much yet still she thrives. She sprouts and blossoms. We're going to have an amazing life here together, the three of us."

"Yes, we will, Fiona. You, Minnie and I. And, all the magical beings and creatures. We're finally in our enchanted house, surrounded by love and magic. We'll have our rough times ahead, but it won't be anything like what we've been through already. We're protected here, Fiona. We're safe from harm. You'll learn the secrets of this land as has young Minnie. You'll remember your past more clearly and we'll go into the future together. I won't leave you again, that I promise."

Standing over the oven, Fiona nestled her back into Sean's belly. He picked her up and carried her to bed where a long overdue reunion awaited them.

Under the covers, their new lives began.

The Letter

IT WAS AFTER midnight and she couldn't sleep. With an ache in her belly, Fiona stood by the bedroom window and looked out over the moonlit grass. All her joy had evaporated. She and Minnie could not stay—it wasn't safe. Again, she needed to run and hide. Sean was right; she should have killed The Black Faerie Prince.

No, he was the new King Custennyn now, and she should have killed him when there was slim chance of success.

Outside a small breeze blew and circled the house—carrying leaves and assorted debris. Listening closely, she heard the new King's voice on the wind.

"This isn't over. I'll come for you, Queen Fiona. Rest and fall into complacency while I gain power and build my empire. But be assured, I'll come back to avenge my father—I'll come back for you and the princess—never, ever will you or anyone you care about be safe from me…"

In a daze, Fiona walked to the library where she collapsed into a chair. The world was shifting and she was unsure of what lay ahead. On the shelves, the books whispered.

No, she knew exactly what the future held.

And, she didn't like it.

She wanted to bury her head in the sand like an ostrich and pretend she never knew. Like all things, though, you can't unknow.

After an hour, she walked around the house like a sleepwalker. With her feet barely skimming the floors, she was almost hovering, floating around the ground floor of the house. Sitting at the kitchen table, she ran her hand across the tabletop; an old barn board lovingly crafted into a beautiful work of art through Sean's hands.

She could feel the magic when she touched it; feel the oil that he so painstakingly rubbed into it to make sure it lasted for centuries. Her eyes misted over. She reached for a piece of parchment and her favorite pen. It was silly but it was a purple pen with a ragged blue feather on it. David had given it to her shortly after they first met and she carried it in her travel bag. That seemed like lifetimes ago.

My dearest Sean.

Gaack! Muttering, she crumpled up the paper.

"That sounded like a bad Hallmark card."

My most beloved.

"Good goddess, that's even WORSE," she said.

She stood and walked to the stove.

Tea.

It was the wee hours of the morning and she craved the warm comfort of tea. As she waited for the water to warm she paced. Unconsciously, her fingers twiddled in such a way that small, erratic sparks flew about.

"Be careful with that, Fiona. You don't want to set fire to anything. After all, you're barely settled in here."

Fiona spun about and scanned the kitchen for the voice.

"Ahhh, it's you Flix. I didn't see you. Why are you up so late, my friend?"

"More like, why are you up so early, Fiona? I take that back. I know why you're up," he said quietly as he hung his head and averted his eyes. "But, who is the *David* you were thinking about?"

Teary-eyed, she turned away to pour roiling water over her tea leaves.

Flix looked out the window at the dark meadow while mindlessly rolling his marbles through his fingers.

"Blueberry and chamomile should do the trick, with a dash of honey from our bees," she mused. As she stirred in the honey she said her silent incantation. "Please give me the strength to do what must be done."

Sitting back down at the table, she tugged a fresh sheet of parchment from its linen sack. The aroma filled her nose, it was perfumed with white sage and patchouli from the garden. It calmed her and would help Sean remember how she smelled.

If only the scent could balance the horror of what I need to say.

"Oh, Flix, how do I do this? How *can* I do this? I have everything here. You, the Fachan, Sean and Minnie. This house is perfect and the gardens are from the scrapbook of heaven. How can I run away?"

Flix turned to her with deep sorrow in his eyes.

"Sometimes, Fiona, we must do what we don't want to do. Sometimes we must sacrifice for the good of all, for the greater good. This world, this mortal world is dark at times, and the ones who bring light have the most to give...and the most to lose."

He turned back to the window and watched fireflies airdance in the tall meadow grasses.

"The most to lose..." he whispered once again.

Fiona let out a sigh and the house sighed with her. She let the pen write the words on its own.

I don't even know where to begin. Sean, you are my love. We've lasted through ages. You found me on that long ago night, cold and soaking wet but with fire in your eyes. You knew long before I did how this would all go. Innocence lost, love rediscovered and kindled strong.

Through deaths and hardships, fire and evils untold.

Out of the darkness and into the light. You've made our

family: Minnie and I, the Fachan and Flix, Luna and all the magical creatures and beings. You've poured your heart and soul into all of this, into us. My heart beats for you; I live and I am because of you.

I know you won't understand. Hell, I don't understand. But here's what I do know.

I must go.

Minnie and I must go. We must go where we can't be found. We must leave no trace. We will travel light, with nothing more than the clothes on our backs and some small provisions. Luna will come with us as well; he will protect us. I trust that you will find us again someday, when the time is right, when the coast is clear. You found me once, twice.

They say the third time is a charm.

Please find me a third time

The night is quiet and dark. The fireflies flutter in the meadow, giving rides to the faeries beneath the moonlight. You sleep soundly; I hear your breathing coming down to me in the kitchen. Minnie tosses in her sleep while Flix keeps watch over me.

All is quiet, save for the fate of man.

When you wake, I won't be here. You'll go to Minnie's room and see her empty bed. I know the fear and panic you'll feel; it's the same as I feel now. Once you've read this letter, I implore you go to the library and read whatever falls into your hand. It will explain everything. It will tell you why I had to leave; why we both had to leave. We do this for you my love, we do this for you.

Sean, please don't hate me. This has to be done. It has to be this way. I trust that you WILL find us when the time is right. Please don't forget about us. Your love will be with me always; it will be my light when I have none. For you I live and breathe; for you I grieve and run into the unknown.

I will not say "goodbye," rather I will simply say "see you soon." May the gods and goddesses protect you and all that you have built. May the darkness not find you and may all remain safe as it is in this moment. Watch for signs, my beloved; listen for the *wind and feel the Earth.*

*I love you. With all that I am and all that I will ever be, I love
you.*
—Fiona

Blinking through weary, tear-stained eyes, Fiona rolled the
parchment and tied it with a purple ribbon. She kissed it once and
left it on the table next to her empty tea cup. Flix looked over and
let a tear fall.

"Take care of yourself, Fiona. Take care of Minnie, too. I'm so
very sorry the world came to this. So very sorry. Make sure Minnie
takes the marbles so we have some idea where you are. So we
know that you are safe. We will come to you when the time is
right. I'll watch over Sean and the Fachan."

Fiona made her way to the window and held out her hand.
Flix ran up and wrapped his arms around her neck. There were no
words to be spoken, only deep sorrow was felt.

"Go, Fiona. Go before it's too late. Go now and may the gods
protect you."

Flix pulled away and went back to the window.

Fiona turned to leave the kitchen and then she turned around
once more—not knowing if she'd ever be back. She blew a kiss to
Flix who caught it and put it in his pocket.

She then slowly made her way upstairs to begin doing what
had to be done.

Standing over the sleeping Sean, she let her nightgown slip
from her shoulders and stood naked in the silver light. She yearned
to reach for him and wake him in the best possible way, but there
was no time. Minnie needed to gather her few essential things.

When Sean woke in the morning, it was required. It was
necessary.

They must be gone.

It doesn't matter what people tell you. It doesn't matter what they might say. Sometimes you have to leave home. Sometimes, running away means you're headed in the exact right direction.
—Alice Hoffman, *Practical Magic*

Printed in the USA
CPSIA information can be obtained
at www.ICGtesting.com
JSHW021750100824
67770JS00003B/100